Model Murder

Chapter One

Detective Chief Inspector Kate Maddox felt a sick lurch
of horror in those first moments of looking down at the
murdered woman. She closed her eyes briefly while she got
a grip on herself, taking deep breaths to fight off waves of
nausea. So much for thinking that she'd schooled herself by
now to take violent death in her stride.

This killing seemed all the more brutal and macabre in
contrast to the peace and tranquillity of its woodland setting,
with sunlight filtering down through a canopy of beech
leaves on a warm September afternoon. A beautiful, vivacious woman had become the victim of yet another sadistic
rapist.

All kinds of emotions were surging into Kate's brain
as separate strands of her horror: revulsion, pity, shocked
recognition. And a blinding fury that men could do this vile
thing to women. Interlaced with all these was something else,
something that made the detective chief inspector instantly
ashamed. A tiny twist of satisfaction that this particular
woman was dead: her potential rival safely out of the way.

You bitch, Kate!

She glanced quickly around, hoping that her face hadn't
betrayed these ambiguous feelings. Fortunately the attention
of her male colleagues seemed focused on the corpse, which
was still partly buried in fibrous leaf mould. The woman's
lovely features were grotesquely distorted, the eyes wildly
staring, the tongue swollen and protruding, while frothy
blood had dried in a crust around the nostrils. Her once
elegant clothes, now stained and damp, had been half torn

1

from her body. A cream silk blouse and the lacy bra beneath it had been ripped apart to expose her breasts. Her lower torso was naked, too, with the skirt pushed up around her waist. One long leg and a slender foot lay bare, with satin panties and a pair of tights draped around the other ankle above a high-heeled black shoe. Incongruously, she was wearing gloves. Clutched in the right fist, mute evidence perhaps of an ineffectual attempt to strike back at her assailant, was a tubular flashlamp.

Kate's sidekick, Detective Sergeant Boulter, as yet unaware of her presence, was scribbling in his notebook. The police surgeon was crouched on his haunches beside the body, completing his initial examination, his every movement recorded by a video operator. A still photographer was busy taking pictures. Various other Scenes of Crime personnel were examining the ground minutely, both inside and outside the protective screens. Several uniformed officers stood around, waiting for instructions, their eyes peeled for any unauthorised person who had managed to sneak through the police cordon and creep up through the trees.

Kate's own arrival at the scene was relatively late in the proceedings. She'd been halfway to Bristol when she received news over her car radio of a suspicious death on her patch. The trip was planned to mark the sixty-eighth birthday of her Aunt Felix – lunch at a pub en route, a visit to the Arnolfini Gallery in the afternoon, then early dinner and seats at the Old Vic for a Pinter play. Only lunch had been achieved before the recall to duty came through.

The stockily built detective sergeant glanced up and saw Kate there.

'Oh, afternoon, ma'am. This is a nasty one we've got here, and no identification so far. There's nothing in her jacket pocket except a tissue, and no sign of a handbag. The bastard probably pinched it as a bonus. Her clothes don't look off the peg, though, so that should help us to – '

'Tim, I know who she is.' Kate's voice was clogged.

'That's a bit of luck.' The colour of his squarish, pink-toned face deepened. 'Sorry ... if she's a friend of yours ma'am.'

'Not a friend, just an acquaintance. Her name's Corinne Saxon.'

2

Boulter frowned. 'Rings a faint bell, but I can't quite – '

'She used to be a top photographic model, but that was some years back. Just lately she's been managing that place Streatfield Park since Admiral Fortescue turned it into a hotel. I met her at the reception given for the launch last month.'

Dr Meddowes had risen to his full-stretch height of five foot four after fastidiously dusting off his nattily suited knees.

'Ah, Chief Inspector! So you've finally managed to get yourself here.'

Kate ignored the sarcasm from this pompous little man, being accustomed to it by now. Dr Meddowes's antagonism, she suspected, was as much because of her superior height as his resentment of women in positions of authority. He was a good police surgeon, she couldn't deny that, but it galled Kate that he had just been appointed regional pathologist. It wasn't going to make life any easier for her.

She raked fingers through her short black hair in a gesture that dispelled all extraneous thoughts and concentrated on the job she had to do.

'What do you have to tell me, doctor?'

He cleared his throat fussily. 'From the bruising on the throat I think it would be safe to say that death was the result of manual strangulation.'

'How long has she been dead?'

He mused at length. 'There are no signs of rigor mortis remaining, and decomposition is just commencing. I would say forty-eight hours, allowing a discrepancy of twelve hours either way.'

'Can't you be more precise than that?'

'No, I cannot. You'll have to wait for my findings when I conduct the post mortem.'

Kate clung to her patience. 'When will that be? Quickly, I hope. If we can have the time of death narrowed down soon, it will save us a great deal of trouble and effort.'

'It may surprise you to learn, Mrs Maddox, that saving the police trouble and effort is not how I see my purpose as a pathologist.'

3

Up yours, too! *But, Kate, you did leave yourself wide open for that little dig.*

She said, with sweet reasonableness and finality, 'I'm sure you'll do your very best to assist us, Dr Meddowes.'

Sergeant Boulter made a face at the doctor's departing back, and said, 'Want me to get someone over to Streatfield Park, ma'am, to make enquiries about when the victim was last seen?'

'No, I'll go myself. We can't take it for granted that the rapist was a complete stranger to her, so the more we can find out about Corinne Saxon the more we'll have to go on. I hope it won't come as too much of a shock to Admiral Fortescue, he's got a bad heart. Just fill me in quickly, Tim. Who was it found the body?' The brush with Meddowes had given Kate a chance to control her emotions and become briskly professional.

'A girl from the boarding kennels just over the hill there. Name of Sally French. She was exercising four of their dogs when they suddenly dashed off and started barking like mad.' The normally dispassionate sergeant allowed himself a moment for sympathy. 'Tough on her to stumble upon this lot. She's only about eighteen, and a real looker.'

Gazing down at the much-abused body, Kate tried to make a mental reconstruction. 'I'd say she was raped and killed right here where she's lying, wouldn't you? Any useful footprints?'

He shook his head. 'Our chaps first on the scene say those dogs had stirred things up more than somewhat.'

'Hmm! Oh, well, Scenes of Crime will find whatever there is to find. What was she doing with that torch she's holding? Was she out walking on her own? After dark?' From what Kate had seen of Corinne Saxon in life, that didn't seem very likely. And who would go strolling in the woods in fancy high-heeled shoes? 'Did she try to bash her attacker with the torch?'

Boulter stepped past the SOC officers, who were painstakingly removing pieces of debris one by one from around the body, and bent to look more closely.

'No sign of adhering blood or hair.' He gently pushed at the torch with the nail of his forefinger. 'She's got it in a grip of iron.'

4

'Cadaveric spasm. Well, I'll leave you to wrap things up here, Tim. First off, I want you to detail a couple of DCs to make enquiries at any house within, say, a half-mile radius. And isn't there a pub somewhere around here?'

'The Green Man. Near the East Dean crossroads.'

'Get someone to ask questions there. One of the regulars might have seen something. By the way, where's the nearest phone box? I need to make a personal call.'

Boulter's sandy eyebrows knit in thought. 'I know.' He pointed over his shoulder. 'Go to the T-junction at the end of this lane and turn left. That's towards Marlingford. You'll find a phone box about half a mile along there, on your right. As a matter of fact, the gates of Streatfield Park are only a few hundred yards farther on, so it isn't out of your way.'

'Fine. See you later, then, at DHQ.' With a nod around at the Scenes of Crime team, she departed.

In less than five minutes Kate was pulling up beside the phone box. She could have wished for a bit longer to prepare herself for this. No question, though, she had to break the news of Corinne Saxon's death to Richard Gower before it reached him some other way.

Those two had at one stage been lovers. It had been many years ago, while Richard was working as a foreign correspondent on a national newspaper, a long time before a sniper's bullet had interrupted his potential career as a top journalist, leaving him with a permanent limp and the need for a less strenuous lifestyle. In those far-distant days, Corinne Saxon was reaching the peak of her success as a photographic model. Kate could well remember how her sensational face and body seemed to be featured in every issue of the fashion glossies. It would have been an ego boost for any man to be chosen to share her bed.

Richard had never spoken of this past affair to Kate until Corinne turned up a couple of months ago. Their relationship had started one summer in Greece, he explained, where he'd been covering a political crisis for the *Monitor* and Corinne was out there on a modelling assignment.

The affair flickered on spasmodically whenever they both

happened to be in London, up to the time Richard was sent to the Far East on a big drugs-trafficking story that kept him there for months on end. Corinne's brief spell of fame at the top of her tree lasted a year or so more, but there was never any further contact between them. Richard had neither seen nor heard from Corinne Saxon until she phoned him out of the blue to say hello and inform him that she was now at Streatfield Park, masterminding its conversion to a hotel. It seemed she'd learned by chance that the owner and editor of the local weekly paper was a one-time flame of hers, and she'd realised that this happy coincidence could be put to good use for publicity. Richard had been very ready to go along with that. The story of Admiral Fortescue's stately home being turned into a luxury hotel provided him with some good copy. Besides (though he hadn't exactly spelled out this aspect to Kate), Corinne was still a very glamorous woman.

Just how glamorous she had bitchily demonstrated at the launch party at Streatfield Park five weeks ago, held for a select gathering of local VIPs on the day before the first hotel guests were due to arrive. Kate had not been expecting to attend the function. She went along in place of Detective Superintendent Joliffe, who was laid low with a sudden viral infection. As the official police representative, Kate had come in for introductions to various people involved with the project. In addition to Corinne herself and Admiral Fortescue, and the admiral's son over from America for the occasion, she met the merchant banker who'd arranged the financing, the architect responsible for planning the conversion, and the building contractor, the latter two with their wives. Mrs Builder devotedly basked in her husband's hour of glory; Mrs Architect, much less devotedly, wanted it clearly understood that the influence of her eminent county connections had played no small part in her spouse's successful career.

It was only natural for Richard and Kate to gravitate towards each other whenever they weren't talking separately to other guests. After enjoying the splendid buffet lunch laid out in the Orangery, they'd strolled together through the various public rooms, admiring the skill with

6

which the alterations and refurbishing had been carried out. Kate's appreciation of good design had sprung from her late husband's enthusiasm. A computer programmer, Noel had worked on a number of projects connected with architecture and had become keenly interested in the subject. Kate always felt, sentimentally, that by fostering her own interest in architecture she was retaining an extra link with her husband and their small daughter she had so tragically lost on that fateful afternoon, now many years ago.

She and Richard were by chance alone in one of the luxurious bedroom suites that were open to view, when Corinne joined them. It was clear to Kate that she had divined the extent of their relationship, and didn't like it.

'Hi, there!' Coming forward gushingly, she took Richard's left biceps in her two hands and pressed it with possessive fondness. 'How's my Big Dick enjoying the party? You and I will have to watch our step today, won't we, with the fuzz in attendance?' The dazzling smile she flashed at Kate was solely for Richard's consumption: two women sharing a friendly little quip. But the look in those violet eyes of Corinne's had carried a different message for Kate, a warning that she could easily snatch Richard Gower away at any time she chose to do so.

Later, that evening at his flat, Richard had voiced his pleasure to Kate that she and Corinne seemed to have got on so well. Only a man could be so bloody dim-sighted.

Now Corinne Saxon was dead. And Richard had to be told. Sighing, Kate climbed out of the car and pulled open the door of the phone booth. Fishing in her purse for a coin, she inserted it and punched out the *Gazette*'s number.

'I thought you were supposed to be in Bristol today,' he said, when she got through to him.

'Richard, listen. Something's happened.'

'What is it?' His voice held concern. 'Are you okay, Kate?'

'It's not me.'

'Felix?'

'No, not Felix. I had to call off the birthday outing and come back. There's been a death, and I wanted to tell you myself before the news reached you from another source.'

'A death? Someone I know, you mean?'

'Yes, I'm afraid so. Corinne Saxon.'

'Corinne! Oh, no!'

'It's true, Richard.' She paused, swallowed. 'I ... I'm sorry.'

He seemed badly thrown, unable to collect himself. 'You mean ... an accident in her car? Poor Corinne, she always did drive much too fast. But Kate, I don't get it. How come you're involved? What's it got to do with the CID?'

'It wasn't an accident. She was murdered. Her body was found just a couple of hours ago in the woods near East Dean. She'd been raped, then strangled. I'm really sorry, Richard, but you had to know.'

There were long seconds of silence from Richard, while Kate wondered what exactly this news meant to him. It was a shock, of course, a fearful shock. Any man with normally decent feelings would be shocked and distressed to learn of the death in such horrific circumstances of any woman with whom he'd once been intimate. But did Corinne Saxon's death mean more than just that to Richard? Without Corinne in his life, now that he'd met her again, did he face an aching void?

Stop it, Kate!

She ended the stretching silence. 'I'm on my way to Streatfield Park now. To break the news, of course, but also to pick up whatever information I can about her to get this investigation off the ground.'

Richard gave a baffled grunt. 'Information about Corinne? How will that help? You said she'd been raped and strangled in the woods.'

'Listen, this conversation is strictly off the record. Understood?'

'I'm not looking for a scoop for the paper, Kate.' His voice was laced with reproach.

'You'll be getting a press release for the *Gazette* in due course. The point is, however much this case might look like an assault by a total stranger, it's a statistical fact that a rapist is far more likely to be somebody who's known to his victim. So I have to enquire into every aspect of Corinne Saxon's life.'

8

'What you're saying is that every man she's ever known is now under suspicion?'

'Got to be.'

'Which includes me.' God, he was bitter.

'Don't be ridiculous.' But there was no protest she could make that would erase the implication of what she'd said. And Richard was suggesting nothing worse than the truth. Inevitably, his name would have to go down on her list of potential suspects. How cruelly ironic! They had originally met because Richard Gower had been a prime suspect in a previous murder investigation, when his car was stolen from outside his flat and used in a deliberate hit-and-run killing. After Kate had finally cleared him of suspicion (to her infinite relief) their friendship had blossomed. Only last night − as so often nowadays − they had been close in their togetherness. But now, suddenly, their entire relationship seemed in jeopardy. Yet she knew, knew with utter conviction, that Richard was not involved in this murder. Any more than he'd been involved that other time.

'There's something you can very likely help me with,' she rushed on, vainly trying to break through the barrier that was all at once between them. 'Corinne's next of kin will have to be informed. Who would that be?'

'I haven't the least idea.'

'But surely ... didn't she ever talk to you about her family?'

'Not a lot that I recall. It was ages ago that I knew her.'

'For heaven's sake, you must be able to tell me something about her.'

'Well, she was born in France, her mother was French. The Lyons area, I think. That's right, because her father was somehow involved in the silk business over there. But Corinne told me that both her parents died when she was quite small. About six or seven, I believe.'

'Did she have any brothers or sisters?'

'No, she was an only child, I do remember her saying that. Then, after she was orphaned, her father's sister took over and brought her up in this country. The aunt was unmarried and very strait-laced, and Corinne never really got on with her. That was in this neck of the woods, as it happens, in Cheltenham.'

'An aunt? I suppose you don't know exactly where in Cheltenham?'

'No, I don't. And it wouldn't do you any good, because she's dead now, too. I happened to ask Corinne recently, while we were chatting, if her aunt was still around. She told me the old girl had pegged out shortly before she got married.'

'Hold on! Are you saying that Corinne Saxon was married?'

'And divorced. It was since the time I knew her, of course, and I only came to learn about it quite by chance.'

'Oh? How was that?'

'If you must know,' he said resentfully, 'I was recently going through some back files of the *Gazette* searching for something, when I stumbled across a news item about the opening of an antique shop at a village somewhere near Marlingford. What caught my eye was a passing mention that the owner had once been married to Corinne Saxon, the well-known model. It went on to say that he and his partner in the new venture planned to marry in the autumn. This was a few years ago, before I took over the *Gazette*. I commented about it to Corinne, but she just laughed and said the marriage had been a total disaster. The man was a wimp.'

'D'you recall his name?'

Richard gave a noisy sigh. 'I suppose I could look it up for you. Shall I send you a photocopy of the paragraph?'

'Yes, do that, soon as you can. Now I'd better get going.'

'You'll be very tied up on this, I expect. There'll be no chance of seeing you for the next few days?'

Was he looking for an out? A good excuse not to spend time with her? Kate said woodenly, 'I want to see you, Richard. I'll need to talk to you some more about Corinne, anyway. It might well be that you can come up with some useful information.'

Again, Kate was horribly conscious of the barrier between them. How could she convince Richard that she was just doing her job? She herself didn't entertain the smallest

10

doubt about him, no matter what the crime statistics might say about rapists being known to their victims.

All the same, once the time of the killing had been pin-pointed, she'd need to establish an alibi for Richard Gower. Otherwise, she'd be shot at by her superintendent (and rightly so) for leaving such an obvious gap in her investigation.

Richard was saying in a withdrawn tone, 'I don't imagine there's anything more I can tell you about Corinne. It was years ago I knew her, and I've not seen all that much of her just lately.'

But exactly *how* much was 'not all that much'?

'I'll call you,' Kate finished quickly. 'I must go now.'

Richard had provided her with information that could be useful. In a murder investigation, *any* information about the victim could prove to be significant. What he'd just told her would have to go into the records, to be mulled over by everyone on the squad, filed, cross-indexed and computerised. Okay, okay, but no way was she going to include the juicy little titbit that the senior investigating officer's boyfriend had once been the lover of the murdered woman. That fact had no bearing on the case.

None at all.

Chapter Two

The gilt-lettered sign at the entrance gates simply stated STREATFIELD PARK, with nothing to indicate that this was a hotel. The driveway ran pencil-straight for three hundred yards, an avenue of clipped yews standing blackly green against the blueness of the afternoon sky.

At the drive's end the mansion stood in landscaped grounds of sweeping lawns and terraces. It was a noble pile of beautiful tawny-grey Cotswold stone, surmounted by a balustrade decorated with Grecian urns. What Kate was seeing was the remodelled version of a more ancient house, undertaken by an eighteenth-century Fortescue. On three stories, finely proportioned sash windows stretched in perfect symmetry from the central pedimented entrance. The Orangery was a later, one-storey addition on the left.

Kate drew up on the expanse of smooth gravel, her Montego looking decidedly meagre beside the cars that were casually parked around − a large, white Mercedes, a couple of shining Rollers, a Porsche and a chrome-yellow Jaguar. She mounted the half-dozen shallow steps just behind an elegant American couple with Ivy League voices. Inside, they turned left to where, through wide glass doors, Kate glimpsed other guests lounging in deep sofas taking afternoon tea.

The reception desk was discreetly tucked away through a canopied archway off the Great Hall. It was staffed by a slimly attractive young woman with a small elfin face and masses of blonde hair piled in a loose coil on top of her head.

'Good afternoon, madam. How may I help you?'

12

Kate introduced herself. 'I wish to see Admiral Fortescue, please.'

'I'm sorry, Chief Inspector, but that will not be possible at the moment.'

'He's not here?'

'The admiral is resting, as he does every afternoon. He must not be disturbed until four o'clock. That is when he takes his tea.' She glanced at her wristwatch. 'In another twenty-five minutes.'

'I'm afraid this is one time he has to be disturbed. Kindly have him informed that I'm here and need to speak to him without delay.'

A moment's hesitation, then the young woman capitulated. A few words were murmured into the phone. After a brief wait, a man in a grey cotton jacket approached Kate. He was fiftyish, thickly built and swarthy. A few wispy hairs sprouted from the top of his domed head but the brows above the unsmiling grey eyes were thick and straggly, and the sagging jowls were stained with dark-blue growth. Not, she would have thought, quite the image for a staff member at a luxury hotel. He spoke in a gruff voice with a strong North Country accent.

'Come with me,' he said, less than civilly. 'I'll take you to the admiral's quarters.'

Kate walked with him along a wide corridor flanked by chinoiserie lacquer cabinets.

'May I have your name, please? And what is your position in the hotel?'

His scowling sideways glance demanded what damned business of it was of hers.

'Larkin's the name,' he grunted. 'Sid Larkin. I'm Admiral Fortescue's personal steward.'

'I see. Have you been with him long?'

'I should say so. I was with him back in the navy.' Which explained his walk, the rolling gait associated with sailors. Accentuated, perhaps, by the effect of the whisky Kate could smell on his breath.

They had reached a pair of doors, walnut embellished with carving. Larkin threw open one leaf, and jerked his head.

'Wait in there, and I'll go and tell his nibs you're here.'

He hesitated a moment before leaving her, and Kate guessed he was speculating about what her presence here meant, but didn't dare to enquire.

She entered a large sitting room that was comfortably furnished with a mixture of modern and antique pieces. Tall french windows overlooked a manicured lawn at the rear of the house with a long view to distant hills. She turned as a door on her right opened to admit Admiral Fortescue. He came forward leaning on an ebony cane, his other hand buttoning the jacket of his dark-grey suit as if he'd just slipped it on. As a younger man, Kate judged, he would have been quite dramatically handsome. He had piercingly blue eyes, accustomed no doubt to looking at far horizons. His face was very lined now, his hair and trim naval beard were iron grey. Five weeks ago, when Kate was introduced to Admiral Fortescue, he had still not fully recovered from heart surgery. He looked little better now, she thought.

'Chief Inspector, please forgive me if I've kept you waiting. I understand that your business is urgent.'

'It is, sir. I'm sorry it was necessary to disturb you, but I'm afraid that I'm the bearer of most unhappy news.'

The habit of cool command had not deserted him. His eyes regarded her with anxiety, but stoically. The only outward sign of nervousness was the clenching of his knuckles over the knob of his cane.

'Something has happened to my son? My grandchildren?'

'No, it's not your family. This concerns Miss Corinne Saxon. I regret to inform you that she is dead.'

'Corinne – dead! That is dreadful. Some kind of accident, I take it?'

'No, sir, not an accident. Her body was found earlier this afternoon in the woods at East Dean, hardly a mile from here. She had been strangled.' Kate withheld any mention of rape at this stage.

The admiral looked stunned, then puzzlement crept into his weathered face. 'There must be some mistake. Corinne set off on Wednesday afternoon for a few days' leave. This woman you found cannot be she.'

'I'm sorry, sir, but it is. I have met Miss Saxon, and you may take it from me that the body found is definitely hers.'

He took moments to accept and believe this, then his whole frame sagged and he sank down into an armchair. He looked pale and quite ill, but he retained the good manners to gesture to Kate to be seated also.

Before doing so, she asked, 'May I get you a little brandy, sir?'

'Thank you, if you would be so kind.'

Near the drinks cabinet, on a Dutch marquetry table set to one side of the french windows, was a collection of cups and trophies. Interspersed with these were framed photographs featuring a younger Douglas Fortescue, snapped in sporting gear and looking in great shape. For a past athlete, his present poor health would be hard to bear.

He took the brandy from Kate and sipped it gratefully.

'Who ... who could have done such a terrible thing? Corinne was strangled, you say. Shocking!'

'You told me that Miss Saxon set off from here on Wednesday afternoon for a few days away. Where was she going?'

He looked slightly agitated by the question. Or was it just that he was still a bit dazed from the shattering news he'd received? 'I'm afraid I can't tell you. Corinne didn't say.'

'Really? Suppose some kind of problem or emergency had arisen? Wouldn't you have needed to know how to contact her?'

The admiral turned his head from side to side in firm denial. 'It wasn't necessary. Corinne had been working extremely hard for several months to get the hotel launched and running. She needed a complete break, away from it all.' He paused, almost as if scanning his reply for flaws. 'Yes, indeed, she was entitled to that.'

'When did you last see her, sir?'

'We lunched together, here, on Wednesday. In the hotel restaurant, that is. Corinne set out directly afterwards.'

'At what time would that have been?'

'Er, let me see. It must have been about two-fifteen. I remember she glanced at her watch and said she had to be going. I sent a porter to bring her car round to the front, and when he came to say it was outside, Corinne stood up

15

at once. The man carried her case out, and I walked with her to the front entrance.'

So she'd been driving, in her own car. Where the hell was it now?

'Can you give me details of Miss Saxon's car, sir? Make, colour, registration number. No vehicle was found at the scene, and I must get my people on to tracing it immediately.'

He frowned. 'It's a Ford, I know that, but I'm not very well informed about the modern range of models. It's a sporty car, bright red, and it has a fold-down hood.'

'An Escort Cabriolet, then.'

'If you say so. Corinne bought it only last month from the Ford dealer in Marlingford.'

'Can you tell me what she was wearing when she left here?'

'Oh, dear! She looked very smartly turned out, but then she invariably did.'

'How about the colour of her clothes?'

He frowned again, then shook his head helplessly.

'Try to visualise her sitting with you at lunchtime,' Kate suggested. 'Was her outfit brown, red, green, blue?'

'Green,' he said, nodding. 'Yes, I'm sure it was green. Some kind of suit, I think.'

Green fitted with the clothing on the body. 'May I use your telephone, sir?'

'Of course.' He gestured to where it stood on the small round table beside his armchair. 'You need to press nine first, if you require an outside line.'

Kate got through to Divisional HQ. 'Bob, I want a systematic search for a red Escort Cabriolet owned by a Miss Corinne Saxon. She bought it from Brownley's in Marlingford last month, so you can get the reg number from them. All divisions, and notify adjoining forces just for the moment. But if we don't come up with something fast, it'll have to go nationwide. That car has got to be found.'

When she replaced the phone, the admiral said, 'You think, then, that Corinne's car was driven away by ... her assassin?'

'It's a strong possibility. Are you quite certain, sir, that

16

you really have no idea where Miss Saxon was going?'

'No, no, absolutely no idea at all.'

Wasn't be being too quick and emphatic with his denial?
'Well, if anything occurs to you, please let me know at once.
My officers will be asking the members of your staff if she
said anything to any of them.'

'They're unlikely to be able to tell you any more than I can,
Chief Inspector.' There was a touch of asperity in his tone.

'We'll see. How about Miss Saxon's next of kin? Whoever
it is must be informed of what has happened. Can you tell
me who that would be?'

The admiral stared at her as if he'd been put on the spot
by her question. 'I ... I don't think she had any relatives.
Not to my knowledge.'

'I'm sure there must be someone she regarded as her next of
kin. Let's hope there'll be an address book in her room.'

'Oh! I suppose that is possible.' He paused, then added,
'Wasn't there anything of the sort in her handbag?'

'Her handbag is missing, sir. We found no trace of it at
the scene.'

He looked surprised and ... what? Relieved?

'Where was Miss Saxon's private accommodation?' Kate
asked. 'I'd like to take a quick look around while I'm here.'

'Er, Corinne had some rooms on the top floor converted
into a self-contained apartment.'

'That will be locked, I presume? Will there be a spare
key?'

'I imagine there must be. In the hotel office, I expect.'

'When I was here on the launch day, I remember having
Miss Saxon's deputy pointed out to me, though I didn't
actually meet him. He'll be in charge of the hotel now, I
imagine?'

'I suppose he will be. Yves will have to be informed about
Corinne.' He sighed jerkily, and blinked his eyes several
times. 'This is very distressing. It's difficult to assemble
one's thoughts. Labrosse, the name is – Yves Labrosse.
He is Swiss.'

'Perhaps your steward could take me to see Mr Labrosse,
sir? I'd better have a word with him myself.'

'Oh, well if you think it's necessary.' The admiral tinkled

a silver bell on the table beside him. The steward entered at once, as if he'd been standing just the other side of the door, listening.

'Ah, Larkin. Chief Inspector Maddox has brought tragic news. Miss Saxon is dead ... murdered. She was strangled, apparently. It is scarcely believable.'

The man's reaction was contrived, theatrical. He recoiled half a step, his eyes widening in horror. Was he just covering the fact that he'd had his ear to the door? Or was his prior knowledge more sinister?

Kate cut short his expressions of dismay by saying briskly, 'I'd like you to take me to Mr Labrosse, please.'

The man glanced at the admiral for permission.

'Yes, yes, Larkin. Do as the chief inspector says.'

'I'll come back and see you later on, Admiral,' said Kate. 'We shall need to talk again.'

Outside, walking along the corridor, she asked Larkin, 'When was the last time you saw Miss Saxon?'

That halted him in his tracks. 'Hey! What're you getting at?'

'Just answer the question, please.'

'You going to be in charge of this case, then?' he asked, showing as much contempt as he dared.

'I shall be heading the investigation, yes. Well?'

He ruminated, sullenly taking his time. Finally he said, 'About half-twelve on Wednesday. She came along to see if the admiral was ready for his lunch.'

'And you didn't see her again after that?'

'No, I didn't.'

'Very well,' Kate said, moving on.

The man was uneasy, and she let him sweat. Later, he'd be questioned at length by one of the as yet unassembled murder squad. And possibly again by her, if his answers were unsatisfactory.

Beside the reception desk, a door led into an office. Larkin threw it open without first knocking, and a woman working at a word-processor looked up sharply in annoyance. She had a long, rather plain, somewhat horsy face. Large spectacles with downward-sloped lenses, intended to add style, gave her an unfortunately dolorous appearance.

'Look here, Larkin, you can't just come barging in like this.' She spotted Kate behind him, and modified her resentment. 'Oh, what is it?'

'Where is he?' Larkin demanded.

'If you're referring to Mr Labrosse, he's in his office.' She addressed Kate. 'Who shall I say wants him?'

'Please inform Mr Labrosse that Detective Chief Inspector Maddox of the South Midlands Police would like a word.' She turned to the man dismissively. 'Thank you, Mr Larkin. That will be all for now.'

He scowled before departing, though whether at her or at the secretary was uncertain. With her hand on the phone, the secretary asked, 'What shall I tell Mr Labrosse it's about?'

'Just say that I want to see him.'

Ten seconds later Kate was ushered into the inner room. It was spacious and tastefully furnished in tones of green, beige and brown. There were two desks, both of them large and opulent. The man who rose to greet her had seen seated at the slightly smaller of the desks. She had seen him before at the launch party, but they had not spoken.

'Chief Inspector Maddox! In what way can I assist you?' He spoke in a rich, firm voice that carried only a trace of a continental accent. Smiling with professional charm, he gestured her into a comfortable chair placed a little to one side. 'It is not a serious matter, I trust? Is one of the staff in some kind of trouble?'

He was, above all, suave. Around forty – tall, dark and very nearly handsome. His subdued grey worsted suit, if bought off the peg, had come off a very expensive peg. A slightly anachronistic touch was the corner of a whiter-than-white handkerchief showing at his breast pocket.

'I'm afraid it's a very serious matter, Mr Labrosse. Earlier this afternoon Miss Corinne Saxon's body was discovered in the woods at East Dean.'

He jerked to attentiveness. 'Her body? You mean that Corinne is dead?'

Kate watched him, noting a complexity of emotions flickering behind the carefully controlled features. 'I'm afraid I do. She had been strangled.'

'*Mon dieu!* How is this possible? When was she killed?

19

Who could have done it? Strangled, you say. How shocking! How brutal!'

'Perhaps you can help me towards finding an answer to those questions, Mr Labrosse.'

'That is my wish, of course, in whatever way I can. But I don't see what you want of me. Corinne set off from here on Wednesday for a brief holiday, but if she was found in East Dean woods she didn't get far. Who could have waylaid her? For what motive? Was it theft, for cash or whatever else she had on her?'

While talking his glance had strayed a couple of times in the direction of the other desk. Corinne's desk, presumably. Was he telling himself that, incredibly, she would never again be sitting there? Or was he mentally sizing it up for his own occupation?

As with the admiral, Kate did not choose to enlighten Labrosse regarding the motive. 'Do you happen to know where Miss Saxon was going? And with whom?'

'She departed alone, Chief Inspector.'

'That doesn't mean she wasn't planning to join up with someone. You haven't answered the first part of my question, Mr Labrosse, about where she was going.'

He gestured in apology. 'I have no idea where she was going. None at all.'

'Isn't it surprising that Miss Saxon didn't say?'

He raised his eyebrows and shrugged his elegantly suited shoulders. 'It was her own concern, *n'est-ce-pas*?'

'According to Admiral Fortescue, she didn't tell him, either.'

His glance sharpened. 'How did the admiral take this terrible news?'

'It was a great shock to him, of course. As I imagine it must be for you.'

'Ah, yes. Indeed, yes. A great shock.' Labrosse had another stab at getting some answers from her. 'Have you any theory yet as to who could have done this dreadful thing? And why?'

'The murder investigation has barely begun,' Kate pointed out. 'And that leads me to another point. I shall need to set up a temporary headquarters. Somewhere as near as possible to the East Dean woods.' She regarded him expectantly. 'Apart from a few cottages and a pub, there is only Streatfield Park within striking distance.'

Labrosse looked appalled. 'We couldn't possibly have a horde of police officers traipsing around the hotel and upsetting the guests. No, no, it's out of the question.'

'I'm sure you could think of somewhere suitably tucked away. We'd be very discreet, I assure you.' Kate's tone and expression was challenging. 'I take it, Mr Labrosse, that you meant what you said about wanting to do all you can to help the police in this unhappy business?'

A faint flush coloured his smooth features. 'Naturally I do. You have my word, Chief Inspector. However, the matter of making facilities available to you is up to Admiral Fortescue. He is the owner of Streatfield Park.'

'I shall certainly ask the admiral's permission before we set up our Incident Room. But he's been in poor health, hasn't he, ever since the hotel opened? I imagine that you, as the assistant manager, would be better placed to suggest somewhere suitable that would cause the least inconvenience.'

Labrosse rubbed his close-shaven chin, not looking at all delighted. After a minute's thought, he said, 'Perhaps the two new squash courts could be given over to you. They're removed from the house, situated at the far end of the stable block. We were planning to have them ready for use some time next week, but I suppose that could be postponed.'

'It sounds ideal. Are the toilet facilities there working yet?'

'Oh, yes. And the changing rooms are finished, too. But there's only one telephone line, and that goes through the hotel switchboard.'

'No problem,' Kate said briskly. 'We'll have our own direct lines installed. I'll get one of my officers to come and look things over right away. And I'll square matters with Admiral Fortescue. Now, Mr Labrosse, I want to take a look around Miss Saxon's private apartment, which I understand is at the top of the house. I'll ask your secretary to find a spare key and take me up, shall I?'

'I'll take you myself, Chief Inspector,' he said, all affability now.

'Thank you, but I have no wish to disrupt the running of the hotel more than is necessary.' In reality, Kate thought that a chat with the secretary might be productive.

Corinne Saxon's apartment, transformed from what had once been attics, was now a penthouse. Set a little back behind the screen of the house's balustrade, the large dormer windows looked out past the Grecian urns and gave a clear view of the grounds and most of what was going on therein. Yet the apartment was completely private, even with its own roof garden that offered possibilities of nude sunbathing or sitting in the leafy shade of tubbed trees. Luxury was the name of the game here, and Corinne Saxon must have judged she was on to a good thing.

The decor was ultramodern, ivory and turquoise, with billowing leather sofas and matching armchairs. A few choice pieces of furniture (on loan from the admiral?) were set around tastefully, and likewise several original oil paintings on the walls.

Coming up in the lift with the secretary, Kate had put her in the picture. Mrs Deirdre Lancing had seemed shocked by the news of Corinne Saxon's death – but not, perhaps, unduly distressed.

'Do you happen to know where Miss Saxon was intending to go when she set off on Wednesday?' Kate asked her, while they stood together in the spacious sitting room.

'I'm afraid not.' She adjusted her large-lensed spectacles with a delicate lift, using the tips of both third fingers. 'She wasn't one to discuss anything personal. Not with the staff, that is.'

'How was she regarded here? Was she popular?'

'Well ...' That one word said a lot, and Kate didn't press the question.

'Did Miss Saxon have any special friends? How did she spend her free time?'

'I really wouldn't know about that.'

'Come now, you must have some idea. Are you telling me

the staff don't talk among themselves about the doings of the management?' Kate smiled encouragingly.

'Well, she must have spent a lot of her time shopping, to judge from all the new clothes she was always appearing in. Then she mixed with the guests quite a bit; in a social way, I mean. Though I suppose that would be regarded as part of her job.'

'Can you give me any specific instances?'

Mrs Lancing considered. 'There's an American couple staying here, the Rubinsteins. They were talking about wanting to visit Bath while they were in the district, and Miss Saxon offered to go with them to show them around. Someone overheard them arrange it. That was last week.'

Kate jotted down the name in her notebook.

'Anybody else?'

'Well, I believe she went to Blenheim House with some guests a couple of weeks ago. I've forgotten their name, they're not here now.'

'Look up the name and address, will you, and let me have it later.' Kate gave the secretary a straight look. 'What about men in Miss Saxon's life? Was there anyone currently?'

Another quick lift of her spectacles. 'There must have been, I should think, but I don't know who.'

'How about phone calls?' Kate pointed to a telephone on a neo-classical writing table. 'Does that go through the hotel switchboard?'

'Yes.'

'So it would be known what incoming calls she received?'

'Well, I'm not sure about that. Who'd bother to remember?'

'If any man called her regularly, it would be noted, wouldn't it?'

She shrugged. 'June Elsted's the one to ask. I'm not on the switchboard often, only as a relief.'

'June Elsted would be the girl I saw downstairs at the reception desk?'

'That's right.'

'Tell me, did you see Miss Saxon at all on Wednesday, before she left?'

'Yes, I did. Just before she had lunch, with the admiral,

she popped into the office. She was short of cash, she said, and asked me for a hundred pounds. I took it from the safe for her. We always keep a large float.'

'What was she wearing?'

'She had on a new outfit. Well, I think it must have been new, I'd never seen her in it before. It was very smart. The skirt was a lightweight wool in a sort of dark olive shade and the jacket was check, in paler toning greens. And under it she wore a cream silk blouse that had little pleats down the front. Black accessories ... a shoulder bag, court shoes with a tiny gilt band on the heels.'

Praise be for observant women! They didn't crop up very often. Mrs Lancing's description fitted exactly with what Corinne Saxon had been wearing when found dead. Which added weight to Kate's interim theory that she had been raped some time on Wednesday, not later.

'Thank you, Mrs Lancing, that's a big help. I'll need a formal statement from you, and from the other members of staff, too, but my sergeant will arrange that. Meanwhile, I'd better have the key to this apartment.'

'Oh, I'm not sure that I ought to —'

'If you please.' Kate held out her hand. 'Are there any other spare keys? Would the hotel passkey open this door?'

'No, that's the only one. This lock isn't in the same series as the hotel ones.'

'Good. Well, I won't keep you, Mrs Lancing. I just want to have a look around up here.'

Alone, Kate gave the room a rapid search for anything that might assist her. The drawer of the writing table was locked, but one of the keys on Kate's own bunch opened it easily. It yielded, among an assortment of items, a book of cheque stubs (mostly payments to clothes stores and boutiques, Kate saw, riffling through), and an envelope containing a couple of bank statements covering transactions over the past three months. A sum credited on the first of each month would be Corinne's salary from the hotel. The amount made Kate blink. Detective chief inspectors weren't paid nearly as much. The only other sizeable credit was another regular one. Four hundred a month. The bank would have to provide an explanation of that.

24

Kate passed on in rapid perusal. A few bills, some paid, some not. A couple of picture postcards, one from Tenerife from someone named Bunny; the other, from the Scottish Highlands, was signed illegibly with a scrawl. There was no other personal correspondence, no letters from friends or possible relatives. She left the little pile on the table and went through to the bedroom.

Wow! A real boudoir, this. The big bed was canopied with pale peach satin, daintily ruched, and similar drapery festooned the windows. The bathroom was adjoining, lavishly appointed.

A beside cabinet produced nothing of interest, the dressing-table drawers only cosmetics and so on. A section of the fitted wardrobes along one wall consisted of sliding trays, each stacked with sweaters, underclothes and accessories, all of good quality. In the hanging spaces were dresses, suits, slacks, coats, jackets. Kate wondered what Corinne had packed for her few days away. The female staff of the hotel would have to be quizzed to see if they could work out which items were missing. Deirdre Lancing should be a good bet for that.

Kate found a folded plastic carrier bag at the bottom of a wardrobe. Back in the other room she stuffed it with the collection of papers she wanted to take away with her. She picked up the phone and pressed 5 for the hotel office. Deirdre Lancing responded.

'Did Miss Saxon keep any personal items in the hotel safe?' Kate asked.

'Oh, no. Nothing like that.'

'You'd be sure to know, I suppose? Might she have put something in there without mentioning it to you?'

'That's not possible. Miss Saxon herself made the rule that I have to keep a strict record of everything placed in the safe.'

'Thank you. What number do I dial for Admiral Fortescue?'

'Oh, number one.'

Appropriate, Kate thought, as she pressed the button. Apologising to the admiral for disturbing him again so soon, she explained the need for an Incident Room that was near to the scene of the crime.

25

'It really would help if we could be accommodated at Streatfield Park, sir. I spoke to Mr Labrosse, who suggested that the squash courts might be suitable.'

'Oh!' The admiral sounded somewhat put out.

'He stressed, of course, that your permission would be required first.'

'Well, if Labrosse has no objection, I suppose ...'

'I'm most grateful, sir. I'll have my officers set things up without delay. There's one other thing. I've been unable to find an address book in Miss Saxon's room, and we need to arrange a formal identification of her body. With no relatives available I would in normal circumstances turn to you, as her employer. But in view of your state of health, perhaps you could suggest someone else.'

'No, no, I will attend to the matter myself. I feel that I should.'

'It isn't necessary, you know, sir. Are you sure you feel up to it?'

'Yes, yes,' he said impatiently. 'What precisely is involved? Where do I have to go?'

'Marlingford. I'll have the necessary arrangements made. We would pick you up and bring you back, of course.'

'That won't be necessary. Larkin can drive me. I shall await your instructions, Chief Inspector.'

There was little more that Kate could usefully do at Streatfield Park for the moment. She returned to her car and drove to Divisional HQ in Marlingford. As she'd anticipated, Sergeant Boulter had already arrived there after finishing at the scene of the crime.

'I suppose you've heard about the dead woman's missing car, Tim? A red Escort Cabriolet. Anything on it yet?'

'Not a whisper, guv.'

'Damn! Where the hell's it got to?' Appearing unexpectedly, Kate had caught her sergeant with his mouth full. Amused, she watched him hastily swallow down a half-chewed chunk of pastry, flakes of which still clung to his lips. 'How have you been filling in your time? Apart from stuffing your face, that is.'

'It was only a sausage roll,' he said, aggrieved.

'And the rest! Well?'

Now Boulter looked pleased with himself, producing his news like a rabbit from a hat. 'I've been on the blower to Wye Division, checking to see if Inspector Massey would be available as office manager. Luckily, he is. He said he'll be here in the morning, first thing.'

'Oh, well done, Tim.'

Male officers with whom Kate could work in complete harmony without the male/female thing rearing its head in one form or another were thin on the Force's ground. Frank Massey was one of the precious few. No chauvinism from Frank, sly or blatant; no assumption that because she was a long-time widow she must be panting to get laid. Frank Massey was content with his own career achievements, and contentedly married. He respected Kate's rank and the intelligence and drive that had got her there. Furthermore, he was a hard worker with a good analytical mind.

'Get back to Inspector Massey, will you, and tell him I've arranged for the Incident Room to be set up in the stable block at Streatfield Park. Two squash courts with changing rooms and toilets.'

'Sounds ideal.'

'I want us to make a start on interviewing the hotel staff and guests first thing tomorrow, Tim. Get things organised sharpish, will you? Admiral Fortescue has agreed to identify the body, so get on to him and fix a convenient time. Tonight, if possible.'

'Will do, guv.'

There was a warmth in Tim Boulter's 'guv' which Kate liked. Nowadays, his use of 'ma'am' was reserved for when others were present, or, ominously, to indicate serious displeasure with his chief inspector. Not another Frank Massey, the sergeant had initially been prickly to work with, and still could be on occasion.

'I suppose it's too much to hope,' she said, 'that the Scenes of Crime lads have found that missing handbag?'

Boulter gave a negative grunt. 'No sign of the second shoe, either. Queer, isn't it? I mean, if it came off in the struggle. But cheer up, guv, I've got one bit of good news that'll help things along. When the body was finally carted

27

away we found that the ground underneath it was dry, as also the parts of the clothing she'd been lying on. Otherwise, her clothes were quite dampish.'

'Ah! Now, what rain have we had in the past two days? None today, and I don't recall any yesterday.'

'Right. The last rain was on Wednesday evening. Quite a heavy shower, but it didn't last long. I was over this way to interview a farmer about those sheep thefts, and we had to take shelter in his barn. The rain started a minute or two before six, and it was all over by half past. Just to be sure, I've confirmed the time with the local met station.'

'Nice work.'

The first real break in the case. Corinne Saxon's body must have been lying where it was subsequently found prior to six o'clock on Wednesday. She'd left Streatfield Park at about two-fifteen. Therefore, she was raped and killed somewhere between those times.

Theories were one thing, but solid facts (so beloved by her superintendent) were something else. This narrowed the investigation down a lot.

Chapter Three

A few minutes after eight that evening, when Kate drove through the archway into the stable yard at Streatfield Park, she found a large van parked there. Men were unloading its contents: office furniture and other equipment for the Incident Room, and all the mass of bumf that was always needed in a major investigation.

Inside the squash courts Sergeant Boulter was supervising the placing of desks, chairs and filing cabinets, aided by the two detective constables who had so far arrived. Even as Kate stood watching, order miraculously began to emerge from chaos.

'Phone lines will be installed by Telecom first thing tomorrow,' Boulter told her.

Kate had spent the past hour at her desk at DHQ in Marlingford, sorting out her caseload to leave her free of other commitments in the days ahead. Needing a clear run on this murder enquiry, she had delegated the jobs she couldn't let hang. Luckily, she had no court appearances scheduled that would demand her presence.

Boulter suggested that she should use a changing room as her personal office. It wasn't too cramped for a desk and chairs, and would get plentiful daylight through a large frosted-glass window. She nodded her approval.

'What about catering facilities for the squad?' she asked him. 'Are you arranging for a mobile van to be stationed here?'

His square face broke into a self-satisfied grin. 'Better yet, guv. I went round to the hotel kitchens and dropped a hint in the head chef's ear that our lads and lassies would be needing sustenance. He insisted it'd be no problem for his staff to lay on grub for us all while we're here.'

Kate grinned back. 'Trust you to get your priorities right, Tim. How much did you have to twist his arm?'

'Hardly at all. So we'll all be feeding on smoked salmon and caviar and game pie.'

'I wouldn't count on it. And for God's sake make sure there's a squeaky clean financial arrangement about the food, or I'll be shot at from on high. Get together with Inspector Massey when he arrives tomorrow and ask him to work out a billing procedure with the hotel office.'

All the equipment had now been put in place and the delivery men were gone. The two DCs were hanging around, wondering about their chances of getting off home.

'Thanks, Vic, Jock, for your help. There's nothing more you can do here tonight, so off you go. Tomorrow we should have a full squad and we'll get cracking. There'll be a lot of interviewing to be done here at the hotel, and I'll issue guidelines on some specific questions I want answered.'

They said good night and left. Boulter cocked a hopeful eye at Kate, but she shook her head.

'Forget it, Tim. You and I still have some work to do. For one thing, I'd like to have another talk with Admiral Fortescue tonight. Check if he's back yet from the identification, will you?' She gestured to the wall phone that connected to the hotel switchboard. 'And while you're about it, ask for a line and ring Julie, to warn her you'll be pretty late home.'

'So this is how the rich live,' said Boulter, gazing around. 'Lucky bastards.' He and Kate were crossing the Great Hall of Streatfield Park on their way to interview the admiral.

'Surface gloss, Tim. They've all got their problems, too.'

A man and a woman had just left the restaurant and were heading for the lift. The woman's dress, flame-coloured and clinging to her figure, left her smooth-fleshed shoulders bare. She was stunningly attractive, and Boulter watched with undisguised lust as the man put his arm around her and they laughed together intimately.

'I wouldn't mind having his problems, guv.'

30

They were admitted to the admiral's suite by the steward, Larkin, who eyed them in silent hostility. Admiral Fortescue was seated before a log fire that blazed cheerily against the autumnal chill of the evening. A dinner tray had been pushed aside, the food only pecked at. It didn't surprise Kate that he'd avoided the restaurant this evening.

'This is Detective Sergeant Boulter, sir,' she introduced, adding, as he made a move to rise to his feet, 'Please don't get up.'

He sank back into his armchair and gestured for them to be seated also. To Boulter's disappointment Kate declined the offer of drinks.

'I'll keep this as short as I can, sir, but you'll appreciate the need to obtain all the information we can as soon as possible.'

'Naturally I'm willing to assist your enquiries in any way I can, but I fail to see what you want from me. Poor Corinne was raped before she was strangled, as I now understand it, so it must be a madman you're looking for. A vicious prowler who saw a beautiful woman and couldn't keep his filthy hands off her.' The admiral held up his own two hands, which trembled slightly. 'My God, I'd like to kill the brute for what he did to her. Prison is too good for his sort. He deserves to die.'

'I can understand your feelings, sir. But the chances are that Miss Saxon's assailant was known to her. That's why I'm anxious to find out all I can about her life and the people she knew. And why I shall appreciate your help.'

'Anything, as I said. Anything!'

'First of all, sir, I'm going to ask if you have any idea who might have perpetrated this crime?'

'Good heavens, no. Her death is monstrous beyond belief. I can't imagine any normal man being capable of such a thing. I'm sure you must be mistaken about it not being a stranger.'

'The possibility of that is not being overlooked,' Kate said, 'though we have reason to think it improbable. So if any name should come to your mind in the next day or two, please let me know at once. Meanwhile, I must set about this investigation by making routine enquiries and gathering

31

all the information I can about Miss Saxon, and about the people with whom she came into contact.'

'Very well. What can I tell you about her?'

'To confirm my earlier conversation with you, Admiral Fortescue, the last time you saw Miss Saxon was at about two-fifteen on Wednesday, when she drove off from Streatfield Park after lunching with you. You said that she was planning a few days away, but you had no idea where she was going. Is that correct?'

'That is correct.'

'How would you describe her mood over lunch? Was it any different from usual?'

He considered that, his face sombre. 'Corinne was always a vivacious woman. She sparkled, that's what was so special about her. Perhaps, on Wednesday, she was a little brighter even than usual. The thought of a short break after a long spell of very hard work would have been pleasing to her.'

'Did she give you any hint − the very slightest hint − that she was joining up with a companion?'

The lines on his face deepened in a frown. 'I don't understand you.'

'Is it likely, do you think, that she planned to spend those few days alone?'

He paused for a moment or two, then said, 'She mentioned nothing to me about a companion.'

'What was it that the two of you talked about over lunch?'

Another short pause. 'We discussed future plans for the hotel. Corinne was full of clever ideas in that direction. She was enlarging upon an earlier thought of hers that we should provide conference facilities for groups of business executives.'

'Please tell me, Admiral Fortescue, why it was you chose Miss Saxon for the job of converting Streatfield Park into a hotel and then managing the hotel for you?'

One, two, three seconds. 'I don't see what it is you're driving at. Why should I not have chosen her?'

'I was merely wondering what her qualifications were. Had she had previous experience in the hotel business? Apart from the fact that she was married for a time, I have no information yet on what she was doing in the years since her modelling career ended.'

Kate kept her gaze on the admiral while she waited. He seemed uneasy.

'Corinne had a remarkable grasp of what is required to make a de luxe hotel successful, even though she had no direct experience in the business. She was full of good ideas.'

'So you just said. But what made you seek her out in the first place?'

'I, er ... I did not seek her out. It was her idea. She made the approach to me.'

'Are you saying that Miss Saxon contacted you out of the blue with the suggestion of turning Streatfield Park from a private residence into a luxury hotel? What made her think you might agree to such a scheme? Did you already know each other?'

'Oh, one could hardly say that.'

'But you had met her before?'

'Well, years and years ago. Just a casual meeting. I had quite forgotten about it until Corinne reminded me of the fact when she first wrote to me.'

'I see. Perhaps you'd tell me about that earlier meeting, sir.'

A quick frown that was intended to show his displeasure of her quizzing. 'I fail to see how this is relevant.'

'As I explained, I am trying to discover all I can about Miss Saxon's life. How long ago was it when you first met her? Where?'

He shrugged in curt resignation. 'It must have been ... nearly twenty years ago. I was commanding an aircraft carrier in those days. We were engaged on a Pacific tour of duty and had called in at Singapore. Corinne Saxon happened to be there at the same time on a modelling job, and she was one of the civilians who were invited to an officers' party we were having on board. I don't recall what the occasion was for the celebration. However, I was introduced to Corinne, and in the course of our social chitchat it emerged that she'd been brought up in Cheltenham and knew this part of the Cotswolds fairly well. As I say, I'd forgotten all about the incident until she reminded me of it.'

'I still don't understand, sir. What made Miss Saxon think that someone like you, whom she had only met casually many years ago, would be prepared to give consideration to such revolutionary plans concerning his family home?'

The admiral was growing increasingly impatient and – it seemed to Kate – uneasy. He smiled with a touch of condescension. 'I realise that it must sound somewhat curious to you, suggesting perhaps that I am too easily influenced. But Corinne – Miss Saxon – was very convincing in her approach to me. She had a way of expressing her ideas with great clarity and enthusiasm. How it came about was this. She had happened to read a feature in *Country Life* about the difficulties faced these days in the upkeep of stately homes. Streatfield Park was mentioned as an example, with an excellent photograph of the house taken from the end of the drive. The article referred to my distress at the thought of the Park passing out of the hands of the Fortescue family. I lost my wife several years ago, you see, and I am alone now except for our son, who has settled in America. Dominic is a corporation lawyer, and doing very well. You may possibly have been introduced to him when he came over for our opening ceremony.'

'Yes, I was.' Dominic Fortescue had been accompanied by his American wife and their teenage son and daughter. They were well-mannered people, demonstratively attentive to the paterfamilias, but Kate received the impression that tradition counted for less with them than present affluence. The hotel had struck them as an excellent way to make some real money out of the Fortescue ancestral home.

'I was anxious to avoid Streatfield Park becoming a problem and a burden to Dominic on my death,' the admiral resumed. 'Yet at the same time I wanted to ensure that my grandson and generations after him should retain control over what I regard as their birthright.'

'I see. And on the strength of reading that article, Miss Saxon conceived her plan to create a hotel out of your spacious home?'

'Exactly so. It wasn't, of course, a totally novel idea to me. Other people in my position had adopted a similar course, and I had already considered the possibility of converting to

34

an hotel – among other possibilities – as a solution to my financial problems. You could say, I suppose, that Corinne sowed the seed in my mind when the ground was fertile, and her enthusiasm persuaded me that it would be a worthwhile venture. As indeed it proved to be, Chief Inspector. Already, even though we have been open only five weeks, the hotel shows every sign of being a triumphant success.'

'Will Miss Saxon's death have a serious effect on that success, do you think?'

'Alas, that seems inevitable. Corinne was the driving force of the whole operation. She was the most charming hostess one could possibly imagine.' He sighed. 'But perhaps we shall manage to survive. I certainly hope so.'

'Will your assistant manager, Mr Labrosse, be able to take on overall control?'

'Possibly. I ... I'll have to talk to him. Corinne told me that he was very experienced in all aspects of the hotel trade and that we were lucky to get him.'

'So it was Miss Saxon who engaged him, not you?'

'Corinne engaged all the staff.'

'And was she satisified with him once he was working here?' Kate asked. 'Was there ever any friction between them?'

The admiral's eyes met hers briefly, then flickered as he glanced away. 'It has to be said that Corinne was something of a perfectionist. She would never tolerate anything but the very highest standards.'

'Are you suggesting that Mr Labrosse sometimes fell short of those high standards?'

'Not at all, no ...' When he began after a momentary pause he seemed to be choosing his words with care. 'The other day – at the beginning of this week, Monday, I think – I overheard what sounded like the tail end of an altercation between them. I asked Corinne about it but she merely shrugged and said that Labrosse, like everyone else, needed a crack of the whip now and then to keep him in line.'

'Didn't you insist on knowing what it was about? A sharp difference of opinion between your two most senior staff.'

'I didn't need to know. Corinne dealt with all matters

concerning the hotel.' His expression changed abruptly. 'Can it be that you suspect Labrosse of — '

Yves Labrosse was just one name on Kate's mental list of suspects; a man in Corinne Saxon's orbit who therefore had to be investigated. There were plenty of other men who qualified — including Richard Gower! Including Admiral Fortescue himself. It was time for the question that had to be put.

'I'm a little further forward in my investigation, sir, than when I first spoke to you. We now know that Miss Saxon was killed between the time she left Streatfield Park and 6 p.m. that same day. Accordingly, my officers will be asking everyone at the hotel, staff and guests, to account for their whereabouts on Wednesday afternoon.'

'Oh, really!' he protested. 'Is that necessary?'

'It's essential to my enquiries. But my officers will be instructed to use the utmost tact.' She smiled at him, as if to make light of it. 'Perhaps you could answer that question about yourself.'

The admiral glared at her, his face suffusing with colour. 'Are you suggesting that I might have — '

'I am suggesting nothing, sir. There is no accusation implied. A vital part of the process of a murder enquiry is the elimination of possibilities so as to narrow down the field. So, for the record, will you kindly tell me where you were between the relevant times on Wednesday afternoon? Between two-fifteen and six o'clock.'

'I was where I am every afternoon these days. Here in my suite, resting.'

'Larkin could confirm that, could he?'

He didn't like the suggestion that his word could be doubted. 'As a matter of fact, no. Wednesday was Larkin's afternoon off.'

'Where would he have been at that time?'

'At the health club in Marlingford. Larkin spends every Wednesday afternoon at the gym. He's very keen about keeping in trim.'

This would be checked out by a member of the squad after Larkin's routine questioning.

'Then is there anybody who could confirm your presence here?' Kate persisted. 'Just for the record.'

He said through tight lips, 'Everybody in the hotel would have known where I was.'

'But you were alone, sir?'

'Yes, alone. Naturally. I told you, I was resting.'

'Alone for the entire time?'

'Well, one of the waiters brought me my tea at four o'clock.'

'The waiter's name, please, sir?' asked Boulter, ready to jot it down.

'Let me see ... it would have been Higgs. Yes, that's right, Higgs.'

'Thank you, sir.'

Kate took a breath. No way could this next question be put discreetly. 'How would you describe your relationship with Miss Saxon?'

He flinched visibly. Kate allowed him a little time to find his answer.

'Our relationship, as you put it, was of employer and employee. A very senior and trusted employee.'

'And that was *all* it amounted to, sir?'

'We ... we were on friendly terms. Corinne was an intelligent woman, and I found her interesting to talk to.'

Kate adopted a patient expression that held only a dash of scepticism. 'You have to look at this from my point of view, sir. A woman whom you had met only once before, many years ago, approached you with a business proposition in a field for which it seems she had no special qualifications. Yet you were persuaded to employ her on an exceedingly generous salary, and provide her with accommodation that can only be described as luxurious. All on the strength of her personality and enthusiasm. Is that a fair summary of what you've told me?'

'I have also told you, Chief Inspector, that my faith in Corinne Saxon has been fully vindicated. The hotel is a great success. She earned every penny of her salary.'

'But I can't help asking myself if the relationship between you was perhaps closer than you have suggested.'

'Madam, you are being offensive.'

37

'I'm sorry, sir, I have no wish to be offensive. But I must insist that you answer the question. Was your relationship with Miss Saxon one of intimacy?'

He said with great vehemence, 'No! There was nothing like that. Absolutely not! Corinne and I ... No, not at all. Beyond the fact that I employed her, we were friends, you might say colleagues. Partners. But that was all. I repeat, Chief Inspector, that was all. I swear it.'

'Thank you, sir. I won't trouble you any more at the moment.'

On their way back to the Incident Room, Boulter said with a chuckle, 'Talk about protesting too much! You wouldn't think the old boy had that much go left in him.'

But Kate shook her head. 'No, Tim, they weren't sleeping together. I believe him about that. All the same, he's hiding something.'

'Why didn't you press him harder, then, guv?'

'He's a man with iron self-discipline. His naval training, I suppose. We'll find out what it is he's not telling us if we play it softly, softly.'

In her newly set-up office, Kate waved Boulter into the second chair.

'Before you and I head for home tonight, Tim, I want to run through exactly what we've got on this enquiry so far.'

'Bloody little.'

'Let's try making a few suppositions, then. See where they lead us.' Kate wanted to find a sense of direction, ready for the report she'd need to make to her superintendent in the morning. Luckily for her, Jolly Joliffe had been tied up all day on a budget meeting at Force HQ, and she had only spoken to him briefly over the phone. Tomorrow he'd be on her back demanding to know what progress she'd made.

'Can we believe, Tim, that within minutes of leaving Streatfield Park for a few days' holiday, Corinne Saxon stopped her car and went for a stroll in the woods, where she was attacked by a prowler? It just doesn't add up. In smart clothes like that? In those high-heeled shoes? And why was she carrying a flashlamp when it would still have been daylight?'

'Maybe she was taken short, guv, and stopped for a pee.'

'I can't buy that. No one would feel the need to walk so far into the woods for modesty's sake. Besides, if she had felt the need for a pee so soon after starting out, I think a woman like Corinne Saxon would have hung on till she got to the nearest service station where she'd have found decent facilities. And what about that damned torch?' Kate absently stabbed the point of a pen at the notepad on her desk. 'I can't accept that she went into those woods alone. Not unless it was to meet up with someone there.'

'That sounds good logic to me,' said Boulter.

'Okay, then, let's concentrate on the idea that the man who killed her wasn't a stranger. Either Corinne had fixed in advance for them to meet there, or she entered the woods *with* him. Either of her own free will – because she didn't realise he was dangerous – or she was coaxed there. Or dragged there.'

'She'd have had to have been carried,' Boulter pointed out. 'There were no signs of drag marks.'

'Right. That torch still bothers me, though.'

'It was quite heavy one. A good weapon. Maybe she took it with her because she was scared of the man, whoever he was.'

'Could be.' Kate frowned in thought. 'Admiral Fortescue was very definite about Corinne not saying where she was going for her few days' break. Significant? Maybe she wasn't planning to go far at all. Maybe she was intending to shack-up with some man right here in the vicinity. Maybe she left her car at his place and they came to the woods in his car. But in that case she surely wouldn't have been scared of him and wouldn't have carried the torch as a potential weapon. And we're back again to those fancy shoes.'

Kate was suddenly caught by a huge yawn, which set Boulter off, too.

'None of it seems to make any bloody sense, does it, Tim? So let's get off home for some shut-eye. But bright and early in the morning, mind.'

Home for Kate now was a ground-floor flat in the newly converted stable block of a large old house near Ampney-on-the-Water. Richard Gower had secured it for her by calling in a few favours. Staying with her Aunt Felix at Stonebank Cottage had worked out fine as a temporary measure when she'd first been promoted to the Cotswold Division. But both of them were women who needed their own space. It was four months now since Kate had moved into her own place, and she still marvelled at her good luck every time she arrived home.

Tonight, she switched on lights and admired her living room, all done in restful tones of green and apricot with white paintwork. She hadn't turned on the central heating yet, so for cosiness she lit the log-effect gas fire.

Five minutes later she'd heated a frozen pizza in the microwave and sliced a tomato salad. With a glass of white wine added, she carried the tray in and flopped onto the sofa with her shoes kicked off and her legs tucked up. She flicked around channels on the TV, but there was nothing that appealed. She found herself thinking how good it would be if Richard were here with her. Soon, she hoped, things would be back to normal between them. But first she had a case to solve.

Imprinted on Kate's memory was a vivid image of the murdered woman lying on the damp woodland floor, her clothing stained and torn, her body violated, her magnificent auburn hair lank and grimy, her beautiful face grotesquely distorted by the brutality of her death. And she recalled, with shame, that brief flash of triumph she'd felt on recognising the victim.

She looked down with distaste at the meal she'd prepared, and shoved the tray to one side. Her appetite had suddenly vanished.

Chapter Four

Despite Kate's example-setting early arrival at the Incident Room on Saturday morning. Frank Massey had already installed himself as office manager. As always, wherever the inspector happened to be, an air of calm and order prevailed.

'Am I glad to see you here, Frank! Now I don't have to keep looking over my shoulder for procedural cock-ups.'

He chuckled. 'Truth to tell, Kate, I was damned glad to get called to this job. It's a handy excuse to keep out of the house for a bit. I'm going to find myself a room at a local pub.'

Kate hoisted her eyebrows. 'Hey, it's not too far for you to travel back and forth each day. I had you tagged as a home-lover.'

'The thing is, Louise has got her parents staying with us for a week or so. Lovely people, of course, but a couple of days of their over-eager company is enough to wear me down. I told them how desolated I was that I couldn't stick around for the remainder of their visit.'

'You hypocritical bastard.'

'You reckon I should have told them the ugly truth?'

A couple of blue-overalled Telecom men walked in, carrying boxes of equipment. Frank excused himself and went to get them organised. Kate saw Boulter at a desk across the room, bent over lists he was making. She called out and beckoned him to follow her into her office.

'You look like death this morning, Tim. Got a hangover, have you?'

'No, I have not got a hangover,' he growled, then tacked on, 'ma'am.'

Kate gave him a sharp look. 'Come on, what's up?'

'Julie isn't bloody home, if you must know. When I got back last night there was a note stuck to the fridge saying she'd taken the kids to her sister Brenda's for the weekend. Not a word to me beforehand, oh no!'

Boulter wasn't getting any sympathy from her. 'Didn't you phone to warn her you'd be late, as I suggested? Or had she already left?'

He coloured right up to his sandy eyebrows. 'There didn't seem any point phoning her. She knows what this job's like. Or she damn well ought to by now.'

'And you damn well ought to know what it's like for a woman being stuck at home bringing up two young children, with a husband who seems to care a hell of a lot more about his job than he does about her.'

Boulter gave her a mutinous glare. 'You'd give me a right rollicking, wouldn't you, if I let my private life interfere with my work?'

Suddenly Kate was swept back years. She had a sharp-focus image of her husband's angry face in the early days of their marriage, when she'd been an eager young WPC in London's Met and had once again ruined their plans for the evening by arriving home late. Even phoning from work to warn him hadn't been good enough for Noel. She could clearly hear, as though it were only yesterday, the bitter rage in his voice. 'When it's a case of me or the job, the bloody job wins hands down every time, doesn't it?'

The job of a police officer demanded one hundred per cent dedication, and it bloody wasn't fair! All the same, Kate warned herself, it wasn't part of her working brief to advise her sergeant on how to save his marriage from falling apart. Nor was her advice appreciated, as she'd discovered in the past. *Why the hell can't you keep your big mouth shut, Kate?*

'There's work to do, Tim,' she said briskly. 'I want to get the squad busy interviewing the staff and guests.'

'I've got everybody listed. The hotel office typed up the names for me.'

'Fine. I'll give the lads a little homily first about bearing in mind that this is a functioning hotel and not making ourselves too intrusive, unless we have to. The guests are paying a lot of money to stay here, and they're entitled to be left free of police harassment.'

Refusing to drop his bad mood, Boulter twisted his face into a sneer. 'I bet some of those rich buggers have a few things to keep hidden. We'd uncover the odd can of worms if we did a bit of digging.'

'It's a rape and murder we're investigating,' she reminded him sharply. 'That and nothing else. There's to be no digging for cans of worms just because we envy other people their wealth. Understood?'

Boulter shrugged disgruntledly.

'Understood, sergeant?'

'Yes, ma'am.'

A tap on the door, and Frank Massey looked in. Sensing an atmosphere, he murmured, 'Sorry if I'm interrupting.'

'That's okay, Frank. What do you have there for me?'

He held out a large buff envelope. 'This has just been brought over from DHQ. It was handed in there by Mr Richard Gower, who said he'd promised it to you.'

Kate took the envelope and spread the contents on her desk. Richard had sent a photocopy of the piece in the *Gazette* about Corinne Saxon's ex-husband and his antique shop. He'd also enclosed prints of some pictures taken by the paper's photographer on the hotel's launch day. The one that had appeared in the *Gazette* (copy of feature enclosed) was of Corinne standing between Admiral Fortescue and Adrian Berger, the local architect who had planned the conversion from stately home to hotel, a good-looking man in his late forties whose enthusiasm for the project had been appealing.

Studying the pictures, Kate was reminded again of how stunning Corinne had looked that day in a white crepe silk dress cut dramatically with one shoulder left bare, tight sleeves to the wrists, and a dragon motif embroidered across the bodice in gold thread. Her gleaming red hair had been caught up in a loose swathe to one side so that soft tendrils just caressed that bare shoulder.

If Corinne Saxon had currently been married, Kate

43

reminded herself, her husband would be the first person she'd need to eliminate from suspicion. Or not eliminate. An ex-husband, even though they'd been divorced for several years, still qualified to be checked out.

'We'll go and pay a call on this man Paul Kenway, Tim, and see what he's got to say for himself.'

Ashecombe-in-the-Vale was one of the Cotswold's loveliest villages, a magnet for tourists. Already, even before nine-thirty in the morning, its wide main street was busy with sightseers, and cameras were much in evidence.

Boulter, spotting a postman emptying the box outside the sub-post office, pulled up alongside him. 'Kenway Antiques, mate?'

The man straightened up and pointed. 'It's the first place on the left over the bridge. There's a sign up. You can't miss it.' His glance followed them curiously as they drove on; he'd scented police, even though their car was unmarked.

Seen from across the river, the gabled building glowed a rich tawny gold in the morning sun, its paintwork glinting white. Built a couple of hundred years ago, Kate guessed. With gardens sweeping down to the river bank, its situation was superb. It was only as they drew closer, swinging in through the double gate and stopping in the small parking bay provided, that she noticed signs of neglect. The painted window frames were cracked and peeling; heavy wooden props shored up the wall on one side.

A hanging sign read *Kenway Antiques, Stripped Pine a Speciality*. Taped behind a small glass pane of the front door, a postcard with felt-pen lettering invited them to enter. As they did so, a bell on a coiled spring was set tinkling.

The aim here was to suggest that this was a lived-in home. Furniture and other pieces were arranged around the hallway and adjoining rooms in a fairly convincing manner, with price tags discreetly placed. But the whole place looked dowdy and depressing somehow. There simply wasn't enough good-quality stuff to support a thriving business.

A woman appeared through a doorway, carrying a feather duster. She was tall and big-boned, in her late thirties, with a mass of dark hair bunched back in a white chiffon scarf.

Her features were good and she could have looked really attractive, but the gloss was missing. Kate noted from the bulge beneath her grubby pink tracksuit that she was about three months pregnant.

'Yes?' Even the tone of voice was lacklustre.

'We'd like to talk to Mr Kenway, please.'

'What about?'

'It's a private matter.'

'I'm his wife.'

Kate introduced herself and Boulter. 'I need to speak to your husband, Mrs Kenway. Is he here?'

'No, he's just popped down to the village for a minute. What is this about?'

Most of the national papers had reported the murder, and the local radio station had gone to town on it. If Mrs Kenway had caught the news bulletins this morning she must surely have guessed why the police had come calling. But the questioning look on her face gave nothing away.

There was the sound of another car drawing up outside. Kate turned to see the driver get out and start walking hurriedly towards the door. He carried a folded newspaper. Entering quickly, he stopped in his tracks at seeing her and Boulter there.

His wife said hastily, as if to stifle anything revealing he might blurt out, 'They're from the police, Paul.'

He immediately paled, the blood draining from his face. He was a thin man standing around five foot ten, and Kate put his age at forty-five rather than the fifty-five he looked. Deep creases tramlined his forehead beneath a rather obvious toupee. He'd been good-looking once, and probably well off financially, too – it was difficult to imagine Corinne Saxon marrying any man who wasn't. But now he had an aura of failure, of lost hope. Scrutinising his features, Kate could see no firmness anywhere; not in chin, mouth, nose or eyes. Right now, his eyes held a look of fear.

'We'd like a word with you, Mr Kenway,' she said. 'I'm Detective Chief Inspector Maddox, South Midlands Police, and this is Detective Sergeant Boulter.'

He didn't speak, but just stared at her. His wife said again, aggressively, 'What's this about?'

Kate nodded at the newspaper he held. 'I take it, Mr Kenway, that you've seen about Miss Corinne Saxon?'

Denial trembled on his lips, but what was the use? He nodded his head with a little jerk. 'I've just this minute read about it.' To his wife, he explained, 'Corinne is dead, Liz. Her body was found in the woods at East Dean yesterday. She'd been strangled. Raped and strangled, it says.'

'Oh, my God! But ... who on earth ...?'

'We know that it must have happened on Wednesday afternoon,' Kate told them. 'We shall therefore be interviewing every man who had any known connection with Miss Saxon, to ascertain his whereabouts at the time. So would you please tell me, Mr Kenway, where *you* were on Wednesday afternoon? Between two-fifteen and six o'clock.'

Both the Kenways seemed to sag under the impact of Kate's challenge. She was content to wait, watching them closely. Finally, it was the wife who gave an answer.

'Paul was here, with me.'

'For the whole of that time?'

'Well ... we closed at five-thirty − just after − and went upstairs. We live on the premises.'

'Is that correct, Mr Kenway?'

If his wife was telling the truth, why was he looking at her with that glazed expression? It was as if he couldn't understand why she should have provided him with an alibi that would get him off the hook.

'The chief inspector asked if what Mrs Kenway says is correct,' Boulter prodded him.

'Of course it is. Of course. My wife and I were here, just as she says.'

'The entire afternoon?' Kate persisted.

'Yes.'

'Who apart from Mrs Kenway could confirm that you were here?'

He took a measurable time to react, then shook his head slowly. 'I can't think of anyone.'

'Presumably you had some customers that afternoon? If you can give us one or two names, we could check with them.'

Another shake of the head.

46

'Any phone calls?'

'I don't remember any.'

'Mrs Kenway?'

'The people who came in on Wednesday,' she said, 'were only chance callers. Tourists, just looking. I didn't know any of them, and nobody bought anything. So you'll just have to take our word for it.' She had pulled herself together now and there was defiance in her tone.

'When was the last time you saw Miss Saxon?' asked Kate, addressing Kenway.

The question seemed to catch him as a fresh assault. He was totally floored, and his wife answered for him.

'It was about a month ago. She came here.'

'Liz!' It emerged as a shocked reproach.

'She's bound to find out, Paul. Very likely she knew already, and that's why she's here.'

'It sounds,' said Kate, allowing this mistaken thought to stand uncorrected, 'as if you don't like the idea of my knowing about it. Why's that, I wonder?'

Kenway seemed incapable of contributing to this dialogue. After an uneasy pause, his wife shrugged her broad shoulders.

'Just that it wasn't a particularly pleasant occasion.'

'Oh?'

'Well, you wouldn't expect it to be, would you? I mean, us two women meeting for the first time.'

'The first time, eh? How did that come about?'

'It had nothing to do with her getting killed, so I don't see what business it is of yours.'

'Everything to do with Corinne Saxon is my business now,' Kate said calmly. 'This is a murder enquiry, Mrs Kenway. I want to know the circumstances of that meeting.'

The woman glanced at her husband in helpless apology, then said, 'Paul got in touch with her. It was the first time they'd been in touch for years. We'd read in the papers about her managing that fancy hotel so we knew she must be doing all right for herself these days. I thought – Paul and I thought – that it was about time we were let off what he had to pay her each month under the divorce settlement.'

Kate recalled Corinne's bank statements and made a stab. 'That four hundred pounds a month?'

'It can't have meant much to her,' Liz said in a falsely casual tone that didn't conceal a deep-felt bitterness. 'Yet to us, saving that amount would have made the world of difference. Paul's had a lot of bad luck since the agreement was made.'

'What sort of bad luck?'

'Well, he and another man had set up in business together, dealing in personal computers and stuff like that. At around the time he and Corinne got married, the firm was doing very well. Then Paul discovered that his partner was making deals behind his back and couldn't be trusted. He agreed to let Paul buy him out, but that meant Paul had to borrow a terrific lot of money. With a huge debt like that the business was no longer making a profit and things were getting difficult. I reckon that Corinne saw the writing on the wall. She made life sheer hell for Paul, and in the end he was thankful to divorce her, even though it meant agreeing to that unfair settlement. Paul and I met soon afterwards, and when I got left this house by an aunt of mine we hit on the idea of running an antiques business from home. Only somehow it's never worked out. People don't seem to have the money to spend these days.' Her hands slipped to her stomach, holding the bulge protectively. 'Now that I'm pregnant, it's going to be tougher than ever for us.'

Born losers, the pair of them!

'But Corinne refused to agree to the monthly payments being stopped?'

'There was nothing really unpleasant when she came. No quarrel or anything.' Kenway had finally kicked himself into the conversation. Like his wife, he was patently trying to play down the episode. 'I just phoned Corinne at Streatfield Park one day and told her I'd like to see her to discuss something. She said okay, and that she'd drop in here when she was over this way. Which she did. Liz and I explained the situation to her, but we couldn't make Corinne see things our way. She took the line that a legal agreement was binding and she wasn't willing to release me from it. So that was that.'

'You felt angry about her attitude, no doubt?'

'Disappointed, naturally, but – '

'No, Mr Kenway, the chief inspector said *angry*,' Boulter

48

intervened, coming the hard man. 'Angry enough, perhaps, to decide to see her again on your own?'

He gazed from one to the other of them, a hunted look in his eyes. 'You surely aren't suggesting that I ...?'

Kate decided to terminate the interview. It would do no harm to leave him to sweat.

'I shall require you to make a formal statement. And you too, Mrs Kenway. At a police station. Someone will be in touch with you to arrange it. That will be all for now.'

Husband and wife stood in silence as the police car drove off. In the deep hush, Liz's voice was low and determinedly challenging.

'Well, Paul?'

He gave her an unconvincing smile. 'Well, what, darling?'

'Oh, please, don't pretend with me. I had to cover for you about last Wednesday, and I want to know why the hell it was necessary.'

'Not *necessary*,' he insisted, 'just helpful. When you told them that I'd been here with you, it seemed a much better idea than just having to say I was driving around looking at antiques, and being unable to prove exactly where I was. So I went along with what you'd said.'

'For God's sake, Paul, do you think I'm stupid? Do you really believe I was taken in by your story about looking around the antique shops that afternoon? I knew all along you were lying to me. I always know if you're lying.' Her voice trembled. 'But now I want the truth — however bad it is.'

His eyes avoided hers. 'You surely don't think that I had anything to do with Corinne's death?'

'How am I supposed to know what to think?' she said on a sob. 'You've been so odd just lately, so mysterious and evasive.'

'Sweetheart, you're imagining things.'

His wife looked up at him, her strained face crumpling in her distress. 'Oh, Paul, why can't you tell me the truth? Why can't you trust me?'

'Please, Liz, don't ask me any more questions. Not now. Give me time to think. Get my mind sorted out. Believe me,

49

there are things it's best for you not to know. One day, perhaps ... but not now.'

The bell above the shop door pinged, and in came a forty-something couple. Their smiles were bright with the apology of people who are only intending to browse, not to buy.

'Good morning,' the man said. 'Er, do you mind if we look around?'

Liz Kenway took a quick, controlling breath. 'Not at all. Please go ahead.' To Paul, she muttered, 'You can't make me forget about this. I'm determined to know the truth. I've got to know.'

On Kate's instructions Boulter drove her first to Divisional Headquarters. He parked the car in the DCI's personal space in the forecourt.

'Be back here in half an hour, Tim.'

'Great,' he said. 'That'll just give me time for a quick snack.'

In her own office Kate made a couple of calls to tender apologies about tasks she was having to postpone. Then she set forth for the superintendent's room.

Knocking and hearing his brusque 'Enter!', she walked in and found Jolly Joliffe on his feet studying a wall chart. Seeing who it was, he promptly stepped to his desk and plonked himself down in his chair. This, Kate surmised, was an attempt to make a point. He'd learned to be wary of her, seeming bewildered by this strange new creature, a *female* detective chief inspector. Kate had endeavoured (with only limited success) to show that she expected the treatment owed to her rank, not the treatment a well-brought-up man of his generation imagined was due to the weaker sex. The strain of acting towards her contrary to his instincts resulted in Jolly switching unpredictably between favouring her with tea served in delicate Royal Worcester china, and addressing her more abrasively than he might have done a male chief inspector.

'Good morning, sir,' Kate said in her brightest voice.

'Aren't you somewhat tardy, Mrs Maddox, in coming to report to me?'

'I've been at Ashecombe-in-the-Vale interviewing the dead woman's ex-husband,' she explained mildly, as she sat down.

He aha-ed, a wintry smile lighting his lugubrious face. 'So that's the answer, is it? Ex with a grudge! Have you brought him in with you?'

'The case is far too wide open for that, sir.'

'Hmph! What else do you have, then?'

Kate related what little else there was as yet. 'I'm very much hoping we'll get a lead on that missing car soon. That would be a big help. And of course I'm waiting to hear about the post mortem and the forensic findings. Hopefully they'll give us something more positive to work on.'

'It's facts I want to see brought to light in a murder enquiry, not a lot of half-arsed hopes and maybes. Solid, indisputable facts. Something we can really get our teeth into.'

'Absolutely,' she agreed, having a job not to giggle.

He regarded her with vexed suspicion, scratching the side of his long nose with one finger. Kate returned his gaze with serene optimism. After a few moments of this eyeball contact, the superintendent waved a dismissive hand.

'Very well, Mrs Maddox, off you go and get on with the job. And bring me a result with all possible speed, eh?'

Humour the old bugger, Kate.

'I will, sir. You can rely on me for that.'

By the time Kate and Boulter returned to Streatfield Park, the Incident Room was fully operational. Both uniformed and plain-clothes oficers plus a few civilian personnel manned the desks and computer terminals. Kate knew that before long information would be avalanching in, all needing to be analysed, stored, and painstakingly cross-indexed.

'A couple of interesting items have emerged from this morning's interviews,' Inspector Massey told her. 'I've put them on top of the pile on your desk.'

'Right. I'd like to have a briefing of the squad this after-noon, Frank. Four o'clock, okay?'

In her office, Kate scanned the paragraphs highlighted by Frank Massey on the two top reports. The first concerned some guests, an American couple named Rubinstein. These were the people, she remembered, whom Corinne had accompanied to Bath (and probably the elegant couple she herself had noticed when she'd arrived at the hotel yesterday afternoon to break the news of the murder). Mr and Mrs Rubinstein had visited Paris before coming to England, and while chatting with Corinne they'd told her how much they'd enjoyed the city. Corinne said she knew Paris well, and added that she was off there on Wednesday for a few days. Then she laughed, and said that as a matter of fact it was a little secret, so she'd rather they didn't mention it to anyone else. Which neither of the Rubinsteins had done, until questioned by the police.

'There's no mention here of any companion,' Kate observed to her sergeant. 'I simply can't believe that she'd be spending time in Paris alone.'

'Nor can I,' said Boulter feelingly, his eyes going to the *Gazette* photographer's pictures of Corinne that were now pinned to the wall. 'A shocking waste, if she had been.'

Kate moved on to the other highlighted report. The hotel receptionist, June Elsted, had spoken of taking a phone call for Miss Saxon late on Wednesday afternoon. The caller was informed that she wasn't there and that she'd be away for the next few days. But on Thursday evening the same man had phoned again and asked for Miss Saxon. Both times he declined to leave a message and had been evasive about giving his name.

'Very interesting.' Kate flicked a glance at Boulter, who was reading over her shoulder. 'Are you thinking what I'm thinking?'

'You reckon he might have been phoning to check if the body had been found yet?'

'Could be.' She looked for the name of the interviewing officer. 'See if Vic Rolfe is around, will you?'

Rolfe, she knew from past experience, was a hard-working detective, reliable and conscientious, but unimaginative. He entered Kate's office wearing a deeply worried expression on his blunt-featured face, as if he expected a reprimand without quite knowing why he might deserve one. He looked relieved at her friendly tone of voice.

'Ah, Vic. This report of yours on June Elsted and the man

who phoned asking to speak to Corinne Saxon. How did she know it was the same caller both times, if he didn't give his name?'

'Er, she didn't explain that, ma'am.'

'Did you get the feeling that she knew the caller's identity?'

Rolfe shook his head slowly, the worry back in place. 'Maybe that's what she meant, ma'am. I suppose I should have asked her. I'll get back to her right away, shall I, and clear it up?'

'No, leave it. Go and get on with your next interview.'

Boulter sniffed when he'd departed. 'Stupid bugger, I'd have given him a rollicking.'

'Just remember, Tim, if he was as bright as you are, he'd have been a sergeant by now.'

'And I'd be a chief inspector if I was as bright as you are, yeah?'

'What, at your tender age?' she said with a laugh as she picked up the phone.

'Miss Elsted? Chief Inspector Maddox here. I wonder if you could get someone to deputise for you on the desk for a few minutes. I'd like to have a chat with you right away.'

'Oh?' She sounded wary. 'What about?'

'If you could just pop over to my office in the squash courts. I won't keep you long.'

The receptionist was plainly nervous as she was shown in. Kate invited her to sit down.

'It concerns the man who phoned asking for Miss Saxon on Wednesday and again on Thursday. It's important that we trace this person, so I want your help. Did you recognise who it was speaking? Or did you just mean that his voice was distinctive enough for you to be sure it was the same man each time?'

'Well ... both, sort of.'

'Please explain.'

June Elsted was hesitant. 'I'd hate saying anything if it turned out that I'd made a mistake. I mean, Miss Saxon being raped like that, and then strangled. I'd feel terrible if I got someone into a lot of trouble with the police when it wasn't him at all.'

53

'You needn't worry, we'll be very discreet. But this is a murder enquiry, June, so you must tell us everything you know that might have a bearing on the case.'

She nodded, still miserable. 'I'm pretty sure it was one of the guests. One of the past guests, I should say. He and his wife stayed here for a few days a couple of weeks ago. Of course, he could have just been phoning to make another reservation. Perhaps he thought he'd do better going direct to Miss Saxon.'

'Who is this man?'

'Mr Arliss. Mr James Arliss. He didn't give me his name on either Wednesday or Thursday, as I told that other detective. But I recognised the voice from when he phoned originally to make a reservation. You see, I entered him in the computer as Mr Arl*ith*, with a *th*. That's what it sounded like. Fortunately, when they arrived it was his wife who came up to the desk while he was giving instructions about the luggage, and of course she said Arl*iss* quite clearly, and I was able to correct the error without her realising that I'd got their name wrong.'

'What you're saying,' Kate said, 'is that he speaks with a lisp?'

'Well, only a slight one. But on Wednesday and Thursday the caller asked for Miss *Thackthon*, like that, and it reminded me of the other man.'

'You're certain in your own mind that it was Mr Arliss, aren't you?'

'I ... I wouldn't want to have to swear it was, or anything.'

'Yes, I understand. Let's assume for the moment that it *was* him. What made you think he might have wanted to make another reservation and imagined he'd do better going direct to Miss Saxon?'

'Well, some people always go straight to the top, don't they?' But she said it evasively.

'I think,' said Kate, giving her a direct look, 'that you can give me a better answer than that.'

'I don't know what you mean.'

'Tell me,' Kate said flatly. 'Come on, now.'

The silence stretched while the receptionist sat looking

cornered. Boulter shifted his feet and was about to say something. But his preliminary throat clearing was enough to trigger her into a babble of words that came out in jerky little spurts.

'I ... I don't want to give you the wrong idea. I mean, it mightn't really have been how it looked. You see, it was only once I actually ... and even then, well, I can't be absolutely sure how serious it was, can I?'

'Just slow down, June, and explain what you're saying.' Kate spoke calmly, encouragingly. 'There was something going on between Mr Arliss and Miss Saxon, right?'

'Yes.' It was said in a whisper. But her voice suddenly gained strength as she continued, and Kate realised she was beginning to enjoy her role as witness. 'Well, it was pretty plain that Mr and Mrs Arliss didn't hit it off very well. At meals, they hardly said a word to one another, just acted polite, and they mostly did quite separate things while they were here. The staff all noticed, it was so obvious. Anyway, I several times saw him and Miss Saxon chatting and laughing together, in the bar or wherever. But then, Miss Saxon did that with a lot of the guests, so I didn't take too much notice. One afternoon, though, Mr Labrosse was off duty and Deirdre — that's the secretary — was away sick. Someone phoned to make an appointment to see Mr Labrosse, so I walked through to the office to check in his desk diary. I had no idea anyone was in there.'

'And?'

'It was Miss Saxon and Mr Arliss. In a real clinch, they were, and it looked as they'd been at it for some time. I just stood there in the doorway, completely stunned, and they broke apart. Miss Saxon was furious, and she yelled at me to get out. I just turned and ran. She could be really nasty when she wanted.'

'Did you tell anyone else about this?'

'No, I didn't dare. I mean, if it had got out among the staff she'd have known it was through me, wouldn't she, and I like my job here. After a few minutes Mr Arliss came out and he stopped by the desk and pressed a ten-pound note into my hand. He winked at me and put a finger to his lips. But it wasn't because of him I kept quiet, it was because of her.'

'I see. Very well, June, you can go now. When you get back to the reception desk, look up Mr Arliss's address for me, please, and call me back with it.'

As the door closed behind her, Boulter said, 'Sounds as if we're on to something with this Arliss guy. Could be he wanted kinkier sex from our victim than she was ready to give him. Shall we pull him in?'

'I'd really like to take him by surprise before he has time to cook up a good story.' Kate considered. 'Thank God it's Saturday, but I can't afford a long wasted journey if he's not at home. He probably lives miles away.'

When the phone rang, Boulter picked it up. 'Oh yes, Miss Elsted, I'll take it down.' He scribbled. 'And the phone number, if you have it.' He jotted that down, too. 'Thanks.'

'How far is it, Tim?'

'We're in luck, guv. Arliss lives at Marlow, less than fifty miles at a guess.' Still holding the phone the sergeant punched out a sequence of digits, waited, then said, 'Sorry, wrong number.' Slamming down the phone, he announced triumphantly, 'He's at home as of this minute, guv.'

'Can you be certain it was Arliss himself who answered?'

'Want to bet? I was listening for it, and he obliged. The guy said, "Four, three, one, thix, theven."'

The phone rang again just as they were about to leave ten minutes later. Boulter answered.

'It's Dr Meddowes for you, guv. Can't be a post-mortem result yet, surely?'

Kate held out her hand for the phone. 'Good morning, Dr Meddowes. Does this mean you've completed your p.m.?'

'Certainly not! You should know that a postmortem cannot be hurried.'

She waited while he huffed and puffed a bit. 'I'm never happy about giving my findings piecemeal, Chief Inspector.' *Never*? He'd been the police pathologist for about five minutes! 'But there is a matter about which I thought you should be informed at this early stage.'

Kate made an uh-huh sound that was meant to convey interest and gratitude.

56

'You'll be getting my full report in due course, but I think this piece of evidence might make a difference to your line of enquiry. So I have decided to put you in the picture without delay, even though my examination of the deceased is not yet complete.'

For crying out loud. Patience, Kate!

'Good of you, doctor,' she murmured.

He paused dramatically. 'This woman, Corinne Saxon, was not raped.'

'*What*? Or do you just mean that penetration wasn't achieved?'

'I mean precisely what I said. She was not raped, and I would further hazard a guess that rape was never his intention. The man meant it to appear so, which accounts for the torn clothing and exposure of naked flesh. And you, my dear Chief Inspector, fell straight into his trap. I suppose, to be fair, it is always difficult for a woman to be properly objective about rape. Even,' he added heavily, 'when that woman is a senior police officer.'

'I'd be grateful, Dr Meddowes,' she said between clenched teeth, 'if you'd tell me what led you to this conclusion.'

'My findings will be presented in detail in my report. But to summarise, there is no sign of bruising in the region of the vulva, no blood staining, no trace of seminal fluid. And no foreign pubic hairs. There is no sign whatever of recent sexual activity. In short, Mrs Maddox, no man could commit rape, nor attempt rape, without leaving a trail of evidence to that effect. There is a total absence of any such evidence in this case.'

Chapter Five

A few stray wisps of white cloud only highlighted the intense blue of the sky. The September sun, lower now than in full summer, laid a coat of shimmering gilt across the English countryside. But Kate and her sergeant were too preoccupied to appreciate the beauty of it.

They'd had to delay setting out for Marlow in order to brief the squad on the new development. Now, as Kate's Montego ate up the miles under Boulter's fast, capable driving, they tried to reassess each of their potential suspects against the discovery that Corinne Saxon had not in fact been raped.

'What I still don't get, guv, is why the hell it was made to *look* like rape.'

'Presumably to mislead us into thinking that she was attacked by a total stranger. But we'd already discounted the likelihood of that, hadn't we?'

'Our chummy, whoever he is, must have felt confident we'd never dream that *he* might have raped her.'

'Right, Tim. He ... or she.'

The sergeant shot her a startled glance. 'You reckon it could have been a woman?'

'That does become a possibility now, doesn't it? A strong woman could have strangled her.'

'A jealous wife, you think? *Mrs* Arliss, rather than Mr?'

'We'll need to check out her alibi, certainly. Or it could equally have been the angry wife of an ex-husband.'

Boulter accelerated past a slow-moving truck. 'That Elizabeth Kenway is pretty hefty. Pregnant, of course.'

'But only three months.'

The Marlow police, with whom Kate and Boulter cleared this intrusion into their territory, gave them directions to the house called Oakleigh, the home of Mr and Mrs James Arliss. It was of recent vintage, probably built for its present owners. Like its neighbours it stood well back from the road, and was nicely separated from the next-door houses by spacious gardens. Kate noted a garage wide enough for three large cars.

'They're not short of a bob or two,' Boulter observed, as they swung in between the white-painted gateposts. 'But then they wouldn't be, if they could afford to stay at a ritzy place like Streatfield Park.'

A man in jeans and a green sweatshirt was clipping a tall box hedge with electric shears. Noticing the car, he switched off and laid the tool down on the grass, then came towards them.

'We're here to see Mr Arliss,' said Kate, getting out of the car.

'That ith me. How can I help you?' The standard English voice was close to Eton and Oxford; but not, Kate judged, quite the genuine article. James Arliss was six foot one or two and well built, with good muscle tone for a man of middle years. His hair, still plentiful, was professionally styled and discreetly tinted, with the temples left grey to add distinction.

Kate introduced herself and Boulter. 'We'd like a few words with you, sir. Perhaps we could go inside.'

Arliss didn't move. 'What ith thith about?'

'It's in connection with Miss Corinne Saxon, sir, of the Streatfield Park Hotel. You were a friend of hers?'

'A friend of hers? Oh, hardly –' He broke off, and began again. 'I heard about Mith Thackthon's death on the radio this morning. A dreadful businith. But what makes you think I'm in any position to help you?' Then he added, as if suddenly aware that they might be overheard in the open air, 'You had better come inthide.'

He led the way into the house through a side door. Kate neither heard nor saw anything to suggest that his wife was around. They passed through a spacious hall and finished up in a smallish room clearly used as a study. He gestured them into chairs, but himself remained standing.

'Now, Chief Inthpector, why have you come to thee me?'

'We are interviewing everyone who had any connection with Miss Saxon recently, sir. You qualify, as a one-time guest at the hotel.'

'Oh yeth, I thee.'

'I understand, Mr Arliss, that you and Miss Saxon were rather interested in one another.'

'Who told you that?' he jerked out.

'It doesn't matter who told me, sir. Are you denying it?'

'Good heavens, it didn't amount to anything.' He made a weak attempt at a smile. 'Mith Thackthon was motht agreeable company. She was very friendly towards all the hotel guethts.'

'Did you ever spend time with Miss Saxon without your wife being present?'

'Now really! I resent that.'

'Please answer the chief inspector's question, sir,' said Boulter.

He pinked around the gills. 'Well, I thuppose I did. Actually, I do theem to recall an occasion when he had a couple of drinkth in the bar while Dawn was upthtairs drething for dinner.'

'Hmm. Why did you telephone Miss Saxon the other day?' Kate asked.

His mouth opened, but quickly closed again.

'Have you nothing to say, Mr Arliss? You telephone Streatfield Park asking for Miss Saxon on Wednesday evening, and again on Thursday. Please tell me why you did so.'

'Oh, that!' he said, with an exaggerated miming of recall.

Kate watched him. Boulter watched him. Arliss sat down behind the desk, leaned back in his chair and crossed his legs to demonstrate how totally at ease he was.

'I was just phoning to, er, to athk about making another reservation at the hotel.'

'For you and your wife?'

'As a little thurprise for Dawn.' He paused before adding, 'It's her birthday the week after next.'

'But you wouldn't speak to anyone but Miss Saxon about it. Why was that?'

'She thaid ... Mith Thackthon thaid that if we ever wanted to book in at short notice, to ring her perthonally and she'd arrange things. Make sure we were given a good thuite and tho on.'

Time to chance your arm, Kate! 'But Miss Saxon was supposed to be in Paris at the time you phoned, Mr Arliss. In Paris with you, Mr Arliss.'

He gaped at her for long moments. 'That,' he said at last, his voice strained to near the point of cracking, 'ith preposterous.'

You're on a winning streak, Kate! Ride it.

'Are you denying that you made arrangements with Miss Saxon for a trip to Paris? Just the two of you.'

He didn't answer, looking cornered. Kate continued, 'What was the real purpose of those two phone calls to the hotel? Was it because you were anxious to ascertain whether Corinne Saxon's body had yet been discovered?'

He jumped to his feet, and his bellowed protest reverberated around the small room. 'No, no, no! You've got it all wrong. Good God, what thort of a monthter do you think I am?'

'Please sit down, Mr Arliss. I just want you to tell me the truth.'

Sinking back into the chair, he shot her an imploring look. 'Can we keep thith private, Chief Inthpector? I mean, I wouldn't want my wife to ... to ...'

'Where is your wife, sir? I shall need to speak to her also.' Kate raised a hand to stem Arliss's horrified objection. 'It's not our intention to make trouble for you, and we shan't reveal any more than is strictly necessary. But that's the best promise I can give you.'

He nodded wretchedly. 'My wife ith away. She's visiting her mother in Scarborough.'

'Give me the address, please, sir,' said Boulter, and wrote it down in his notebook.

'How long has your wife been in Scarborough?' Kate enquired.

'She went there latht Thaturday. Her mother had an operation, and Dawn went up to be with her.'

'When will she be returning?'

'Not for another week at leatht, I imagine.'

If this checked out, it would be one suspect eliminated from the enquiry. Kate said next, 'Tell me about your relationship with Miss Saxon, please, sir.'

He gestured with his hands to signify helplessness. 'I thuppose it was that girl, the retheptionist, who told you? I knew she might be a problem, but Corinne laughed and thaid she'd put the fear of God into her.'

Kate waited, her face expressing nothing beyond a calm determination to get at the truth.

'Corinne was a very thpecial kind of woman, Chief Inthpector. Damned attractive, of courthe, but more than just that.'

'You and she embarked on a sexual relationship while you and your wife were staying at the hotel? Is that correct, sir?'

'Well ... I thuppose you could say – '

'Yes or no, sir?'

'Well, we did, but only on the one occasion.'

'How did this projected trip to Paris come about?'

He looked down at his hands. His fingers were twisting restlessly. 'Corinne thaid she had thome time off due to her, and we left it that I'd get in touch as thoon as ... an opportunity occurred. When Dawn had to visit her mother, I thought – '

'How exactly did you make the arrangements?'

'I, er, I phoned Corinne. The previous Thursday. We fixed it then.'

Kate nodded. 'Go on.'

'I thaid I'd make all the bookings, and we agreed that we'd each drive to Heathrow theparately. That theemed the best way. When Corinne didn't show up at the coffee shop where we'd arranged to meet, I became anxious.' He paused and made a face. 'The truth is, I wath afraid she'd thtood me up. After I'd been waiting for over an hour I phoned Streatfield Park, and they told me that Mith Thackthon had gone away for a few days. I didn't know what to make of it. I hung around hoping that she'd thtill turn up and we could take a later flight. Finally I gave up and came back home. The next day I phoned Streatfield Park again from here, just in cathe she'd returned there by then; in cathe there'd been thome kind of mix-up and we'd mithed each other.'

'And what have you been doing since?'

'Well, I've just thayed at home. I'd told my offith that I would be away for a few days, so it theemed best not to return there. Anyway, I wanted to be here in cathe Corinne phoned.'

'Where is your office, sir?' asked Boulter.

'In Reading. I'm a partner in a firm of chartered account-ants.' He gave the name and address for the sergeant to note down.

Kate said, 'Miss Saxon was killed some time between her leaving the hotel at about two-fifteen on Wednesday, and six o'clock that same day. I must ask you to account for your movements between those times, Mr Arliss.'

'For God's thake,' he exploded, 'you can't imagine that I had anything to do with her death.'

'At this stage of our enquiries,' Kate said soothingly, 'my aim is to eliminate possibilities. We are asking every man who was in any way connected with Miss Saxon to account for his movements during the relevant times. But I must advise you, sir, that considering the special nature of your relationship with the deceased, your full co-operation in telling us what we need to know would be very much to your advantage.'

Arliss glared at her resentfully for a moment, then nodded his acquiescence. 'I set out from here at about two-thirty.'

'Was anyone at home when you left?'

'No, my wife is away, as I told you?'

'Perhaps a domestic help? A gardener?'

'No, our cleaning woman only comes in the morning, and we don't have a regular gardener. Dawn and I like to do motht of the garden work ourthelves.'

'Would a neighbour have seen you leave? Anyone?'

'I doubt it. There's a good deal of thpace between these houses, as you must have theen, and it's always quiet on a weekday afternoon.'

'Did you drive directly to Heathrow? Or did you stop anywhere on the way?'

'No, I didn't thtop. It would have taken me about forty

minutes, and then I parked the car and went to the terminal building.'

'Did you check in your luggage?'

'No, I only had hand luggage.' Before Kate could speak again, he rushed on eagerly, 'I thtill have the airline tickets. I can fetch them now. That will prove to you that I was there.'

Kate shook her head. 'Possession of the tickets isn't proof that you were ever at the airport. You must see that.'

Arliss pressed his lips together in a grimace. 'I thuppose not.'

'What did you do once you reached the terminal building? What precisely?'

'Let me thee. First I vithited the men's room, then I went thtraight to the coffee shop where Corinne and I had arranged to meet. After a while, though, I began to grow anxious and I walked over to the check-ins to thee if by chance she'd misunderthood where I'd thaid to meet. Then I hurried back to the coffee shop in cathe she'd arrived in the meantime.'

'You remained at the coffee shop for how long?'

'About an hour and a half, all told, though theveral times I made a quick reconnoitre of the check-ins, and twice I enquired at the information desk if there was a message for me. I waited around until long after our flight had left, hoping against all the odds that she'd just been delayed by traffic or thomething. We could have taken a later flight.'

'All the time you were at the airport, did you speak to anyone who might remember you? Apart from the information desk.'

'I thuppose the staff at the coffee shop might remember me. I was sitting there a long time, and I bought theveral cups of coffee.'

Some hope he'd be remembered, considering the number of people they served each day.

'If you story is to be substantiated, Mr Arliss, you must try to give us something to go on. Think hard, did you get into conversation with anyone we might be able to trace?'

He nodded, looking unhappy. 'As a matter of fact, while I was waiting there an acquaintance of mine came over to join me. We chatted for a few minutes, then his gate number came up on the thcreen and he left.'

'What time was this?'

'I really can't say. His flight was to Bruthelth.'

'This gentleman's name, please, sir,' said Boulter.

'Ian Pollock.' Arliss looked at the sergeant in dismay, then at Kate. 'Is it really nethessary for you to thpeak to him about this?'

'Yes, but it won't be necessary to tell him what it's in connection with. Give the sergeant his address, please.'

He did so reluctantly. 'That's his offithe. He's a tholicitor. I'd rather you didn't go to his home. His wife and mine play bridge together.'

Kate regarded him thoughtfully across the desk. 'Mr Arliss, if you're telling me the truth and you *weren't* involved in Miss Saxon's death, then someone else *was*. In view of your special relationship, you must be particularly anxious to assist the police in tracking down her killer.'

'I only wish I could help.' He breathed deeply as rage seemed to build up in him. 'A vicious thex-maniac like that hath got to be caught.'

'We now know that Miss Saxon was not in fact raped,' Kate told him. 'Nor was she in any way sexually assaulted. It was made to appear so by the killer *after* her death.'

Arliss stared at her incredulously. 'Why on earth ...?'

'To put the police off the scent, presumably. So now we're looking for someone who knew Miss Saxon and who had some motive for killing her that was quite unconnected with rape.'

'It wasn't me,' Arliss said earnestly. 'For heaven's thake, Chief Inthpector, what pothible reason could I have had for killing Corinne?'

'Then try to help me find who did. Cast your mind back. Did Miss Saxon ever say anything to you, directly or indirectly, about any other relationship she might have had? Think hard. In your conversations with her, she may have let slip something.'

Arliss hesitated, then shook his head. 'No, I can't think of anything.'

But he has thought of something, Kate!

'Are you quite sure, sir? You don't need to concern your-

65

self about possibly making trouble for someone who's quite innocent. It's for me to make sure that doesn't happen.'

'No, really, there's nothing I can tell you.'

Kate allowed her disbelief to show. But she only said, 'Very well, I won't press you any further just now. But perhaps later on you may recall some odd remark she made that with hindsight strikes you as being significant. Please give the matter very careful thought, and if anything occurs to you get in touch with me at once. If I'm not available, leave a message and I'll get back to you.'

'Here's the phone number of the Incident Room, sir,' said Boulter, holding out a scrap of paper.

Arliss took it, in a daze, and looked at Kate uncertainly. 'I am telling the truth, I didn't kill her. You do believe that, don't you?'

'My personal opinion, Mr Arliss, has no relevance one way or the other.'

Driving away, Boulter said, 'You don't think he did it, do you, guv?'

'I'm inclined not to. But even if he was at the airport that afternoon, it still doesn't prove his innocence. It's possible that he drove to the Cotswolds first and killed Corinne before going to Heathrow to establish an alibi. All the same, we'll see what that man Pollock has to say, and have questions asked at the airport coffee shop and information desk. Also, contact the Yorkshire police and have his wife checked out.'

On their way back to Streatfield Park they stopped at a roadside café. Boulter, predictably, ordered a large platter of ham and eggs and French fries. Kate surprised herself, and him, by ordering the same. She felt ravenous. The last time she'd eaten anything more than just a snack, she realised, was yesterday lunchtime with her aunt, en route to Bristol. Which reminded her that she must find a moment to ring Felix some time today.

Within minutes of their return to the Incident Room, a PC looked in to inform Kate that a Mr Hammett was asking to see the officer in charge.

'He say's he's got some information on that missing Escort, ma'am.'

'Good. Wheel him in, Mike.'

Men, Kate had found, reacted strongly when confronted by a chief inspector who was female. In a variety of ways. The man who was shown into her office, fair-haired, fortyish and running to fat, seemed tickled pink.

'Well, well, so this is the high-powered lady copper everyone's talking about,' he said with a chuckle. 'Got looks too, haven't you, as well as brains?'

She indicated a chair. 'Your full name, Mr Hammett?'

With a well-practised pluck he produced a card from his breast pocket and handed it to Kate. *Gregory Hammett*, she read. *Sales Executive, The Pinnacle Double-Glazing Company.*

'When I heard that you'd set up your headquarters at Streatfield Park, I was thinking it would be in one of their posh suites.' He glanced around her makeshift office critically. 'I can't say I'm much impressed by this.'

'Sorry to disappoint you, Mr Hammett. Now, I believe you have some information about the red Escort we're looking for. Do you know where it is?'

'Haven't got the faintest.'

'Then what do you have to tell me?'

He leaned back in his chair and crossed his legs, savouring the importance of the moment.

'I popped into the Green Man down the road for a quick half just now, and the landlord told me you people had been asking a lot of questions about last Wednesday, the day you reckon that woman was raped and strangled.'

Kate didn't correct him about the rape. 'In the light of what occurred, we're looking for anything that might seem unusual or suspicious. We're particularly trying to trace her car.'

'I don't hold with rape,' he said virtuously. 'Oh, I know that some women damn nearly ask for it, but ... And killing her afterwards! It's just not on. So I thought I ought to come straight to the police. I mean to say, it's one's duty, isn't it?'

'Very public-spirited of you,' Kate said dryly. 'Now let's get to the nitty-gritty. The red Escort, Mr Hammett. You've seen it somewhere, have you?'

'I should say so!'

'Where was that? And when?'

'On Wednesday, that's when. Wednesday afternoon. It must've been happening at that very moment. Him raping her, I mean. Only how was I to know? My God, it's a shaker, isn't it?'

'Tell me about the car.'

'Well, I was on my way to see a punter over Verdley way to give him a price for one of our de luxe patio installations. I took that lane as a short cut, and there the car was, just sitting there. One of those Escorts with a fold-down hood. Bright red, brand spanking new, too. I remember thinking what a neat little job one like that would be for the missus when I get my next bonus. Myself, I need something a lot bigger, of course.'

'What time was this, Mr Hammett?'

He looked pleased with himself. 'Guessed you'd ask me that, so I figured it out for you ready. My appointment was for six o'clock when the guy would be home from work, and I arrived bang on the dot. Always do. Make a point of it. So it must've been seven or eight minutes before that when I drove along the lane and saw that car.'

It didn't tie in. Corinne Saxon had left Streatfield Park at around two-fifteen − that much was certain − and the drive from there to where her body was found would only have taken her a few minutes. So had she driven somewhere else before her fateful arrival at East Dean woods? Or had her car been left standing at the roadside for several hours after her death? In which case, had the killer come back for it? Or was it someone else who'd driven it away? Or had Corinne been killed elsewhere, and her body taken to be dumped in the woods, using her own car?

Gregory Hammett hadn't finished, though. 'When I went back along that way about an hour later,' he added, 'the car wasn't there.'

'Can you pinpoint the time more precisely?' Kate asked him.

'Well, let's see. I popped into my local for a noggin before going home, and I remember that *This Is Your Life* was just starting on the TV in the bar. I hung on for a few minutes to see who it was going to be.'

68

'That means the Escort was driven away some time between a few minutes to six and a few minutes to seven,' she said. He nodded. 'Must've been.'

'That means the Escort was driven away some time between a few minutes to six and a few minutes to seven,' she said. He nodded. 'Must've been.'

'Tell me, was it drawn right up on the grass verge, or what?'

'No, it was on the tarmac. The lane is a fairish width at that point, so there's room enough for a car to park without causing any obstruction.'

'Did you notice anything else that might possibly help me?'

'Not a blind thing. If I'd had the faintest glimmer of what was going on I'd have been in there after that bastard like a shot, I can tell you.'

'Very well, Mr Hammett, thank you. I'm most grateful to you for coming forward. This information will be very useful to us.'

He looked smug. There'd be an embroidered version of how he'd been such a big help to the police told tonight in the Green Man. And at his local pub. Kate stood up. 'If you'll just come with me, I'll get someone to take down a statement from you and ask you to sign it.'

'Anything to oblige.' As he stood up too, he gave Kate a sharp glance. 'Do you live around here, Chief?'

'In the neighbourhood,' she said cautiously, wondering what was coming.

'It just occurred to me, with the winter not far off, you might be interested in our new all-PVC sealed units range. I could offer you a very competitive price.'

Kate laughed out loud, oddly enough liking the man a mite better for his sheer bloody nerve.

'Not just now, Mr Hammett.'

'Oh, well, you've got my name and address if you should change your mind.'

Chapter Six

The afternoon briefing was unproductive. Kate could sense a marked relief among the men on the squad that it was no longer a case of rape they were dealing with. Most men felt edgy concerning rape; uncertain, ill at ease and out of their depth. Not blazing with anger, like the women officers.

Among a number of informative items pinned to a board were some of the photographs of Corinne Saxon that Richard Gower had provided. As the briefing broke up, a young WPC went to have a closer look. A minute later she came over to where Kate was talking to Inspector Massey and Sergeant Boulter. She looked flushed with excitement.

'What is it, Pippa?' asked Kate.

'That dress she's wearing, ma'am.' The girl twisted round and pointed at the board. 'I've seen it.'

'The picture appeared in the *Gazette* a few weeks ago. Was that where you saw it?'

'No, I mean today. I've seen the dress today.'

Kate jerked to full attention. Boulter, though, wasn't so impressed. 'You saw one just like it, you mean?'

They were two women together now, pitying his male ignorance.

'It's a model dress, sergeant,' said Kate. 'Not a mass-production number.' She looked back at WPC Hamilton. 'You're quite sure it was the same one?'

'Oh yes, ma'am. I had a good look at it. I was on foot patrol in Marlingford High Street this morning, and I glanced at the window of that Nearly New Boutique on the corner near the library. I've bought one or two things there for myself, only

70

most of their stuff is out of my price bracket, even though it's second-hand. The assistant was just arranging this dress on a stand in the window, and I watched her for a minute. Feeling sick with envy, to be honest.'

'Did you go in and ask about it?'

'Not when she pinned the price tag on. Eighty-five quid!'

Kate glanced at her watch. Already past five. 'Would the shop still be open?'

'I expect so, ma'am. Up to five-thirty, I should think.'

'Come on, then, Pippa. Let's get going.'

The Nearly New Boutique was a small shop a few doors away from the public library, with a hairdressing salon above it. The central doorway and both windows had small bouffant sunblinds, with the name scripted in flamboyant gold leaf.

'It's gone!' Pippa exclaimed in dismay, pointing to the left-hand window.

'Never mind,' said Kate. 'We'll ask inside.'

Fortunately, the shop was empty of customers. The woman who came forward to greet them was large-boned and an inch or so taller than Kate's five foot eight. She toned down her somewhat gaunt features by softly styled hair and a pair of pink-rimmed fashion spectacles.

Kate introduced herself and the WPC. 'Are you in charge here?'

'I'm the owner.'

'Your name, please?'

'Mrs Sanderson-Browne — that's Browne with an *e*.'

'This morning,' said Kate, 'my colleague spotted a dress in your window. White silk crepe with a dragon embroidered on the bodice. It's not there now. Have you sold it?'

The woman had been eyeing Pippa's uniform with a certain distaste, but now she sensed a sale and beamed.

'That particular model has been sold, and no wonder, at the snip of a price I was asking. But I have plenty of other very attractive dresses. I'm sure I could fit you up. It's for some special occasion, is it?'

Kate dashed her hopes. 'I'm not here to buy. This is official police business. I'd like to know how you came to acquire that particular dress.'

71

'Why?' She bridled. 'There's nothing wrong, is there?'

'I'm afraid there almost certainly is.'

'Oh, dear! Well, it was brought in here and offered to me, like most of the things I sell. I don't have to go looking for stock. I turn down far more than I buy.'

'Who brought it in, Mrs Sanderson-Browne? And when?'

She ruminated, fingering the tie of her silky blouse. 'It would have been, let me see, Thursday. No, I tell a lie, it was yesterday. Friday morning. I'd just been along to the bank, so it would have been around eleven o'clock. The woman had never brought in anything before, but she had some nice things. Very nice things, in fact. I hope you aren't going to tell me they were stolen?'

'Are you saying that you bought some other items from her, too?'

'Oh, yes. Several.'

'Then I'd like to see them, please.'

Resentfully, she went around the shop plucking things from racks and display stands. When she'd finished there was quite a pile on her glass-topped counter. Almost everything tallied with the list of items missing from Corinne Saxon's wardrobe that she was presumed to have packed for her trip.

'We'll have to take all these things with us,' Kate said. 'We'll give you a receipt, of course.' Cutting across the outraged protest, she went on, 'What can you tell me about the woman who sold them to you?'

'Not very much. She was short and dumpy, a bit on the common side, to be frank. She told me the clothes belonged to her sister, something about her getting married again and going to live in the tropics where they wouldn't be suitable. I remember thinking the two sisters can't have been very much alike, because the one I saw wouldn't have come within a mile of getting into these things.'

'Yet you accepted her story without question?'

'Now listen, I can't be expected to go into the credentials of everyone who walks into this shop. I paid out good money for these things – in cash – so what's going to happen now?'

'That depends. Think carefully, please, is there anything

you remember about this woman that might help us trace her?'

'I told you already, I didn't know her.' But there was a note of uncertainty in her voice and Kate persisted.

'Was she local, do you think? Was her face in any way familiar to you?'

Mrs Sanderson-Browne considered, while fastidiously plucking an invisible speck from the sleeve of her blouse.

'Well, since you ask, I did get a slight feeling that I'd seen her around somewhere. But for the life of me I can't remember where. Maybe she works in a shop.'

'What kind of shop might it be? Try to visualise her against a background.'

Her head-shaking suddenly yielded to a triumphant nod. 'Hold on, I think I've got it. Not a shop, a market stall. Yes, that's it. I've seen her at the Thursday markets here in Marlingford. I close for lunch, you see, and I usually go along to the market for fresh fish and vegetables. Her stall is right up at the end, near the Electricity showrooms. I've never bought anything from her, though.'

'What sort of things does she sell?'

'Knick-knacks and bits and pieces. Bric-a-brac, I suppose you'd call it.'

'Right. We'll need a written statement from you, Mrs Sanderson-Browne, covering everything you've told us. Someone will be in touch on Monday to arrange it. The only other thing I need now is the name and address of the customer who bought that white silk dress.'

'Oh, dear! You don't have to trouble her, do you? I mean, she buys a lot of things from me. I'd hate to see her in any way upset or embarrassed.'

'We'll explain that it's not your fault. But we must recover the dress. It's stolen property.'

The Thursday market in Marlingford was a much-cherished tradition owing its existence to a charter granted by some long-ago monarch. Nowadays, it was controlled by the local council; but Kate couldn't hope that the official responsible would be found at his office at this hour on a Saturday.

'I want the name and address of this woman stallholder,

Pippa, and I want it now. Someone at DHQ can dig it out for us. If the market manager can't be contacted at home, then they'll have to get hold of someone else who can open up the Town Hall and look through the records. While we're waiting for the information, I think you and I have earned ourselves a cup of tea, don't you?'

There were several officers sprinkled around the DHQ canteen who eyed them with interest as they sat down with their teas at a table near one of the windows. Kate could see that Pippa was both nervous and chuffed to be sitting there with a chief inspector. She was twenty-two or three, a pleasant-looking girl with curly fair hair. Though not tall, she had well-coordinated movements that suggested she'd put up a good show in a dodgy situation.

'It was very sharp of you spotting that dress,' Kate commended her. 'Small things like that can make all the difference in an investigation.'

A faint surge of colour came to her face. 'I do hope it leads to something, ma'am. This is the first murder enquiry I've been on. It's very exciting.'

'How long have you been in the Force?'

'Three years now. Before that I worked in an insurance office, but it was deadly dull.'

'Are you ambitious, Pippa?'

'You mean about getting promotion?'

'Yes.'

'I'm going to have a stab at the sergeant's exam the minute I'm eligible. My boyfriend says I must be crazy. He reckons this is no career for a woman.' She looked confused. 'Oh, I didn't mean – '

Kate smiled. 'Your boyfriend isn't the only man around who takes that view. Is he in the police, too?'

'No, he's an electrical engineer.'

'Well, let me tell you something, Pippa. No career is *right* for a woman, not the police nor anything else. It's the woman who has to be right for the career. You do whatever you want to do. And aim high.'

'Thanks, ma'am. I know it's good advice. I'll tell Derek what you said.'

'He'll probably say that I'm trying to interfere in your life.'

'Oh no, he won't, he'll damn well take notice. I'll make him take notice.'

Kate spotted a PC enter the canteen and scan the room. He started over in her direction, a piece of paper in his hand.

'Good, here's the information we're waiting for. Drink up.' Draining her own teacup, she reached for her shoulder bag and stood up. 'Stick at it, Pippa, and you'll get there. You've got the makings.'

Chapter Seven

Mermaid Crescent was only one of several colourful street names that had been chosen by the local council for an estate of extremely colourless houses. To reach it, Kate turned the car by the water works into Hydrangea Grove, then drove along the length of Pearblossom Avenue. The house she sought was one of a terrace of four, all faced with a reconstituted imitation of Cotswold stone. The front garden of number 16 was particularly unkempt, with seeding weeds everywhere.

Kate and WPC Hamilton got out of the car and approached the front door. The woman who answered the bell could perhaps be described as plump and cuddly. Just at present, her thickly made-up face wore the irate expression of one torn away from a television game show, the sound of which belted from the living room.

'What d'ya want?' she demanded of Kate. Then she clapped eyes on Pippa in uniform standing beside her, and exclaimed, 'Oh, my Gawd! Billy,' she yelled over her shoulder, 'it's the bleeding fuzz.'

The television was switched off and a moment later a man in a woollen vest and braces appeared in the doorway behind her. Even shorter than his wife, and slightly built, he had the look of a jockey who'd been caught by the stewards doping the horses.

'Mr and Mrs Billings?' Kate enquired.

'Yeah,' the man grunted. 'What d'yer want? I ain't done nothing.'

'Acutally,' said Kate, 'it's Mrs Billings I want to talk to.

I'm Detective Chief Inspector Maddox, and this is WPC Hamilton. May we come in?'

He didn't budge, just jerked a thumb at his wife. 'She ain't done nothing, neither.'

'No, I ain't done nothing.'

'Do you want us to conduct this interview on the doorstep?' asked Kate. 'With the neighbours having a good listen?'

'Oh, all right then, you better come in.'

Their living room, a through room from front to back, could only be described as gaudy. Garishly patterned wallpaper, patterned carpet, and patterned Dralon on the overstuffed three-piece suite. A massive television set stood in one corner. Also, Kate noted, *two* video recorders and a camcorder, and a top-of-the-range midi system. She let Billings observe her interest in these items, and he shifted his feet uneasily.

'Listen,' he said. 'They was all bought legit.'

Kate ignored him. 'Mrs Billings,' she began, 'yesterday morning you took some items of ladies' clothing to the Nearly New Boutique in Marlingford High Street. I'd like to know where you got them.'

'Got them?' she parried.

'How and when you acquired them'

'Well ... they was mine.'

'You told the woman at the shop they were your sister's.'

'That's right. She give them to me.'

'I see. What is your sister's name and address, please, so we can ask her where she got the things from.'

'She ... she's gone away.'

Kate sighed ostentatiously. 'We can still get in touch with her, can't we? Wherever she happens to be now. So just tell me how to reach her.'

The woman went dumbstruck. Kate said, 'Why play around? There isn't any sister, is there?'

'I ... I ...'

'Suppose you tell me the truth.'

Husband and wife exchanged scared glances. Kate could read their minds. The cops wouldn't be here if they didn't already know most of it, would they? Stood to reason. Put you away as soon as look at you, those bastards. Play along a bit, and they might go easy on you.

'We didn' know that woman'd been done in,' said Billy. 'We never saw 'er at all, honest to God. Just the car.'

'Just the car,' his wife echoed.

'A red Escort?' said Kate, her pulses quickening.

'Yeah. Just drew up there, it was, at the side of the road in them woods. We pulled up and had a gander. Called out to see if anyone was around, we did. But no one answered.'

'No one answered,' his wife concurred.

'This was last Wednesday?' Kate queried. 'What time?'

Billy scratched his right buttock. ''Bout half six. That right, Olive?'

''Bout half six.'

'Was it raining at the time?'

'Had bin. It'd stopped by then. I said to Olive, crying shame it was, the way that lovely little motor had got all wet inside with the hood down.'

'You were driving along that lane near East Dean at about half-past six on Wednesday evening, and you saw a red Escort parked at the side of the road. There was no one in sight. Correct? So what then?'

'Listen,' Billy said urgently, 'if we tell yer, you can't go nicking us on anything to do with that rape and her getting strangled. That weren't nothing to do with us. I told you, we din't even know she was there. Her body, I mean. Dead and everything.'

'If we'd known,' said Olive with a rare burst of original thinking, 'we'd have scarpered. Oh, yes!'

'We'd have scarpered,' echoed her husband.

'So am I to understand, then, that you drove the car away?'

'Well, it was asking for it, weren't it? Just sitting there waiting to be pinched.'

'Were the keys in the ignition?'

'Yeah, they was. But even if they hadn't bin, that wouldn't've stopped me.' His professional pride was at stake. 'Blimey, the day I can't start a motor without a key, I'll hand in me chips.'

Kate bypassed the issue of his apparent regular involvement in car thefts. Just now she had a higher priority.

'I presume,' she said, 'there was a suitcase in the Escort, and when you saw the quality of the clothes it contained, you reckoned you could raise a bit of cash?'

'It seemed a wicked waste not to,' said Olive, a sentiment with which her husband agreed.

'A wicked waste, it would've bin.'

About to ask if there had also been a handbag in the Escort, Kate paused. The Billingses might deny it on principle, thus limiting the amount of trouble they would be in. But the presence or otherwise of the handbag could be crucial. Kate framed her question with care; in court it would have been disallowed as leading the witness.

'You also found the victim's handbag in the car, of course?'

'Just sitting there, it were,' said Billy.

'Where, exactly?'

'Shoved in the stowage bin on the door.'

'On the driver's side?'

He nodded glumly.

What woman would leave her handbag in an open, unlocked car? If she left the car for any reason she'd take it with her, or at least lock it away in the boot. *She was killed in her car, Kate!* That was almost certainly it. Killed in her car and her body carried into those woods.

'Where is the handbag now?' she demanded. 'Do you have it here?'

'No!' they both shrilled. 'It ain't here. We ain't got it.'

Damn! 'So where is it?'

'We chucked it away, din't we?' Billy muttered. 'Olive was going to keep some of the stuff, make-up and suchlike, but when we heard last night about that woman getting done in and you was looking for the car, we got the wind up. We drove over Linchmere way and chucked it in the gravel pit there. Shoved a brick inside and tossed it in the water.'

'Did you keep anything? Anything at all?'

'Well, we hung on to the cash, naturally.'

'Naturally! 'How much cash?'

He exchanged a quick look with Olive. 'Only about twenty quid. Just over.'

Kate gave him a disbelieving stare. Corinne had drawn money from the hotel safe just before setting out.

'Don't you mean just over a *hundred* pounds?'

'Oh, all right, then,' he agreed sulkily.

That missing shoe could prove a clincher to her new theory.

'Was there a shoe in the car?' she asked. 'Just one. Black. High-heeled?'

'Yeah, there were. It'd got itself stuck under the clutch pedal, and I had to stop to hook it out. Afterwards, I searched around for its partner, but it wasn't nowhere in the car. So I brought it back with me, thinking Olive might have found the other one in the stuff she'd brought home in our car. But she hadn't, so we threw it in the bin.'

'Will it still be there?'

Olive shook her head. 'Emptied Thursday.'

Sod it! Small hope of finding that shoe now, but the motions would have to be gone through. An unpleasant job at the refuse tip for some luckless police officers.

'You'd better come with us, you two,' Kate told them. 'We'll want statements from you both. And you'll be taken to that gravel pit to show us the exact point where you threw the handbag into the water. I badly want that handbag. And the car, of course. That's got to be tracked down.'

'Huh, you'll be lucky,' said Billy. 'It'll have gone by now. Vanished.'

'Vanished?' exclaimed Pippa Hamilton, mystified.

'Out of the country by now. Might be anywhere.'

Kate explained to the WPC. 'That's the way these ringers often work. They line up a buyer for a specific model of car somewhere abroad, then get one pinched to order by someone like our friend here. The cars are shipped off in no time at all. I presume,' she said to Billy, 'that you'd been told to be on the lookout for an Escort Cabriolet?'

He grabbed at that as a sort of justification. 'A red 'un, too, they wanted. That's why it seemed a real gift from 'eaven, parked there just asking to be drove away. Olive and me were on our way to visit her mum in hospital, but it

80

wouldn't have seemed right, somehow, not to have grabbed a wonderful chance like that.'

'We all get our gifts from heaven,' said Kate, and grinned at Pippa. 'You'll agree with that, won't you, constable?'

'Does this mean you're going to do me for the car?' Billy muttered sullenly.

'You and Olive both,' Kate assured him. 'For the car *and* the suitcase *and* the handbag *and* the money. But thankfully not by me; I've got bigger fish to fry. Come along, let's get moving.'

A small convoy of vehicles bumped down a rutted track to the disused gravel pit. Two police cars — in one of which were Billy and Olive Billings — a Land-Rover carrying the police diver and his assistant plus all their gear, and Kate and Sergeant Boulter bringing up the rear in her Montego.

There was no moon, just a glimmer of starlight which gave ghostly substance to the wraiths of mist lying low across the water. On the way, Kate had remarked on the mildness of the evening for September, but down here she felt a dank chill in the air as she got out of the car.

The Billingses were led along the water's edge, arguing between themselves, until they finally agreed on the spot where they had thrown in the handbag.

'About here, it were,' Billy declared. 'Must be.'

'Must be,' Olive confirmed.

They all stood around stamping their feet and hugging their arms while the diver and his mate made preparations. Finally, the rubber dinghy was inflated and on the water, the diver clad in full regalia. Kate watched him submerge into the dark water, and shivered.

'Rather him than me,' said Boulter beside her.

The water was deep and murky. The light from the diver's powerful handlamp glimmered for a while, then was lost. They waited for hours, it seemed. Kate began to lose hope. She went over to join the Billings pair. They too looked anxious now, as if they'd been banking on the recovery of the handbag to vindicate their crimes.

'Are you sure you pinpointed the right spot?' she asked.

'Dead sure,' said Billy, sounding uncertain.

'Dead sure,' his wife agreed, no less doubtfully.

'Well, I hope for your sakes that you're right.' Though quite what she meant by this threat Kate didn't know.

Another tense ten minutes, then the underwater light shivered into view; the surface swirled, and the diver's head reappeared. He held something aloft, waving it triumphantly.

Brought ashore, the handbag was a soggy mess, the leather slimy and disgusting. A stench arose from it.

'God!' said the diver. 'The muck down there. All sorts, you'd never believe.'

'No bodies, I suppose?' Boulter joked.

'If it was bodies you wanted, Tim, you should have said.'

The sergeant had spread a plastic sheet on the ground, while someone shone a light for him. Undoing the clasp, he tipped out the handbag's contents. The usual woman's things, apart from the hefty stone placed inside by the Billingses. What interested Kate most was the wallet, a passport, and a small leather-bound notebook.

'What's that, sergeant? Has it got addresses in it?'

Gingerly, Boulter opened the little book. 'Job to see, ma'am. It's totally sodden. I doubt if this is going to be much help to us.'

'Okay, we'll get back to the Incident Room. If we can't get any information out of it ourselves, we'll pass it over to the lab.' She turned to the diver. 'Thanks, Alec. Sorry it was such a mucky job for you.'

'I've done a lot worse, ma'am.'

'See, we *was* right,' said Billy virtuously.

'We *was* right.'

'So you were,' said Kate. 'But you needn't look so smug about it. You're lucky not to be charged on a much more serious charge than theft. Whatever the court hands out, you should count yourselves fortunate.'

At the now almost deserted Incident Room, Kate and Boulter examined the handbag's contents anew. The wallet, robbed of cash, contained what one would expect − credit cards, driver's licence and certificate of insurance. The notebook, limp and sodden, was totally indecipherable.

'Definitely a forensic job,' said Kate. 'Come on, Tim, it's off home for us.'

He looked grim. No Julie waiting at home for him tonight, of course. 'Reckon I'll catch the last half-hour at the boozer,' he muttered.

'If you do that, Tim, mind you walk home. Or take a taxi. Hear me?'

He shot her a look that was charged with venom. Venom against her or the absent Julie? Both, probably. He'd worked well all day, but now that the strain of the job was temporarily lifted he looked as if he might fall to pieces. Kate had a feeling that if she uttered a single word on the subject of his wife, Boulter would either start yelling at her to mind her own bloody business, or she'd have him sobbing on her shoulder. She couldn't afford to let either happen.

She stood up, buttoned her jacket and slung her bag over her shoulder.

'Go straight home, Tim,' she advised him earnestly. 'Get yourself something to eat, then hit the sack. That's what I intend to do.' She walked out before he could answer.

Once home, Kate remembered something she ought to have done by now. Luckily it wasn't too late. Her aunt never went to bed early.

'Kate!' The eagerness in Felix's voice pricked her niece's conscience. 'I'd have phoned *you*, but I knew you must be hellishly busy.'

'I've just this minute got home. Sorry about yesterday, Felix. We'll do your birthday outing some other time.'

'Don't worry about it, girl. How're things going on the case? I read all about it in the paper this morning. Sounds a ghastly business.'

'It is pretty horrible. I met Corinne Saxon once, you know. At that big do to mark the opening of the hotel.'

'Oh yes, of course, I hadn't thought. You were there with Richard, weren't you? Funny he didn't mention that to me.'

'*When* didn't he mention it?' Kate asked suspiciously.

'At lunchtime, at the Wagon and Horses.'

A Saturday meeting at the Chipping Bassett pub had become a little ritual that Kate and her aunt both enjoyed, whenever Kate's workload allowed. Richard sometimes joined them. So it wasn't in the least odd that those two had chanced to meet up. All the same . . .

'What was he doing there?' Kate demanded. 'He must have known that I'd never be able to make it today.'

'The man is entitled to enjoy a drink, damnit, even without the pleasure of your company. Likewise me. I must say, though, Richard was very taciturn. I mentioned this murder enquiry you're on, and he just looked at me daggers and clammed up. Have you two had a row?'

'Something like that.' Kate certainly wasn't about to fill her aunt in with the details.

'Well, make it up fast. Life's far too short to waste time in quarrelling.'

'Ah, the sagacity of the sere and yellow.'

'Don't knock it, girl. When you reach my advanced years and look at all the missed opportunities in life, it makes you feel angry. You young people don't appreciate a good thing when you find it. Why you and Richard can't admit that you're ideal for each other, I just do not know. If you had a grain of commonsense, Kate, you'd get on the phone to him this minute, and — '

'Do me a favour,' Kate interrupted. 'Spare me the agony-aunt bit. Whatever's up with you tonight? You're not usually given to maudlin rambling. My advice to you, Auntie dear, is to screw the cap back on that bottle of Scotch and get yourself off to bed.'

Chapter Eight

Sunday morning Boulter was at the Incident Room ahead
of her, scowling his face off. No need to ask if the errant
Julie had had a change of heart and returned to the nest.
Exasperated, Kate felt a longing to bang their two silly heads
together.

'Morning, Tim. Has the postmorten report been sent over
yet?'

'Arrived a few minutes ago, ma'am,' he told her with a
cheerless grimace.

'Give it here, then,' she said, and headed for her office.

The report was a wordy document, as pompous as its
author, Dr Meddowes. A few minutes later Kate called
Boulter in.

'You've read this, Tim?'

'Not yet. Didn't have time.'

'I've just struck something I wasn't expecting. It seems
that Corinne Saxon gave birth at some stage.'

'Did she, now!' Give Boulter his due, that small piece
of information was enough to spark his interest. He'd
immediately seen the possible implications.

'The child might not have survived, of course,' Kate went
on. 'In which case it's probably unimportant from our point
of view. But if there's a child of hers still around somewhere,
it could be significant. I think we'd better go and talk to
Kenway again.'

'Like now, you mean, guv?'

'Why not? Get it cleared up. Anyway, it's time we had
another go at him about his shaky alibi.'

On this fine Sunday, the village of Ashecombe-in-the-Vale had even more tourists milling around than the day before. Kate wasn't surprised to find there were customers at Kenway Antiques. When she and Boulter entered the house, both the Kenways were talking to an elderly couple who seemed interested in a stripped pine kitchen dresser. The arrival of the police was clearly unwelcome. The Kenways exchanged glances, looking apprehensive.

Kate said quietly, 'We'd like a word as soon as possible, Mr Kenway.'

'Er, yes, of course.' He muttered an apology to the customers, leaving them to his wife. 'You'd better come upstairs.'

The furniture in the living quarters was of distinctly lesser quality than in the display rooms below. In fact it was all pretty shabby. The walls needed decorating and the sofa and chairs cried out for re-upholstering. One corner of the room was used as an office. A battered filing cabinet and desk and chair. On the desk stood a typewriter so ancient it might well have fetched a price in the shop as a genuine antique. Clearly, Kenway and his wife were existing on a shoestring. Saving that regular monthly payment of four hundred pounds to Corinne was going to make a world of difference to them. Kenway didn't invite them to sit down. Presumably he hoped to be rid of them quicker that way.

'When I talked to you yesterday,' Kate began in a bland voice, 'you were unable to suggest anyone who might be able to verify your claim to have been here with your wife last Wednesday afternoon. Have you had any further thoughts on that?'

His eyes flickered nervously. 'No, there isn't anyone.'

'You were both here for the entire afternoon?'

'That's right. As Liz and I told you before.'

'You're quite *certain* of that, sir, are you?' Boulter queried, with one of his intimidating glares. '*Wednesday* afternoon, we're talking about. Neither you nor your wife went out for any reason?'

'No, definitely not. I ... I don't see why you won't accept that.'

86

We might, Kate thought, if you weren't so obviously concealing something. She said, 'If you want to change your story in any way, Mr Kenway, this is the time to do so.'

He seemed suddenly to come to the boil with indignant anger. 'You can't seriously be suggesting that I did away with Corinne. What possible reason could I have had for killing her?'

'For the saving of four hundred pounds a month, perhaps.'

'That's a monstrous thing to say.'

'But it's a fact that you won't have to pay the money any longer. Which is quite a considerable benefit to you. So I'm afraid that unless you provide us with some real proof of where you were that afternoon, your name will remain on our list of suspects.'

He was silent for extending moments, glaring at her sullenly. Then he muttered, 'I was here, I tell you. Liz and I were both here, and you'll never be able to prove otherwise.'

'That remains to be seen,' Kate said. 'Now, on to another matter. The postmortem examination of Miss Saxon's body has revealed that she gave birth to a child at some time.'

Kenway looked totally flabbergasted. 'No, that can't be right. Unless ... you mean since the divorce?'

'Are you saying that it wasn't your child, sir?' Boulter asked.

'Of course it wasn't.'

'Why of course?' said Kate.

'Because Corinne flatly refused to have a baby, that's why. I kept on and on at her about could we start a family, but she just wouldn't listen. She said she'd no intention of being lumbered with kids.'

Believable! It tallied with Kate's assessment of Corinne Saxon's character.

'The evidence of the pathologist,' she said, 'is that the birth wasn't recent. Therefore, if it wasn't during the time you were married to her, it's likely to have occurred at some earlier date. Are you sure she never said anything to you about having had a child? Did you never suspect the possibility from something she let drop?'

'No, never. I had no idea.'

'I want to find out more about Corinne Saxon's life in those earlier years before you were married. What can you tell me, Mr Kenway? How did you come to meet her?'

'We first met at a hotel in Cheltenham. The Angel. She was there in the cocktail bar.'

'Alone?'

'Yes, and I was alone, too. She was stunningly attractive, and I thought she looked vaguely familiar. But I didn't realise who she was. A couple of times she gave me a friendly glance, and after a bit I went over and told her I was sure we must have met before somewhere. She laughed and said that it was a terribly corny line, but then she said maybe I'd seen her on the cover of a magazine. She told me her name, and of course I recognised it. That was the start. After that we went out together most evenings. I was doing pretty well in those days, so I could afford to take a woman to the best places.'

'What was she doing in this part of the world?'

'She was staying at her aunt's house, near the Spa. She told me the old girl was ill in hospital, and because she'd brought Corinne up after her parents died, Corinne felt a sort of responsibility towards her. She gave me the impression that she was still being very successful in her modelling career, and I wasn't to know any different. She said she'd cancelled all her professional engagements to come and be with her aunt.'

'Her aunt died, I understand?'

'Yes, about six weeks after we first met. By that time I was head over heels about Corinne, and I was scared to death she'd go back to London and I'd never see her again, so I asked her to marry me. It was only later on I realised she'd been expecting to inherit a lot from her aunt. She knew the house was only leased, but she didn't know that the old lady's income came almost entirely from annuities that died with her. So all there was for Corinne was a few hundred pounds and the furniture.'

'She saw you as a fat meal ticket?' Boulter asked brutally.

Kenway flinched, but he didn't show offence. 'I imagined that Corinne would continue with modelling work, but she never did. I was glad, really. I could support her, and I didn't like the idea of her being away for days at a time. Even so, she went off to stay in London on a few occasions – to go shopping, she said, and look up her old friends.'

'Where were you living in those days?' asked Kate.

'In Cheltenham, in a very fancy new block of flats. Corinne found the place and I didn't need much persuading, even though the rent was astronomical. As I said, I was doing pretty well at that time. Then things began to go downhill with my business, so we had to move somewhere cheaper. Corinne hated that. She never stopped blaming me for letting her down. In fact,' he added with a burst of feeling, 'she made my life sheer bloody hell from then on. In the end, I was only too glad to get out of the marriage, even on the terms Corinne demanded. I became a free man again.'

'Those friends of hers in London,' Boulter said. 'Do you know who they were?'

'I haven't the least idea.'

'You seem to know remarkably little about the woman you were married to, Mr Kenway,' Kate observed.

'It was the way Corinne wanted it, and I was so happy to have her I didn't let it worry me. Not at first. Later, it became obvious that she'd been using me all along, right from the start. There was never any closeness between us, not ever. Now, though, I have a real marriage, and I thank God for it.'

There was a slight sound from the doorway. Unnoticed, Liz Kenway had come upstairs and she must have overheard his last remark. With a little catch of breath that was almost a sob she ran forward to her husband and touched her lips to his cheek. Then she stood there beside him, her hand finding his. Together in their closeness, they faced the police.

Don't go soft on them, Kate!

'Mr Kenway,' she said directly, 'did you kill Corinne Saxon?'

He flinched again, and Kate saw his wife's grip on his hand tighten. But he answered steadily, with no more than a slight tremor in his voice.

'No, Chief Inspector, I did not. And I believe you know that I did not. I could never do such a dreadful thing.'

89

'How about you, Mrs Kenway? Did you kill her?'

'How dare you accuse my wife?' Kenway flared.

'Please, sir,' Boulter cut in, 'allow the lady to answer for herself.'

'Of course I didn't kill her. What a suggestion! I hated Corinne, I'm ready enough to admit that, and I'm not sorry that she's dead. But I'd never have dreamed of killing her.'

'It sounds as if,' Boulter remarked when they'd returned to the car, 'they were expecting us to take their word for it, just like that.'

'Innocent people do,' Kate reminded him. 'They just can't appreciate how the situation looks to us.'

'That was quite an act they put on, wasn't it? The loving couple.'

'Was it an act, Tim? I'm not so sure. All the same, they weren't telling the truth about Wednesday afternoon. I think we'd better have questions asked in the village, and specially the neighbouring houses, to see what emerges.'

A message awaited Kate at the Incident Room that Mr James Arliss has phoned. Would she ring him back? She made it her first job.

'Ah, Chief Inthpector, you athked me to let you know if I thought of anything.'

'And you have?'

'I'm not sure it will help you, but ... well, on the one occasion I was with Corinne in her private apartment at the hotel, she received a phone call. I didn't think anything of it at the time, except ... well, it was annoying.'

'In what way annoying?'

Blushes don't usually travel well along telephone lines, but this one came over loud and clear. 'We were, if you, er, underthtand me ...'

'Quite so. Carry on, please, Mr Arliss.'

'Corinne took the call in the other room, the thitting room, tho I didn't hear every word. Not that I was really lithening.'

'Do you know who the caller was?'

'No, I don't, but it was obviouthly a man. The gist of the conversation seemed to be that she was telling him not to keep pethtering her. She thounded quite irritated.'

There's gold here, Kate, so keep digging! Never mind that Arliss was clearly lying in pretending that he'd only just remembered this phone call. No man could have 'forgotten' an interruption like that at such a deflatory moment. Alternatively, Arliss might be inventing the phone call (though she didn't think so). In which case, *why*?

'Did you get any hint of who it could have been?' she asked. 'Did Miss Saxon use his name at any point?'

'Well, I'm not sure. It was only the once she thaid it, and —'

'What name was this?' Kate broke in urgently.

'The point is ... I can only tell you what it *thounded* like.'

'The name, Mr Arliss.'

'It was Ram. But I might have got it wrong, of courthe.'

'She called him Ram? R-A-M?'

'Well, yeth.'

'Just the once? And no other name of any kind was mentioned? Perhaps the name of a place?'

'No, just that one name, as far as I heard.'

'Tell me what you can remember about Miss Saxon's side of the conversation.'

'At first she was talking quietly, so I couldn't really hear. She thounded impatient more than anything. Exathperated. But then she thuddenly exploded at him.'

'Exactly what was it she said?'

'I've been thinking about that. As far as I can recall, it went something like this: "Just get the hell out of my hair, will you? Can't you get the message, Ram, it's over? *Finito.* Tho bloody well stop bothering me!" Then she thlammed the phone down.'

'What comment did she make when she came back to join you?'

'She was laughing, but I have a feeling she wasn't really amused.' Arliss swallowed audibly. 'She just thaid, "Don't *you* get to be a bloody bore, Andy, when I give you your marching orders."'

'Andy? Why did she call you Andy when your name is James?'

'Oh! The fact is, my second name is Andrew.'

'I see. Tell me, Mr Arliss, do you have the slightest idea who she might have been speaking to? Can you make a guess?'

'I'm afraid not. I've no idea who it was.'

'Very well. If anything further does occur to you, please get in touch with me at once. Meantime, I think you'll like to know that this morning I have received a report from Yorkshire. The police there are entirely satisfied that your wife was in Scarborough at the relevant times.'

He made a grunting sound. 'Dawn mentioned on the phone last night that they'd been round to question her. She was very puzzled, naturally, but I managed to convinth her that it was just a matter of routine police enquiries.'

A handy phrase, that, routine police enquiries! Kate hung up and called Boulter in.

'We've very possibly got our man, Tim, except that we don't know who the hell he is.' She relayed her conversation with Arliss.

'Ram?' the sergeant repeated thoughtfully. 'Convey anything to you, guv?'

'It's an abbreviation, I suppose.'

'Ramsbottom?' he suggested. 'How many Ramsbottoms have we got on our suspect list?'

'Listen, have a run-through on the computer to see what name-links it comes up with. Of course, it could well be that he's not a local man. This Ram guy could easily be someone from her past, not a recently ditched lover. We've simply got to get more information about Corinne Saxon's background before she turned up at Streatfield Park.'

'We're trying every lead we can think of, guv.'

'Well, try harder. I think I'll slip across to the hotel and have another word with Admiral Fortescue. I've always had the feeling that he hasn't come totally clean with us. It's just possible he knows something that would point us to the identity of our Mr Ram.'

'The coppers have found out what happened to her car,' Larkin announced breathlessly, spotting Labrosse coming out of the hotel library. 'Someone bloody nicked it.'

The Swiss stopped in his tracks and stared. 'How do you know this, Sid?'

'That Maddox woman was telling the admiral. Heard her, I did. She said it was nicked by a bloke working for one of those organised car-theft set-ups. He just happened to spot it parked in that lane and grabbed his chance. She reckons the car will have been whipped out of the country by now.'

Labrosse began chuckling. '*Mon dieu*! We never thought of that explanation. Very convenient, too, except for the worry it's caused us wondering where on earth it had gone. Did the police inspector have anything else to say?'

'She was going on about them following up all kinds of leads, but it sounded like a proper load of flannel. Oh yes, she asked the old boy if the name Ram meant anything to him. Which it didn't.'

'Ram? That means nothing to me, either.'

'Nor me.'

Labrosse chuckled again. 'Let us hope it keeps the police guessing for a nice long time.'

'Yves, don't you think we should − '

'Relax! We have nothing to fear. And how many times must I tell you not to call me Yves? One of these days someone will overhear you. You're just the admiral's steward, and I'm the manager of this hotel. Mr Labrosse to you. Remember that in future, Larkin, and keep your place.'

He strode off along the empty corridor. Larkin watched his departing back with troubled eyes. Bitter eyes.

Towards the end of Sunday afternoon Kate sat in her makeshift office with a cup of tea that had just been brought to her. Through the narrow slit of the open ventilator she had a view of the clock on the stable tower. Its gilt hands glinting in the sunlight said four-fifty-two. Which made it three minutes slow, she saw, glancing down at her wristwatch.

Earlier, there had been a flurry of excitement when the computer had thrown up two names that might possibly have been abbreviated to Ram. Both proved to be dead ends. Herbert *Ram*sden was a local vicar, on file because he'd been invited to the hotel's launch party. Not only was he a pillar of the community, but discreet enquiries had established that

93

he'd spent the afternoon of Corinne Saxon's death conducting a funeral service, afterwards adjourning to the home of the deceased for baked meats with the family. Then there'd been Hi*ram* G. Ledbetter, from Milwaukee, a guest with his wife at Streatfield Park for a few days just after the hotel opened. The Milwaukee police department came up speedily with the information that on the day of the murder Hiram G. had been right there at his home in town, resting up a broken ankle sustained on the golf course.

So what now? Kate took a sip of tea every now and then. The thought she'd held at bay all day had begun to gnaw at her brain. She still needed to talk to Richard Gower, because he had known the murder victim. Had at one time been intimate with her.

Kate didn't suspect Richard, of course she didn't; she never had done. Even so, it had come as a relief, when the time limits of Corinne's death were established, to realise that Richard had an excellent alibi.

Wednesday was press day for the *Marlingford Gazette*, which meant that each Wednesday afternoon Richard prowled anxiously between his editorial office and the machine room where the ancient Crabtree clanked painfully, as if each revolution would be its last. It was Richard's constant fear that one of these weeks there'd be a major breakdown before the print run was complete, and (so his foreman printer complained) he fussed like an old mother hen until the last copy was safely off the press at approximately 6 p.m.

Nevertheless, she couldn't indefinitely postpone her talk with Richard. Now that she needed to widen the investigation by delving deeper into the victim's life, he was an obvious person to interview. Yet she shrank from the thought of discussing Corinne Saxon with Richard. She dreaded his hostile reaction when she raised the subject.

Don't be so bloody gutless, Kate Maddox!

Reaching for the phone, she punched out Richard's home number. No answer. Just on the off-chance, even though it was Sunday, she tried the *Gazette*'s number. Nothing. Shrugging, she gave her attention to the new batch of routine reports, but her mind was made up now. Half an hour later she tried Richard again. And later still, yet again.

When Kate finally arrived home, the first thing she did was to try him once more. Talking to Richard had suddenly become imperative. Her last attempt to reach him was just after midnight.

Kate awoke at six-thirty on Monday morning with a thick head, like a hangover she hadn't earned. The sky in the east was an ominous red and the air coming in through the open window felt clammy. Maybe a jog would revive her, she thought, and get her brain thinking straight.

She dragged herself out of bed, pulled on a tracksuit, and slipped out into the silent morning. By the time she returned, twenty minutes later, the threatened rain had begun and she was soaked to the skin.

The phone started ringing just as Kate stepped under the shower. Sod's law! Dripping wet, she went to the nearest extension, which was in the bedroom. Before she reached it the ringing stopped. Damn and blast! If she returned to the shower, whoever it was would probably call again. Resignedly, she rubbed herself dry and got dressed.

A slice of wholewheat toast and Oxford marmalade. No butter. Plus a mug of strong black clear-the-brain-cells coffee. She'd taken her first bite of the toast when the phone rang again. Okay, Mr Sod, I get the message.

Today's going to be a real bitch, Kate!

Picking up the phone, she mumbled her number through a mouthful of half-chewed toast. An irate voice exploded in her ear. Richard.

'Kate! Where the hell have you *been* all this time? I've been trying to get you since just after seven.'

'What the hell business is it of yours where I've been?'

'I tried the Incident Room at Streatfield Park, and you weren't there.'

'So I wasn't there. And I wasn't here.'

'Cut it out, Kate, this is serious. Felix is in a really bad way.'

Alarm clutched at her throat. 'What do you mean? What's happened?'

'A full-scale abdominal crisis, peritonitis, that's what's happened. Those bloody gallstones of hers. She's in the operating theatre now.'

'Oh, my God! Where? At the Peace Memorial? I'll get there right away.'

Twenty-five minutes later Kate hurried in through the hospital's automatic glass doors. As she crossed to the information desk, Richard came forward to meet her.

'What's the latest news?' she gasped.

'Nothing new. She's not yet out of theatre.'

They sat down on two orange plastic chairs in the waiting area, and Kate demanded, 'How come you're here? When was she admitted? Why wasn't I informed? Sooner, I mean.'

'Because Felix wouldn't allow you to be told. I wanted to phone you when she was brought in last night, but she insisted that you'd got too much on your plate just now.'

Typical! Kate should have felt grateful for this consideration. Instead, she felt resentful that her aunt had turned to Richard instead of her.

'Tell me about it,' she snapped. 'How was it you came to be involved?'

'Because I took the trouble to find out how she was. On Saturday lunchtime I saw Felix in the Wagon, and — '

'Yes, she told me.'

'You mean you actually talked to her,' he said, with an accusing glare, 'and you didn't register how sick she was?'

That cut deep. She should have guessed something was wrong when Felix sounded so maudlin and unlike her usual self on Saturday night. Instead, she'd put it down to one or two whiskies too many. She'd been too bloody preoccupied with the job to spare enough attention to her elderly aunt.

'Felix did sound a little ... strange on the phone,' she admitted repentantly. 'But I didn't realise there was anything really wrong. She said nothing to me about feeling ill.'

'You know damn well that she's had this bloody gallbladder trouble for years. Her doctor's kept on and on at her about having it seen to.'

'I thought she had things under control — as long as she watched her diet.' But she remembered, guiltily, the acute attack her aunt had suffered while Kate had been temporarily living with her after being transferred to the Cotswold Division. The nausea and vomiting, the obvious pain. Felix had tried her best to play it down, of course; and

96

afterwards, after she'd been to see her doctor, Kate had too easily accepted Felix's assurance that the problem had been solved.

'Did she ring you, Richard, to ask for your help?'

'No. I called round last night to see how she was. God, it's lucky I did! I felt a bit concerned about her after seeing the state she was in on Saturday. So as soon as I got back from spending the day with those friends of mine in Bath, I thought I'd give her a ring. There was no reply, and that worried me. I couldn't believe she'd feel up to going out for the evening. Anyway, I decided I might as well drive round to Stonebank Cottage to check she was okay. She didn't answer the doorbell, but there was a light on in the living room. When I peered in through the window I saw Felix lying on the floor, doubled up in pain. I broke in and called an ambulance. I would have called you, of course, except that she begged me not to.'

'I wish to God you had.' Kate felt sick with guilt. Pelting through her mind were all the things that Felix had done for her after her mother's early death − the consoling, the supportiveness, the wise advice through all the crises of growing up. And the very first time, in any important way, she might have repaid some of her outsize debt to her aunt, she hadn't been there. The job stood in the way. That was why Felix hadn't allowed her to be contacted − the bloody job.

'If anything happens to her,' she said, 'I'll never be able to forgive myself.'

Richard's voice gentled. 'Nothing's going to happen to her. She'll be okay.'

'How can you know that?'

'Felix is a tough old biddy. She'll come through this all right.'

They went on waiting. Somewhere along the line, Kate remembered that she ought to have called in to report where she could be contacted. She found a phone and explained to Sergeant Boulter what had happened.

'That's tough luck, guv. I do hope Miss Moore will be okay. She's a really nice lady.'

'I didn't realise you knew her, Tim.'

'Well, I don't suppose she registered my name, but I met her on the job five or six years ago, when I was a DC.'

'Oh?'

'Some kids had been on the rampage and smashed the panes in her greenhouse, and I was sent to see her about it. She invited me in and we chatted and she fed me tea and cakes. We never did catch those kids.' Boulter chuckled. 'I always had a feeling she knew who they were all along and wouldn't let on.'

'Sounds like my aunt!' Kate pulled her mind to the case. 'Anything new, Tim?'

'Not a lot. Arliss's alibi has been checked out, as far as being at the airport is concerned. The girl at the information desk remembered him. But he could still have done it – just – if he'd already been in the vicinity of Streatfield Park at around the time Corinne Saxon set out.'

'Hmm! Well, ring me here at the hospital if anything urgent comes up. It looks as if I'll be hanging around for a while yet.'

Kate returned to sit with Richard, and she was glad he insisted on waiting with her. They didn't speak much, but she found his presence comforting. After what seemed an endless stretch of time, a doctor came to inform Kate that surgery had been satisfactorily completed.

'You can see your aunt when she comes round. But only for a few minutes. She'll be pretty woozy.'

Felix appeared to be asleep, but at the sound of Kate's voice her eyelids fluttered upwards.

'So you're here, girl. How did you know?'

'Richard called me – eventually.'

'He shouldn't have done,' Felix said, frowning. 'I told him not to bother you. I shall be all right, Kate, don't worry, and there's nothing you can do by being here. You've got far more important things to attend to.'

'Oh, bugger that! They'll have to do without me for a while.'

'Silly girl.'

'And you are a silly old woman,' said Kate, bending to touch her lips affectionately to the pale, weathered cheek. 'Don't you dare scare the hell out of me like that again, d'you hear? It's all right, nurse, I'm just leaving. I'll be back to see you this afternoon, Felix.'

Outside, Richard walked her to her car. 'They told me no other visitors till tomorrow,' he said, 'so I'll come round to see her then.'

'I've got to talk to you, Richard.'

'I'm listening.'

'Officially, concerning Corinne Saxon.'

'Are you cautioning me?' He gave a taut, bitter smile.

Kate made an exasperated face. 'We badly need information about Corinne's earlier life, before she turned up at StreatfieldPark.'

'You want me to attend for an official grilling? With the doughty Sergeant Boulter wielding his tape recorder?'

'It doesn't need to be formal. You say where.'

Richard didn't reply. Kate unlocked the door of her car and stood waiting to get in. At last he said, 'I'll be home this evening from six o'clock onwards. Drop by any time it suits you.'

Chapter Nine

Bad news from the forensic laboratory. After only a single day's immersion in the filthy water of the gravel pit, Corinne Saxon's diary was virtually indecipherable. The lab people would continue to apply every known technique to try and unlock its secrets. But the prognosis was gloomy.

There was one tiny bit of good news, though. Some figures written on the flyleaf in a different hand from Corinne's and with a different type of pen could partially be made out. Six digits, three of which were clear, one could be a five or a six, one a two or a seven. The final figure was unreadable. From the first two digits it was recognisable as a local telephone number.

'Get someone to work out the possible permutations, Tim, then ask Telecom to provide a list of all the subscribers matching that list of numbers.'

For lunch Kate had a meal on a tray in her office, provided by the kitchens of Streatfield Park. A small, delicious avocado and watercress salad, a portion of game pie (how right you were, Tim!) and a dish of late raspberries with cream. Plus a pot of coffee that was light years away from the muck served in the canteen at DHQ.

Refreshed, she felt ready for the result of the numbers game. There was quite a list of possible variations. All but two, though, appeared to be totally unconnected with Corinne Saxon. They'd have to be checked out, of course, but that job had a fairly low priority. Of the two numbers that remained, one was that of a market gardener who regularly supplied organically grown produce for the hotel. Kate had often bought salad stuff from the roadside stall by his smallholding, and considered him a very unlikely candidate for an intimate relationship with Corinne Saxon. The other possibility looked more promising, being the residential phone number of the architect who'd worked on the conversion of Streatfield Park, Adrian Berger.

On Kate's office wall were the photographs Richard had sent her, taken by the *Gazette*'s photographer at the launch party. One showed Berger in a group. As she recalled, he'd been a pleasant, affable man. Good-looking, too. Nearly fifty, he was of medium height, with a small bristly moustache, tanned skin and bright sky-blue eyes that darted around alertly. Not surprisingly, he'd been on quite a high that day, what with the congratulations being showered on him and the champagne flowing like water. Standing beside him, his wife looked coolly supercilious, as if accepting the homage to her husband as no more than her due.

Thoughtfully, Kate buzzed for the action report on the original interview with Berger. DC Cowan, who'd gone to see him on the Saturday, had reported that he appeared very upset indeed about Corinne Saxon's death, especially at the fact that she'd been brutally raped first (as it had then been believed). Questioned on his whereabouts at the time of the killing, he'd at first taken offence, then given the name of a junior partner at his firm. The two men had spent the entire afternoon at a cottage near Larkhill, which they were modernising for a client.

Kate picked up the phone. 'Is Nick Cowan around?' she asked.

'Yes, he is, ma'am.'

'Send him in, will you?'

DC Cowan had chalked up several years' experience in the CID. A six-footer and natty dresser, he was a man who fancied himself with women. There'd been one occasion when Kate had had to slap him down hard, since which time he'd been wise enough never to step out of line with her. His manner now as he entered her office was cautious, with an undertow of resentment.

'Something wrong ... ma'am?'

'Not that I know of,' Kate said equably, waving him into a

chair. 'I just wanted a word with you about this chap Adrian Berger, the architect. Is there anything you can add to your report, Nick? Any impressions of the man?'

'A bit of a wimp, I thought,' he said contemptuously. 'He seemed really shaken up by the Saxon woman's death. He must have realised it made him look pretty feeble, and he apologised for it.'

'Apologised?'

'Muttered something to the effect that as they'd been working together such a lot, it'd come as a terrible shock to him. Almost in tears, the man was. And the fact that she was raped, well, he just couldn't seem to believe it. As if that sort of thing doesn't happen. Christ, some of these middle-class bods seem to live in another world from the rest of us. You'd think he'd never picked up a newspaper in the past ten years.'

'Hmm!' *Work at this, Kate! It's worth spending time on.* 'His alibi about being with a partner of his that afternoon at a cottage they were converting – were you entirely happy with it?'

Cowan's shrug rejected the implied criticism he read into her question. 'I don't see why not. The partner – what was his name, Pascoe – confirmed everything Berger had told me. The cottage used to belong to an old girl who died a few months back, and Berger negotiated to buy the place for his brother-in-law who'd been wanting to find a house in the country for when he retires next year. It needs a lot of work doing, enlarging and so on, and Berger's firm is handling that. Apparently the whole roofline has got to be rebuilt, and that other guy, Pascoe, is a whizz at roof design. The two of them were there all Wednesday afternoon.'

'So you were quite satisfied? No doubts at all?'

Cowan frowned. 'No, not really.'

'Come on, Nick, out with it.'

'Pascoe seemed a mite jumpy, that's all. He's fairly young, mid-twenties, and I put it down to nerves. I also checked with their office and got confirmation that both men were out all that afternoon. It seems that Pascoe had told the staff he'd be at the cottage, in case he was wanted.'

'Where *he'd* be? Not *they*?'

'Berger hadn't said where he was going, just that he'd be out. But that was quite normal. He doesn't always tell them where he'll be.'

Kate mused. 'The fact that you double-checked with their office at that early stage of the investigation suggests to me that you had a few reservations about their story.'

'It was just to do a thorough job. Is that wrong?'

She nodded at him. 'Okay, Nick. Tell the switchboard to get Berger on the phone for me, will you? Or if he's out, to ask his office have him ring me ASAP.'

Within a couple of minutes Adrian Berger was put through to her. He sounded like a busy man disturbed at a very difficult moment. Impatient, yet worried.

'There's a small matter concerning the death of Miss Saxon that you might be able to help us clear up, Mr Berger. I wonder, would it be possible for you to come and see me right away? At the Incident Room in the squash courts at Streatfield Park.'

His tone was resentful. 'I've already made a statement to one of your officers, Chief Inspector. I don't think there's anything I'll be able to add to it.'

'I won't keep you long.'

'Well, I suppose —'

'Let's say in half an hour, shall we?'

He murmured something Kate didn't catch, to a colleague or secretary, presumably, then said with a point-making sigh, 'Very well, in half an hour.'

He arrived ten minutes late. When he was shown into her office, Kate remembered him vividly. He was a man with a powerful aura, but the affability was lacking today. The darting eyes were looking everywhere except directly at her. At Kate's invitation, he sat down in an abrupt movement and crossed his legs.

'How is it you imagine I can help you, Chief Inspector?'

'For reasons I won't bother you with, Mr Berger, a diary belonging to Miss Saxon was found immersed in water. As a result, the paper has been virtually reduced to pulp and the writing cannot be deciphered. But we have been able to make out part of a telephone number written on the flyleaf, and this could possibly be your residential number.'

He straightened, sitting bolt upright. There was a note of sarcasm in his voice. 'That's hardly surprising, because it *is* my number. I jotted it down for her myself. Really, Chief Inspector, if you'd asked me about it on the phone I could have told you there and then and saved wasting all this time.'

'*Why* did you write your number in Miss Saxon's diary?'

'Why?' A lock of his dark hair had fallen across his forehead, and he brushed it aside impatiently. 'Because Corinne Saxon was the sort of client who expected people to be at her beck and call. My home number happens to be ex-directory, and she was annoyed when she couldn't get hold of me one evening. I don't like being bothered at home, but she was too good a client to upset, so I wrote the number on the flyleaf of her diary.'

'I see. You must have had a great deal of contact with Miss Saxon these past few months.'

'Almost daily,' he agreed. 'What of it?'

'You will have known her better than most people. Can you think of anyone who might have killed her?'

'No, I can't. She could be irritating, of course, as I've explained, because she was such a perfectionist. But she was a charming and delightful woman, so it's impossible to think of her having any enemies.'

A smoothie, this one, Kate!

'Mr Berger, did *you* kill Corinne Saxon?'

He looked stunned; then his expression became contemptuous.

'Is that meant as a serious question?'

'Perfectly serious.'

Berger snorted a laugh. 'If I *had* killed her, I'd be likely to answer yes, wouldn't I?'

'You might be best advised to do so. Because the truth will emerge in the end, make no mistake.'

'Well, I'm sorry to disappoint you, Chief Inspector, but I didn't kill Corinne Saxon. I couldn't possibly have killed Corinne on Wednesday afternoon because I was elsewhere at the time. Furthermore, I had no reason to kill Corinne, and no wish to kill her. So if I've now answered all your questions, perhaps you'll allow me to get on with my interrupted day.'

104

'By all means, Mr Berger.'

He departed with (over-the-top?) jauntiness.

Kate stole time from her busy schedule that afternoon to
drive to Marlingford to visit her aunt in hospital. En route
she stopped off to buy a bedjacket, a couple of nighties
and a few toiletries. It distressed her to find Felix looking
so pale and wan as she lay flopped back against the pillows.
She was too exhausted to say more than a few words, and
the deep-etched lines on her face betrayed every one of her
sixty-eight years.

In the evening, Kate went again for a longer visit. This time
she found the patient greatly improved. Felix was sitting up
alertly and in a bossily confident mood.

'What a ridiculous fuss everyone's making about my little
problem.'

'If you'd had your little problem seen to years ago,'
Kate observed dryly, 'there'd have been no need for a
red alert and all systems go. I've been thinking, Felix.
Making plans. You could always come and stay with me
while you're convalescing, of course, but I thought you'd be
more comfortable in your own home. So instead, I'll come
and stay with you at Stonebank Cottage for a bit.'

'You certainly will not, girl.'

'Don't be so difficult. You can't cope on your own. Not
at first.'

'I won't be on my own. I've already made other arrangements, Kate. The younger sister of one of the nurses here
is going to come and stay with me for a couple of weeks.
It will fit in very neatly before she starts her own training.
Nice, bright, young girl by all accounts.'

'My God, you're a fast worker! Barely come round from
the anaesthetic and you're making detailed plans.'

'I knew what you'd be like, girl. I refuse to be a drag
on you.'

'Felix, you'll never be a drag on me.' Kate spoke with
sincere affection. 'I'd have loved to come to Stonebank
Cottage and cosset you for a while.'

There was a glint of tears in her aunt's eyes at this untypical
moment of emotion between them. But she blinked away such

weakness and said briskly, 'Well, you won't get the chance now, will you? But here's something you *can* do for me. I'm booked for the gymkhana at Iliff on Saturday, and there are a number of other dates in the next week or so that'll have to be cancelled, too. You'll find all the details in my book, by the phone.'

Leaving the hospital, Kate drove to Chipping Bassett and spent nearly an hour at Stonebank Cottage, checking that everything was secure, throwing out food that would go bad, collecting together a few items that Felix wanted, and telephoning to cancel her aunt's upcoming engagements as an equestrian photographer. Then she drove on the few hundred yards to where Richard lived.

Borough House was one of the architectural delights of the small town. Creeper-clad right up to its castellated roofline, the charming sixteenth-century building had been converted a few years ago into eight flats. Until Kate had acquired a place of her own, she had envied Richard his spacious living quarters and mused over what she could do with the various rooms. As for Richard, so long as he had moderate comfort and someone to come in and keep the place clean, he seemed satisfied.

Parking her car in Duck Lane, she walked around to the entrance and up the flight of stairs, solid oak with wrought-iron banisters. Richard opened his front door to her ring.

'At last! I'd begun to think you weren't coming, Kate.'

'It's not much past nine,' she said, on the defensive. 'I had to visit Felix this evening, and then she wanted me to collect some things for her from Stonebank Cottage.'

They walked together into his living room, but they both remained standing.

'How's Felix doing?' he asked.

'Oh, getting back to normal. She's already started bossing me around again.' Kate paused. 'She's very grateful to you, Richard, for all that you did. And so am I, of course.'

He shrugged. 'For Christ's sake, it was no more than anyone would have done.'

'You mean,' she said bitterly, 'what I should have been around to do myself.'

106

'Oh no, spare me the guilt trip!' His stance challenged her. 'Why don't you get on with what you've come to say? I suppose you're here to ask me for my alibi for when Corinne was killed?'

'I already know your alibi. You were where you always are on a Wednesday afternoon. At the *Gazette*, sweating blood until the last copy comes off the press.'

'So why,' Richard demanded sarcastically, 'all that crap the other day about every man who'd ever had anything to do with Corinne being under suspicion?'

'I was merely explaining the police viewpoint. Personally I never had the least suspicion about you – and you damn well ought to know that. However, it's an academic point now. Since the time of Corinne Saxon's death has been narrowed down to Wednesday afternoon, there's no possible question that you could have been at the scene then.' Deliberately, Kate flopped down on the leather chesterfield. 'Aren't you going to offer me a cup of coffee? I could do with one.'

Richard wouldn't relinquish his grievance so easily. 'Sure you don't want to check with my staff that I really was at the *Gazette* that afternoon? And then check their bank accounts to see whether I bribed them all to back up my story?'

'Oh, bollocks!'

Richard retreated to the kitchen, but Kate got up and followed him. It would be easier to talk when he was occupied with doing something than when they were just sitting.

'The postmortem's thrown up something interesting about Corinne,' she said. 'This is not for publication, Richard, not yet, but it seems that at some point in her life she gave birth to a child.'

Kettle in hand, he shot her a furious glance. 'Well, it certainly wasn't mine.'

'I didn't imagine it was. But – think about it – did Corinne ever give you any hint that she'd once had a pregnancy? I mean, either just recently or when you knew her way back?'

'Never. Does it matter?'

'As it happens, yes, it does. For one thing, it's odds on that the child is still alive, somewhere.'

'Well, I can't help you. How about her ex? Could it have been his?'

'I'm pretty certain it wasn't – judging from his shocked reaction. He told me he'd always longed for children, but Corinne was adamantly against it. The evidence suggests that the birth took place some time ago, so if it wasn't while she was married, it must have been before that. I'm trying to piece together a picture of her life, Richard. These past few weeks, did she talk to you about the old days at all? Did she refer to people she'd kept in touch with since that time?'

He gave an impatient sigh. 'Listen, since Corinne turned up at Streatfield Park we only had a couple of meals together and the odd few drinks. Mostly, our conversation was about the sort of publicity she wanted me to give the hotel in the *Gazette* as quid pro quo for the ad space she was taking in the paper.'

'You must have reminisced, brought back a few sweet memories?' *What the hell line of questioning is this, Kate?*

Richard fitted a filter paper in the cone, spooned in coffee, and dribbled water from the kettle. He didn't answer until he'd put the kettle down again.

'You seem to think that our little caper way back was the great passion of both our lives. For God's sake, Kate, back then I was just your average horny young guy who spent most of his waking hours thinking about sex and how I could manage to lay a girl that night. When Corinne drifted into my life, it was like winning the pools. Better than. She was the sexiest creature I'd ever encountered, and she made it clear she had the hots for me, too. The next few weeks is like a hazy dream in my mind – even at the time it was somewhat hazy. Then suddenly the magic was all gone. We dragged things out for a bit, but at that sort of age there's nothing colder than yesterday's love affair. While it was still going on, though, we didn't waste time discussing our mutual backgrounds.'

Kate felt a lot more cheerful. But she wasn't through yet. 'I got an impression that Corinne's recollection was a little more vivid.'

'What makes you say that?'

She pulled a face at him. 'Big Dick!'

108

'Oh,' he said, looking a bit sheepish. 'Well ...'

'You may well give me "well". You were as fatuously pleased with yourself the other week as you must have been when she first coined the epithet. Men!'

Richard's temper, too, had markedly improved. He was grinning. The aroma of coffee, as he poured it out and carried two mugs into the living room, was delicious.

'Kate, do we have to talk about Corinne?'

'Yes,' she said, following him. 'We do.'

'But there's so little I can tell you. Honestly.'

'Oh, come on! You two must have knocked off for a breather every now and then. You must have talked about something.'

'I've already told you the few things I know.'

'Who did she mix with in those days?'

'It was more a matter of who she let mix with her. A top model is way up in the popularity stakes.'

'Anyone special? Apart from yourself?'

'There were always men hanging around her. She used to scoff to me about them, the way they kept trying it on. Corinne was a person who liked to choose her friends for herself.'

'And her lovers?'

'And her lovers. Me, I just got lucky. I always realised that.'

'So you don't think there'd be anybody from that era who could still be harbouring a grievance?'

'Enough to kill her? God, no. It's all ancient history, Kate — for all of them as much as for me, I'm sure.'

'What about girlfriends? Were there any other models around when you knew Corinne?'

'Several. They were a pretty bitchy lot with each other. There was one, I recall, Corinne seemed quite pally with. She hadn't made the big time like Corinne, which perhaps explains it.'

'What was her name?'

'Search me. No, hang on, it was Mitzi, I think.'

'Last name?'

'No idea. I doubt if I ever knew it.'

'Oh, well, I expect we can track her down, if need be.'

109

Kate drank the last of her coffee. 'You haven't been a lot of help, Richard. If you really can't think of anything else about Corinne, I'd better be moving.' She stood up.

Richard stood up, too. 'Kate, don't go.'

The barriers suddenly came down with a crash. 'I mustn't be late,' she temporised. 'It's going to be another heavy day tomorrow.'

'No problem. I'll set the alarm nice and early. And I'll boil you an egg for breakfast.'

'Really?' She gave a slow smile. 'Now that's an offer I can't refuse.'

'There's more.'

'What? Is there no end to your mad generosity?'

Richard reached out for her, put his arms around her, and the jokery stopped.

Some time in the small hours of the night, Kate drifted awake. Beside her, Richard was breathing gently, his breath fanning her hair. His flesh, where they touched, felt wonderfully warm. Outside it was raining, the steady patter on the window panes increasing her sense of closeness to him.

Contentedly, she let her mind wander. Stupid to have gone all uptight about Richard's once-upon-a-time relationship with Corinne Saxon. For God's sake, Corinne would have been just one of a whole string of women in his early life, and she didn't feel jealous about the rest of them.

Big Dick! Huh! Maybe, Kate thought with an inward grin, Corinne made a habit of handing out that sort of sexual flattery to her lovers. Andy? Andy? She wouldn't mind betting that Arliss had suppressed the first half of his nickname; it would have been Randy Andy for sure. Otherwise, why home in on his middle name? How about Ram? Well, Ram by itself could be construed as a sexy nickname. But the HOLMES computer had failed to make a productive link between Ram and one of the names on their suspect list.

Corinne must have had a reason for calling the man Ram, damn it. A connection of some sort, however vague, that might have grabbed her fancy. Corinne was an ex-model, still a glamorous woman ... she was quick-witted ... she was half French. Kate's thoughts lingered there. French. Some connection between the man's name and a French word?

Methodically she considered, clicking through the suspect list one at a time like a slide projector. At Adrian Berger, she stopped, her mind sizzling. Berger had a French shape to it, could easily be pronounced as a French word, *Bear-zhay*. But what the hell would it mean?

Knowing she wouldn't get back to sleep again until this problem was solved, she jogged Richard awake. As he came to he reached out for her, misreading her intention. But Kate disentangled herself and rolled away from him, leaning out to switch on the bedside light.

'Richard, do you have a French dictionary?'

'*What*?'

'A French dictionary. I need to look something up.'

He flopped back on the pillows, muttering to himself. Then he said, 'This reminds me of *Tristram Shandy*.'

'Oh?' Her mind was distrait. 'What are you on about?'

'It was at just such an inappropriate moment that the mother asked the father if he'd remembered to wind the clock before coming up to bed. He retorted − let me get it right − "Did ever a woman since the creation of the world interrupt a man with such a silly question?"'

Kate glared at him. 'Richard, this is important. I'm not in the mood for literary allusions. Have you got a French dictionary?'

'Of course.'

'Then kindly fetch it for me.'

With an enormous protesting sigh, he slid out of bed and disappeared naked into the next room. A minute later he was back.

'Here you are. I'm agog to know what can be so momentous that it can't wait till morning.'

Kate, riffling through the pages, found the entry she was looking for. *Berger (substantive, masculine) − shepherd.* Shepherd . . . sheep . . . ram. Yes, a logical train of thought. She read on. *Berger* also meant *swain, lover.* How deliciously apt! As Kate closed the book with a snap, elation was rippling through her.

'Aren't I going to get an explanation?' Richard demanded grumpily.

'Not now. And I apologise for the interruption. Where were we?'

Chapter Ten

First thing on Tuesday morning, phoning from Richard's flat (a fact she discreetly kept to herself), Kate gave instructions to have both Adrian Berger and Vincent Pascoe brought in for questioning. Each of them was to be picked up at home, before leaving for work, and driven separately to Divisional Headquarters in Marlingford.

Sergeant Boulter, as she had also instructed, reported to Kate at her DHQ office at nine sharp, having first collected the files on Berger and Pascoe from the Incident Room.

She asked him, 'Have our two chummies arrived here yet?'

'They have. Berger's as truculent as hell, and Pascoe's shaking in his natty shoes. I was able to tell them, with hand on heart, that I hadn't a clue what they were here for. What's it all about, guv?'

Even the cold clear light of morning hadn't shaken Kate's conviction that she was on the right track concerning Berger. She told Boulter about the inspiration that had come to her during the night. The sergeant, though, looked far from impressed.

'Sounds a bit of a long shot to me, guv.'

Granted. But Kate had learned to trust her instincts. 'Take my word for it, Tim, giving the man a nickname like that is exactly the sort of thing that Corinne Saxon would have done. Always a sexy innuendo with her.'

'Always? Which other men did she dub with a sexy nickname that we know about?'

You've brought this on yourself, Kate! Damn it, she wasn't about to reveal Richard's nickname to anyone. What mileage her male colleagues would get out of that juicy little item. Big Dick! She shuddered.

'Well, James Arliss, for one,' she said crisply.

'Oh?' Boulter was immediately alert. 'What did she call him?'

'Well, you see, his middle name happens to be Andrew, so she called him Randy Andy.'

Boulter chortled. 'He admitted that to you? I didn't notice it in your report.'

'Well, Arliss didn't actually tell me. I figured it out for myself.'

The sergeant tilted his head musingly. 'A guy wouldn't really mind, would he? I mean, it's dead flattering. What put you on to it, guv? The connection between Ram and Berger, I mean. You know French, do you?'

'Not according to my school reports. But Corinne Saxon was born half French, remember, and lived over there for several years. It suddenly struck me that the name Berger could be pronounced in a French way, *Bear-zhay*. So I looked it up in a French dictionary, and − bingo!'

From Boulter's expression she could see he was miles from being convinced.

'Tim, if we can bust Berger's alibi, then we've got him. So I want to hammer him and Pascoe, keep on at them until one or the other breaks. Neither is aware that the other is here, I take it?'

'No, guv. They're being held separately.'

She went first to see Vincent Pascoe, who was being kept waiting in one of the stark interview rooms on the ground floor. He was a tall, slender young man with intelligent brown eyes. He was trying to put on a bold front, but failing sadly.

Kate introduced herself, then sat down across from him at the small table. Pascoe watched nervously as the sergeant went through the motions of setting up the tape recorder, breaking the seals on the twin cassettes and explaining the regulation procedure. Kate waited in silence, ostensibly glancing through the file of reports she'd brought in with her. Boulter identified time and place and those

114

present. Kate allowed a brief interval, then commenced briskly.

'Mr Pascoe, you informed one of my officers in a previous interview that you spent the whole of last Wednesday afternoon at Yew Tree Cottage, in Larkhill, working on some architectural plans for its conversion.'

'That's right,' he concurred. 'I was there all the afternoon. There were lots of measurements to be taken and sketches to be made.'

'I'm not disputing your presence there,' Kate said. 'But you also stated that Mr Adrian Berger was with you during that time.'

'Well ... he was.'

'*All* of that time?'

Pascoe swallowed, his Adam's apple bobbing. 'Mr Berger joined me there a few minutes after I arrived.'

'A few minutes after? How many minutes, exactly?'

'Oh, about five, I should think. We'd arranged to meet at the cottage at two o'clock, which was when I arrived.'

'So Mr Berger got there not later than about five past two? Let's say ten past at the latest. Is that what you're telling me?'

He nodded confirmation. Boulter gestured towards the tape recorder, and Pascoe enunciated faintly, 'Yes, that's correct.'

'And you both remained at the cottage until what time?'

'It must have been about a quarter to six, or a bit after. Mr Berger said he wanted to look in at the office, but I drove straight home.'

'Was it raining then?' asked Boulter.

Pascoe looked lost for a moment, then his face cleared. 'On my way home it started to come down quite heavily. I had to dash round from the garage to the front door, not having a mac.'

The last couple of answers had the ring of truth. But it wasn't so much Pascoe's movements she was interested in. The big question was whether or not Berger had been with him for any or all of that afternoon.

Kate held out the top sheet of paper from her file. 'Mr Pascoe, this is the statement you gave the other day to one

115

of my officers. Please read it through, and consider carefully. If you want to change it in any small detail, I suggest you do so now before it's too late.'

She watched him go pale as he read, but he braved it out. 'Why should I want to change anything? I've told the truth.'

'If you're trying to protect Mr Berger, you'd be well advised to stop right now. Otherwise, I shall be forced to consider whether you and he were implicated together in the death of Miss Corinne Saxon.'

Pascoe's hands came up in a protesting gesture, as if to ward off her attack. 'No, that's not true. Neither of us had anything to do with her death. Absolutely not, we're completely innocent. I swear it. You've got to believe me.'

'How can you be so certain of Mr Berger's innocence?'

His reply to this challenge – to Kate's intense interest – wasn't an indignant protest that Berger couldn't possibly have committed murder that afternoon because the two of them had been together at the relevant time. Instead, after a gap of several tense seconds, he muttered, 'It's ridiculous to suspect Adrian. He ... he *couldn't* do a terrible thing like that.'

'I suggest,' said Kate, 'that the reason for your certainty is that Mr Berger somehow persuaded you that he'd had nothing whatever to do with the murder.'

Pascoe stared back at her, wide-eyed, obviously fearful about what he was getting himself into.

'Why should he have done that – persuaded me? I ... I mean, he didn't need to. It stands to reason.'

'I agree that he wouldn't have needed to persuade you of his innocence if he'd been with you while the murder was taking place. The question is, *was* he with you?'

'Of course he was. I ... I've already told you.'

'Indeed you have, Mr Pascoe. But were you telling the truth?'

While he was stammering his way out of that, Kate decided to let him sweat for a while. Signalling to Boulter to make a break in the recording, she said, 'I'm going to have a talk with Mr Berger now, to see what he's got to say about all this.'

116

'You mean,' said Pascoe, looking startled, 'that he's here, too?'

'Oh yes, he's here helping us with our enquiries, just as you are.'

Kate deliberately took a moment to shuffle the papers back into the file. As she rose and turned to leave, Pascoe asked, 'How long are you going to keep me here?'

'As long as it takes to get at the truth, Mr Pascoe.'

A uniformed officer came to stand just inside the door. Kate and Boulter walked along the corridor to a second interview room. Berger, seated at the small table, sprang to his feet as they went in.

'At last! I really must protest, Chief Inspector. It's bad enough to be brought here in this peremptory way, but to be kept kicking my heels like this is quite disgraceful. I've a damned good mind to make a formal complaint.'

'That is your right, of course, if you wish to do so.' Once again, Kate waited while Boulter went through the preliminaries of taping the interview. Then she said, 'Mr Berger, I'd be interested to know why Miss Corinne Saxon called you Ram.'

As she'd intended, that stopped him in his blustering tracks. If Berger suspected the truth − that it was only inspired guesswork on her part that identified him as the Ram who'd talked to Corinne on the phone in James Arliss's hearing − he might deny it. And she had no kind of proof, nor ever would have. As it was, by great good fortune, he assumed she must somehow know it for a fact. All the same, Kate had to admire the man's coolness.

'Oh, that!' He shrugged elaborately. 'It was something to do with the meaning of my name in French, I think.'

Kate felt a frisson of excitement. She was convinced now that she'd found her murderer.

But proving it is going to be something else, Kate!

She didn't pursue the nickname aspect. It had served its purpose.

'How did you persuade your junior partner, Vincent Pascoe, to provide you with an alibi for the afternoon Miss Saxon was killed?'

Berger was again badly shaken. She could read his speeding

117

mind: just how much did this woman know? What might Pascoe have let slip? Then his expression changed. He'd decided to continue with his bluff.

'What the devil are you talking about? As I told you before, I spent the afternoon at a cottage at Larkhill, with Vincent.'

Kate glanced at Boulter. 'Sergeant, is Pascoe still sticking to that story? Has he been made to understand the seriousness of perjury?'

Boulter picked up his cue. 'Perhaps I'd better just go along the corridor and make sure he fully understands the consequences, ma'am.'

Berger started. 'Have you got Vincent here, too?'

'Indeed we have,' Kate confirmed.

His eyes narrowed and he adopted a reproachful tone. 'Chief Inspector, Vincent is only a young chap. It simply isn't ethical to use threatening tactics with him. If you convey to him that by telling lies he can in some way save himself from trouble with the police, he might well be tempted.'

'Don't worry, Mr Berger, our intentions are the exact opposite of that,' Kate told him. 'Sergeant, I think I'll come with you and talk to Mr Pascoe myself.'

Vincent Pascoe had certainly been sweating during their absence. Kate felt a fleeting pity for the young man as the two of them entered. He was on the verge of breaking down. Kate took a seat, and Boulter reopened the proceedings on the tape recorder.

'Mr Pascoe,' she began. 'I want you to listen carefully while I spell out a few things to you. The enquiry on which I'm currently engaged is not a trivial matter, but a case of murder. A particularly horrifying murder, too. Now, I have reason to believe that you gave the police a false version of events on the afternoon of Wednesday last. That in itself is a serious matter. But if you persist in the falsehood, you'll put yourself in an even worse position. And you won't in the end help Mr Berger — if that is indeed what you're trying to do. Because, believe me, the truth is eventually going to emerge.'

Pascoe burst out in a fever of urgency, 'Adrian didn't do it. I know you think he might have done, and that's exactly

118

why he asked me to . . . ' He trailed off as the realisation hit him that he'd said the wrong thing.

'Tell me about it,' Kate urged him gently, and gave him time to gather his courage together.

At length, Pascoe said in a low voice, 'He really didn't do it, I swear he didn't. But he knew things might have looked bad for him, if he wasn't able to give you a proper alibi for the time it . . . it happened.'

'Where *was* Mr Berger then, if not at the cottage with you?'

'I don't know where. But he wasn't . . . well, not where you seem to think. He didn't commit that murder and make it look like rape and everything. It can't have been him, not possibly. Adrian just isn't that sort of man.'

'Tell me about it,' Kate said again. 'All of it. From the beginning.'

'Well, on Friday evening, after . . . after the body was discovered, Adrian phoned me at home and asked me to meet him. He was very upset, and he said that the police were certain to question him because he'd had such a lot to do with Miss Saxon over the conversion of Streatfield Park.'

He suddenly dried up, and Kate prompted him. 'Why should that have bothered him, if all he had to do was to explain where he was at the time of her death?'

'Because he *couldn't* explain. Don't you see, he'd have been compromising someone else.'

'And what made you agree to perjure yourself for his sake?'

'I felt I had to. Adrian told me — he was completely frank about it — that he'd been very foolish and indiscreet in having an affair with a married woman. But he said that if it were all to come out there'd be a nasty scandal which could have serious repercussions on the firm, so that all of us on the staff would suffer. So he asked for my help. I'd been at Yew Tree Cottage all Wednesday afternoon, alone, and he explained that all I had to do was to say that he'd spent the afternoon there with me. It didn't seem much to ask; I mean, Mr Berger's always been very good to me, and it would save him a lot of trouble and embarrassment . . . and everyone else at the firm . . . ' Pascoe gave her a forlorn look.

119

'I didn't realise it was going to get out of hand like this.'

'People seldom do when they start lying to the police.'

'What's going to happen now?'

'That depends. Did Mr Berger tell you who the woman was? The one he claims to have been with?'

'No, he said it was best that I didn't know.'

You bet it was best, Kate!

'Now, Mr Pascoe, I shall want you to give one of my officers a full and detailed statement about what you have outlined to me. Meanwhile, I'm going to talk to Mr Berger again.'

'Are you going to ... I mean, will you have to tell him that I've told you?'

'Obviously.' She stood up. 'I hope you realise, Mr Pascoe, that you have seriously hampered the police in their enquiries and wasted a great deal of our time.'

Out in the corridor, Boulter said with a hint of admiration, 'It didn't take you long to get him spilling the beans, guv.'

Kate smiled inwardly. Compliments from her sergeant came but rarely. 'Berger made the mistake of thinking that Pascoe would be as accomplished a liar as he is himself.'

'So it looks like the end of the road?'

'I doubt it. Berger is going to be a lot tougher to break than Pascoe was. We've still got no hard evidence that Berger was anywhere near the scene of the murder.' She raised her eyes aloft, towards the superintendent's office on the floor above. 'No solid facts.'

Berger greeted her return with an air of supreme confidence. Marred only by the fact that, had he really been as innocent as he claimed, he should have appeared more indignant than sarcastic.

'Back already, Chief Inspector! Having failed dismally, no doubt, in your attempt to bludgeon poor young Pascoe into giving you the story you want to hear.'

'Actually,' she said, 'Mr Pascoe has confirmed what I already believed to be the case. I felt sure he wasn't someone who'd willingly cover up for a murderer.'

'What the hell do you mean? What's the silly young fool been telling you?'

'In essence, that you were not with him at Yew Tree Cottage

120

last Wednesday afternoon. That he felt obliged to help you out by concocting a false alibi for you. So I'm afraid the game is up, Mr Berger. I'd like the truth now.'

'Very well. I was ... somewhere else that afternoon.'

'The point is, where?'

He was silent, debating the odds. Finally he muttered, 'Where I was is no concern of yours.'

'It's very much my concern, and you know it. So tell me.'

He adopted, somewhat painfully, an air of candour. 'I assure you, Chief Inspector, that where I was had nothing to do with this case. I was not murdering Corinne Saxon, nor anywhere near East Dean woods. If you insist on knowing, well, I was with a lady whose identity I cannot reveal.'

'In the circumstances, her anonymity is not possible. Who is she?'

'There is no way I'm going to tell you that. It would end her marriage if this came out. I have given her my word that nothing will induce me to reveal her name, and I intend sticking to that.'

'Nothing, Mr Berger? Suppose your refusal results in a charge of murder?'

His face lost colour, but he retained his aplomb. 'That's ridiculous. Totally absurd. How can a perfectly innocent man be charged with murder?'

Kate knew that as long as Berger stuck to his story, there could be no question of charging him. What evidence did she have? Just that Berger was the 'Ram' who'd pestered Corinne Saxon on the phone. From Vincent Pascoe she only knew where Berger had *not* been at the time of the crime, not where he actually was. Her own conviction that she'd found her killer was based on nothing that would be acceptable to the Crown Prosecution Service.

Kate still persisted for a while, hoping she might open up a crack in his armour. But Berger remained stubbornly confident. So confident, indeed, that he never even hinted that he wanted his solicitor present. At length, she had no option but to give up and let him go. For the moment.

When Berger departed, self-assured to the last, Kate said to her sergeant, 'We're going to put everything we've bloody

121

well got into nailing him. Turn the whole squad onto gathering data about Adrian Berger: his domestic life, his business contacts, his friends and enemies. Somewhere out there is the proof we need.'

But such a concentration of effort never happened; it was overtaken by events. When Kate and Boulter reached the Incident Room they were greeted by Frank Massey, looking harassed for once.

'There's been a second murder, Kate. Just five minutes ago a chambermaid found Yves Labrosse in his room. Dead from a blow on the head.'

Chapter Eleven

By normal standards, the suite occupied by Yves Labrosse would have to be described as luxurious. At Streatfield Park it rated merely as run-of-the-mill. A spacious sitting room, with a bedroom plus adjoining bathroom through an archway; nice décor, nice furnishings, nice pictures on the walls. While Dr Meddowes made his on-scene examination and the SOC team were busy, Kate and Boulter absorbed what could be seen without touching anything and possibly destroying evidence.

The dead man lay in a crumpled heap on the floor. Blood had oozed from an ugly wound at the back of his head, matting his dark hair. He was dressed in the immaculate way Kate had always seen him — a beautifully tailored grey wool suit with pristine white shirt and grey silk tie. There was something different about his attire, though, which she couldn't pin down for the moment.

Labrosse had been struck from behind, it would appear, while seated at a small rosewood writing table. The murder weapon was there on the carpet, a silver-gilt candlestick with a heavy octagonal base. Presumably it had been snatched by the killer from one end of the mantelpiece, since its identical partner stood at the other end. Nothing else in the suite appeared to have been disturbed. A thin smear of blood covered the length of the candlestick, and Kate surmised that when the weapon came to be examined they'd find it had been wiped clean of fingerprints. With what? No sign of any bloodstained cloth.

By all the laws of logic, the second murder had to be

linked with the first. Two entirely unconnected killings of top personnel at Streatfield Park was beyond credibility.

So where the hell, Kate thought despondently, had all her brilliant intuition and deduction got her? Maybe, after all, Adrian Berger had finally told her the truth. Maybe his false alibi had been given, just as he claimed, for chivalrous reasons, in order to protect a lady's reputation (and also, of course, to protect himself and his firm from the wrathful vengeance of his well-connected wife). Maybe Adrian Berger was entirely innocent so far as Corinne Saxon's murder was concerned.

Stuff that, Kate!

Except – and what a bloody big except it was – Berger couldn't also have killed Yves Labrosse. And why not? Because he'd been at DHQ when it happened, being questioned by her. Labrosse was seen alive at approximately ten o'clock, and discovered dead at seven minutes past eleven. Seldom could the time of death in an unwitnessed murder be pinpointed with such accuracy. The medical opinion on the matter of timing was superfluous, but Kate didn't tell Dr Meddowes that. The pompous little man was in a jovial mood, savouring the grandness of his new role as regional pathologist. Having pronounced Labrosse dead, killed less than an hour previously by a blow on the head from a blunt instrument, he was inclined to linger and relish Kate's difficulties.

'*Two* murders to solve now, dear lady. You're not finding the responsibility of it all too onerous for you, I trust?'

'I'm coping, thank you,' she said sweetly. 'How about you, Dr Meddowes?'

'Me?' He looked mystified.

'I was wondering how you felt you were measuring up to your higher status, doctor. You've not got in above your head, I trust?'

Kate regarded his huffily departing back with satisfaction. 'Right, Tim, you know the drill. I'm going to have a word with Admiral Fortescue. Shan't be long.'

The 'drill' consisted of opening up a whole new murder enquiry. Re-interviewing everyone they'd already questioned and reconsidering everything the police had so far uncovered, to see how it could be interpreted now that Labrosse too was dead. Just when she'd fondly been thinking there was light at the end of the tunnel.

Kate knocked at the door of the admiral's suite, and was confronted by a darkly doubtful Larkin.

'Admiral Fortescue is very upset,' he told her in his North Country brogue. 'He's not well enough to see you now.'

'I'm sorry, but I'm afraid I must talk to him right away.'

The manservant nodded sullenly. 'I'll go and tell him that.' He withdrew into the room, leaving the door just ajar. Kate heard a low murmur of voices, then the admiral called in a quavery voice, 'Please come in, Chief Inspector.'

He was seated in his usual armchair, looking paler and altogether frailer than she had ever seen him. Which wasn't really surprising, with his managers falling like ninepins. He might even be wondering if he too were in danger.

At his invitation, Kate seated herself. Larkin hovered in the background as if standing guard over his master, and he didn't get dismissed. Perhaps the admiral felt in need of moral support from his long-time steward.

'The death of Mr Labrosse has complicated matters, sir, just when I felt I was nearing a solution to Miss Saxon's murder.'

'Yes, yes, it's a terrible thing. But does this mean, Chief Inspector, that you thought you had identified Corinne's killer?'

'Things seemed to be moving in that direction,' Kate said, without enlarging. 'But now I have to consider whether the two killings were perpetrated by one and the same person. So I am faced with having to re-question everyone who had any kind of connection with both victims.'

'The same person, you think?' Admiral Fortescue considered for a moment, then nodded his head. 'Yes, I suppose that would be a logical assumption.'

'At the same time, of course, I have to keep every possibility in mind. Have you yourself any thoughts as to who might have had a motive for killing Mr Labrosse?'

'None, Chief Inspector. None whatever.'

125

'Are you quite sure?' He'd seemed to dismiss her question too readily. 'Please think very carefully.'

Choosing his words now, the old man said slowly. 'I don't think one could say that Labrosse was universally popular among the staff. He was, perhaps, a little too abrupt in giving instructions. But that would hardly constitute a motive for killing him, would it?'

'Has he ever had to dismiss any employee, who might since have harboured a grudge against him? Perhaps against Miss Saxon, too?'

'Oh no, there's been no such incident, I'm thankful to say. The staff engaged by him and Miss Saxon have all proved to be satisfactory, and they all appear to be happy working here. As far as one can judge.'

'So you can't think that any of the staff would have a reason to want to kill either of the victims?'

'Absolutely not.' The admiral glanced round at the surly figure who stood hovering behind his chair. 'Have you any thoughts on the matter, Larkin?'

'Me, sir? Can't say I have, sir.'

Kate left it there. She had already established in connection with Corinne's death that it would be possible – not easy, but possible – for an outsider to enter the hotel and move around without being challenged. Another possibility was that one of the guests might have had a motive for killing Labrosse and perhaps Corinne, too. She made a mental note to pay particular attention to the guests whose stay had spanned both deaths.

'I shall now have to ask you both,' she went on, 'to account for your movements in the period during which Mr Labrosse met his death. That is, between ten o'clock and eleven-seven.'

'I was here, of course,' Admiral Fortescue said sharply. 'I don't usually leave my rooms until lunchtime, and not always then.'

'And how about you, Mr Larkin?'

'I was here, too. With the admiral. Where else d'you think I'd be?'

'So you can each vouch for the other?'

'That's right,' said Larkin.

126

'Do you agree with that, sir? You can confirm that Mr Larkin was here, too?'

The admiral frowned, as though unable to grasp the reason for her insistence. Then he nodded in irritation, 'As Larkin says, yes. Yes, indeed.'

Sid Larkin stepped forward. 'Now look here, miss, you can see the master isn't well. You shouldn't be bothering him like this.'

'This is a murder enquiry,' Kate replied with a quelling glare. 'I shall ask whatever questions I consider necessary at this time.' She turned back to the admiral. 'What are your intentions regarding the hotel, sir?'

'My intentions?' He gave her a lost, bewildered look. 'I . . . I really don't know what is to be done. This has been such a shock, coming on top of Corinne's death. I haven't had an opportunity to consider the matter.' He shook his head regretfully. 'I cannot see that I have any choice but to close the hotel − for the time being, at any rate. The guests will have to be asked to leave. Indeed, a number of them will probably wish to do so now.'

'Couldn't the hotel tick over for a while? At least for a few days? I'm very anxious that you shouldn't take a hasty decision to close, sir. There will have to be further questioning of the staff and the guests, and it would be more convenient to have as many as possible still on the premises.'

'I see. Well, I suppose . . .' He seemed in something of a daze, all his former air of authority gone. Kate could well understand that the continuance of the hotel must seem of little importance to him in the present circumstances. 'I'll talk to the chef and the housekeeper, Chief Inspector, and see what arrangements can be made to keep going.'

'Thank you.'

Back at her office in the Incident Room, Kate instructed Boulter, 'Get someone to go through the hotel's files and let me see all correspondence relating to Labrosse − letters about his appointment to the job here and so on. Has anything useful emerged from the search of his rooms?'

'Nowt. He doesn't seem to have had any outside contacts.'

'Get the desk in his office searched, too. There might be something there.'

The phone rang, and it was Richard.

'Listen,' she said before he could speak, 'I'm up to my eyeballs right now. There's been a second murder.'

'My God! Who?'

'The manager here, Yves Labrosse.'

'Labrosse! That's very interesting. I'd better come and see you now, Kate.'

'Didn't you hear what I said? I won't have a minute to spare, not for days. Possibly even weeks.' Her voice had grown shrill – from despair. There was nothing she would have liked more at that moment than to be with Richard.

'Okay, keep your wig on! Kate, I've just come across something that might be significant. Even more so now that Labrosse is dead. I'll come over right away, okay?'

Within fifteen minutes Richard was ushered into her office. His limp seemed very noticeable as he came forward and dropped into the spare chair.

'Bloody leg,' he grumbled. 'Means there's more rain on the way.'

'Can't you take something for the pain?' Kate asked sympathetically.

'Already have done,' he said with a grimace. 'Now then, here's my little offering.'

From an envelope he'd been carrying, he shook out a couple of photographs and a cutting from a newspaper. Curious, Kate reached for them. The photos, just snapshots, depicted a much younger Corinne Saxon. In one she was in a small group that included Richard (looking suntanned and devastatingly attractive) at an open-air café. The second was a beach snap with just one other girl. Caught sunbathing on the sand, they were laughing up into the camera. Kate unfolded the newspaper cutting, which was yellow with age. It showed the same two girls in the same situation, but this time in a more studied, seductive pose.

Richard said, 'I know you felt a bit let down when I couldn't fill you in more about Corinne in the early days. So I did a search through masses of junk at home that any sane man would have chucked out yonks ago and dug out this stuff. The pictures were taken in Greece, when I . . . knew Corinne.'

128

'In the biblical sense!' *Stop it, Kate!*

'That newspaper pic, have you noted the legend beneath it?'

She hadn't. It read: *Fun in the Grecian sun. An off-duty shot of model girls Corinne Saxon and Mitzi Labrosse enjoying the beach.*

Kate looked up swiftly. 'Labrosse? Mitzi Labrosse? Is she the one you mentioned as being Corinne's friend?'

'That's the one.'

'So what's the connection with Yves Labrosse? I take it Mitzi wasn't married then? Labrosse was her maiden name?'

'I shouldn't imagine she was married.'

The phone on her desk rang. It was Boulter. 'Thought you'd like to know, guv, that there's nothing whatever on file regarding Labrosse's appointment to the job here.'

'Nothing? No contract? No exchange of letters?'

'Not a blind thing. It must have all been arranged verbally – or the evidence destroyed.'

'Did you ask the secretary about it? Deirdre Lancing.'

'Yep. All she knows is that Miss Saxon spoke of someone coming soon as assistant manager, and the following week Labrosse arrived.'

'Strange! Tim, something very interesting has cropped up. Come in as soon as Mr Gower leaves, will you?'

Kate put down the phone and looked across at Richard. 'Didn't you tell me that Mitzi was French? Not Swiss?'

He shrugged. 'She could've been Franco-Swiss. I just remember her and Corinne prattling away in rapid French every now and then.'

'Did Corinne seem to know Mitzi from the past, from her childhood years in France?'

'It's possible,' he said thoughtfully. 'Certainly she and Mitzi were pretty close, as close as someone like Corinne would ever be likely to get with another female. Come to think of it, there did seem more to it than the normal sort of friendship between two girls in the same line of work.'

Kate pressed him further, but nothing else emerged. 'Okay, Richard, thanks. Get back to me, will you, if anything more occurs to you that I could use?'

'Will do.' He rose to his feet, awkwardly and painfully. 'When do I see you, Kate?'

'I wish to God I knew.'

'You have to sleep somewhere tonight,' he reminded her dryly. 'At my place you'd have an excellent selection of dictionaries and reference books on hand.'

'Get outa here, Gower.'

Boulter came in the instant Richard had left. Kate filled him in with what she'd learned.

'We've got to discover more about the Saxon-Labrosse connection, Tim. Get all the manpower we can spare at work on that aspect. Try to track down this Mitzi Labrosse. She's probably married by now. Talk to the various model agencies to see what information can be got out of them. And get on to the French and Swiss police to dig out what they can for us about the Labrosse family. If necessary, go over there yourself. I can't really spare you, but ...' She gave the sergeant a warning glare. 'If it's *absolutely* necessary!'

It was what Tim Boulter really liked, she knew — being handed an assignment to work on himself rather than dogsbodying for her. He departed, looking mighty chuffed. Kate sighed in anticipation of the fresh avalanche that was about to hit her, the mass of reports flowing from the re-interviews, of which all but point one per cent would be totally irrelevant. Her job was to spot the little nuggets of gold among the dross.

The receptionist and the secretary, she mused, had probably known Yves Labrosse better than anyone else on the staff. Kate decided it would be useful to talk to both these women herself. She sent for June Elsted first, and while waiting for her to arrive she took the chance to eat a sandwich the ever-thoughtful Frank Massey had sent in for her.

The receptionist came in, looking pale, upset and not a little scared. Smiling, Kate tried to put her at ease.

'Sit down, June. This is a very nasty business, and I know you'll want to do everything you can to help me. First, I'd like to get things clearer about what happened this morning. You did see Mr Labrosse earlier on, I take it?'

A nervous dip of the head. 'Yes. He did his usual tour

around once breakfast was under way, checking that everything was in order. He stopped at the desk and we talked over one or two small problems, then he went through to his office. I didn't see or hear anything more of him until about ten o'clock, when he came out and walked across to the lift. I suppose he must have been on his way up to his room, where he ...' She choked back a little sob.

'Did he speak to you at that time?'

'No, he just nodded as he went past. Smiled actually. It struck me that he was looking rather pleased about something. As if he'd just had some good news.'

'Oh? Have you any idea what it might have been?'

'None at all. It can't have been about the bookings, because we've had several cancellations since Miss Saxon was killed, and some of the guests have cut short their stay.'

'Was it normal for him to go up to his room at that time of day?'

An emphatic shake of the head. 'Not at that time, no. Sometimes just before lunch he would go upstairs, like when we had that very hot spell a couple of weeks ago and he wanted to change his clothes. Mr Labrosse was always fussy about his appearance – he liked to look immaculate at all times, and of course it gave such a good impression to the guests. Anyway, apart from something like that, he usually spent the whole morning in his office, or in the kitchens, or around the reception rooms somewhere.' She gazed at Kate forlornly. 'I don't know how the hotel can keep going without Miss Saxon or him.' Not unnaturally, June was thinking about her job.

'Hopefully,' Kate said, 'Admiral Fortescue will find someone else to take charge. Meantime, the best thing is for everyone to keep on doing their respective jobs as well as possible in the circumstances. Tell me, June, what did the staff in general think about Mr Labrosse? Was he well-liked, would you say?'

The receptionist was immediately wary. 'He wasn't what you'd call popular. With him everything had to be just so. I suppose that's fair enough, in a smart hotel like this. But he was always sort of aloof from the rest of us. Never the least bit friendly.'

Changing tack, Kate said, 'You know Mr Berger, the architect, I suppose?'

'Yes, he's here a lot. Not so much now, of course, since most of the work has been done.'

'Always on business? Or socially sometimes?'

'Oh, on business.'

'Could there have been anything more than a purely professional relationship between him and Miss Saxon?'

'Well, I didn't think so.'

'Did he ever visit Miss Saxon in her private apartment?'

'Never, as far as I know. I think it would have been talked about if he had.'

That figured. Berger would have been anxious to avoid any gossip over an affair with Corinne − and thence the probability of messy repercussions. That much was certain, from the arguments he'd used to persuade Vincent Pascoe into giving him a false alibi for the afternoon Corinne Saxon was killed. So where had he and Corinne met for their trysts? Another hotel? The Cotswolds wasn't exactly the sort of area where you could book a hotel room for a few daytime hours. And in this locality there'd be a big risk of their being recognised.

'Might the two of them have met away from Streatfield Park sometimes, do you think? Did anyone ever mention seeing them together, perhaps? Think hard, please.'

'Well ... oh no, it can't have been anything.'

'Tell me about it.'

'I did once see them together away from here. It was one evening about six weeks ago, a few days before the hotel was opened. My boyfriend was driving me to visit his married sister who lives at Larkhill. Just before we reached the village, we were passing an old cottage and I saw Miss Saxon and Mr Berger coming out of the front door. Both their cars were parked in the driveway round at the side.'

'Did they realise you'd seen them?'

'Oh, yes. You see, I gave them a wave, automatically, without really thinking. Next morning Miss Saxon explained to me that Mr Berger was having the cottage modernised for a relative of his, and he'd asked her to give him some advice on the décor.'

One of those little nuggets of gold, Kate! Why the heck hadn't this emerged earlier? Still, she had it now. After getting June to establish the date and time of this encounter as accurately as possible, Kate let her go. Sergeant Boulter was fully occupied with the French connection, so she called in Inspector Massey and explained the latest development to him.

'I want to organise a house-to-house in the area around Yew Tree Cottage in Larkhill. Will you set it up for me, Frank? I'm looking for corroborative evidence that Berger and Corinne Saxon used that cottage for their rendezvous. As things stand, Berger could still insist that Corinne was telling June Elsted nothing but the truth about going there with him to give advice about the décor. But if those two went to the cottage on a number of occasions, someone in the local community must surely have seen them.'

Yves Labrosse's secretary, Deirdre Lancing, seemed even more upset about his death than the receptionist was. It was clear she'd applied fresh make-up before coming over to the Incident Room to see Kate, but she hadn't been able to conceal the fact that she'd been weeping. Her eyes were reddened and puffy, and the droopy-lensed glasses gave her a ludicrous appearance.

'I want you to tell me about this morning, Mrs Lancing,' Kate began. 'Everything you can remember. Were you already in the office when Mr Labrosse made his first appearance of the day?'

'Yes,' she whispered. 'I start at nine, and he came in just before nine-thirty.'

'What did he say?'

'Just . . . just good morning, as usual. He glanced through the mail and took a few letters that would need his attention into his own office. I heard him on the phone once or twice — I don't know who to — then after a while he brought out a tape for me to type up for him. Answers to the letters and so on.'

'Just routine correspondence, was it?'

'Yes.'

'All the same, I'd like to read those letters in case they

133

contain anything I ought to know about. Now, the phone calls he made – you said you didn't know who they were to. But wouldn't he have asked you to get them for him?'

She shook her head. 'Mr Labrosse always preferred to dial himself. And internal calls you dial and receive direct.'

'So he might have been talking to someone in the hotel?'

'Yes, he could have.'

'When he came out of the office the final time, did he say anything to you?'

Deirdre Lancing lifted her spectacles delicately. 'Just that he wouldn't be away long, if anyone wanted him.'

'But he didn't say where he was going?'

'No, he didn't.'

'Was that unusual? Did he normally keep you informed where he'd be?'

'Well, yes. Normally. In case he was wanted.'

'What was his demeanour?'

'How do you mean, his demeanour?'

'His mood, then. Did he seem pleased, angry, regretful or what?'

'Quite pleased, I suppose. He was sort of smiling to himself.'

'And that was the last you saw of Mr Labrosse?'

Her eyes pooled with tears, and she bowed her head. 'Yes.'

Kate asked the same question she'd already put to June Elsted. 'Was Mr Labrosse popular among the staff here?'

Mrs Lancing raised her head again, surprised and to a degree hostile. 'He was management. Most of them don't understand that someone in his position has to insist on proper discipline. Make what might seem like harsh decisions sometimes.'

'So a number of the staff resented his authority?'

'I suppose you could put it like that.'

'Did he make any real enemies among them?'

'No!' she protested. 'Just, well, you always get grumblers, don't you?'

'Anyone in particular?'

The woman shook her head quickly.

'Was there any special incident that caused an upset among the staff?'

Again a negative response, and Kate knew there was no point in pressing this line of questioning at the moment. She said smoothly, 'I'd like you to think about it, Mrs Lancing, and maybe you'll remember something that could be significant. Meanwhile, what was your personal opinion of Mr Labrosse?'

'Well ... ' She was instantly on her guard, like a woman who knew it would be only too easy to betray her feelings. *She fancied Labrosse, Kate!* That explained the depth of her distress.

'He was wonderful at his job. I ... I admired him for that, of course. He could easily have run the hotel single-handed, without Miss Saxon, but I doubt if she could have done half as well without him.'

Kate decided to rub in salt to see what it produced. You couldn't always be nice in this job!

'Was there a woman in his life, Mrs Lancing?'

'No!' She was wounded. 'Nothing like that.'

'Come now, Mr Labrosse was a good-looking man, in the prime of life. It's only natural to suppose that he must have been having a sexual relationship.'

'Well, you're wrong.' Acid resentment now. 'He wasn't the sort of man who spent his time chasing after women.'

Which statement − quite unintentionally, Kate felt sure − provided her with a new line of thought. She made her approach cautiously.

'He must surely have had some friends,' she said in a casual tone. 'Was he friendly with any of the men on the staff? Or any man who wasn't on the staff, come to that?'

'Not exactly friendly.' Sullen, but quite unsuspecting.

'What do you mean by "not exactly"?'

Deirdre Lancing shrugged. 'It wasn't what you could call *friendly*, but it always annoyed me the way that man Larkin used to barge in to see Mr Labrosse whenever he pleased, and never got put in his place. I suppose it was because he's the admiral's personal steward and wasn't under Mr Labrosse's supervision.'

135

Labrosse and Larkin! Smooth and rough. Well, it happened, and propinquity accounted for a lot. This certainly explained a few things. Kate had no wish to alert the secretary to the direction of her thinking. She thanked Mrs Lancing pleasantly for her help, and the woman departed.

Alone, Kate pondered her next move. She recalled that Admiral Fortescue hadn't given a prompt reply when she'd asked if he could vouch for Larkin's presence in his private quarters during the period in which Labrosse was killed. He and his surly manservant probably didn't spend much of their time together in the same room, so had the admiral merely been assuming Larkin's presence elsewhere in the suite? It was scarcely conceivable that he would knowingly cover up for the man.

Straight away, she went across to the hotel to talk to the admiral again. As before, Larkin admitted her and stood hovering, making no move to leave the room. But this time Kate dismissed him.

'I wish to speak to Admiral Fortescue alone.'

He departed sullenly. Kate waited until the door had closed behind him, then said, 'When I asked you earlier, sir, you confirmed that Larkin had been here in your private quarters during the period in which Mr Labrosse had been killed.'

'I did, Chief Inspector.'

'Presumably he wasn't in this room the whole time, so how can you be sure that he didn't leave the suite for a while?'

The admiral regarded her with dismay. 'Surely you don't suspect Larkin of ... of ...?'

'I'm just trying to clarify a point, sir. Kindly give me your answer to the question.'

He shook his head in sorrowful resignation. 'Larkin was in and out of this room. Part of the time I was taking my morning bath, and he knows I always require him to be within call then, in case ... well, in case I should get into difficulty. And for the rest, I could hear him moving about next door, vacuuming and so forth. Larkin was here, Chief Inspector. He was definitely here. So please put out of your mind completely any suspicion you may be harbouring about him.'

'I see. Would you ring for Larkin, please, sir?'

The manservant answered the bell at once, and Kate said, 'I want to see you in my office over at the squash courts, Mr Larkin. In ten minutes.'

'What for, miss?' he demanded truculently.

'I'll explain when you get there.'

The admiral looked at her unhappily. 'Chief Inspector, please! I really must protest.'

'I have a few more questions to put to Mr Larkin,' she told him, 'and the Incident Room is the best place. I won't keep him any longer than necessary.'

Ten minutes later, when Larkin was shown into her office, he looked badly shaken. He sat awkwardly in the chair facing her across the desk, while his stubby fingers nervously smoothed down the few wispy hairs across his balding head. Kate guessed that he'd topped up from the whisky bottle for courage.

She began, 'Did you know Mr Labrosse before he came to work at Streatfield Park?'

'No, I didn't. Why should I have done?'

'Yet in the short time he was here, you two became very close. How did that arise?'

He glared at her. 'Don't know what you're talking about.'

Kate let out an audible sigh. 'Please don't let's waste time fencing with each other. You and Labrosse had a sexual relationship, right?'

Larkin looked as if he were about to deny it, and for an instant Kate feared she might have read the signs all wrong. But then, with a shrug of his hefty shouders, he said gruffly, 'That's not a crime, is it?'

'No, it isn't a crime. And I'm not trying to make any kind of moral judgement. It's facts I'm interested in. Just facts.'

'Can't see it matters to you, one way or t'other.'

'Of course it matters. Yves Labrosse has been murdered, and I'm looking for someone with a motive. Did you two quarrel?'

Kate sat back in her chair, giving him time to consider his position. It took a full minute. His voice, when it came, was harsh and cracked.

'I never killed Yves. Why the Christ should I want to

137

kill him? Okay, him and me got together, I'm not saying different. Right from when he first arrived, we sort of clicked. But to try and make out I had a motive for killing Yves, that's crazy.'

'Are you saying that you and he never quarrelled?'

'Not what you could call *quarrelled*. We had the odd ... well, difference of opinion. Who doesn't?'

'What sort of things were these differences of opinion about?'

Hesitation. 'Yves was a cut above me, and he bloody didn't let me forget it. He'd proper bawl me out sometimes for what he called not remembering my place.'

'You can't have liked that much.'

Sid Larkin said with a flash of spirit, 'When you're just a bloody nobody, you have to get used to it.'

This wasn't getting anywhere. Kate switched tactics. From preliminary reports she knew that a mass of fingerprints had been found in Labrosse's room; a number of them the victim's own, the remainder as yet unidentified. But the murder weapon itself, the silver-gilt candlestick, had been very carefully wiped clean of all prints, just as she'd suspected.

'I shall require you to give us your fingerprints,' she said, 'for comparison with prints found in Labrosse's room.'

For a moment or two Larkin looked startled. Then he gave an off-hand shrug.

'Well, my prints would be there, wouldn't they? I'm not denying that I've often been in his room.'

She tried a bluff. 'Suppose we find they match with prints on the murder weapon?'

Larkin snorted. 'I don't even know what the murder weapon was.'

'Don't you? Very well, I'll tell you. It was a candlestick. One of a pair from the mantelpiece.'

'Well, then, it couldn't have my prints on it, because I've never touched those things.'

Damn, it hadn't worked! There was nothing solid enough to hold him on. She needed above all to break the alibi that he'd been with the admiral when Labrosse was killed.

'Very well, Mr Larkin, that'll be all for now. I'll be wanting to see you again, though.'

138

He rose to his feet, his face and balding skull flushed red with anger.

'I never killed Yves,' he spat. 'And you've no cause to treat me like this. It'd be nice and easy for you to nail me, wouldn't it? Oh, yes! All wrapped up nice and quick, case solved, and never mind the poor sod you get sent down for something he didn't do.'

Kate managed to get to the hospital that evening for a quick visit. Thankfully, she found her aunt was continuing to make good progress. She was away from the Incident Room less than an hour all told, but when she arrived Frank Massey warned her that Superintendent Joliffe had turned up and was waiting in her office.

Had taken possession of her office, more like! She found Jolly's large frame overflowing the chair behind her desk with his long legs, crossed at the ankles, projecting through the knee-hole. On his face was an expression of held-in impatience. Kate guessed that he'd hurriedly adopted this pose on hearing her voice outside the door.

'So here you are at last, Mrs Maddox!'

'I just popped out to visit my aunt in hospital, sir.' Why the hell did she let him put her on the defensive? 'Surely you were informed, when you arrived?'

'Yes, yes. I trust the good lady is making satisfactory progress?'

'Thank you, sir. She is.'

'The same cannot be said for you, alas. Rather than solve one murder, Chief Inspector, you have landed us with a second one. The ACC is most put out.'

'I'm sorry about that, sir. I didn't do it on purpose.'

But humour of any kind was wasted on Jolly Joliffe. She proceeded to outline the facts about Labrosse's death, his relationship with Larkin, and the information she had gathered from Richard Gower.

'Hmm! This friend of yours, Gower, is quite a mine of information, isn't he?'

For the simple reason that he had once been Corinne Saxon's lover. *Skate over it, Kate!*

'I certainly have reason to be grateful to him in this case.'

139

'No doubt. I trust, Mrs Maddox, that you don't allow your gratitude to lead you into making him some sort of quid pro quo.'

'Perhaps you'd explain that remark, sir?'

The superintendent seemed unaware of the dangerous note in her voice. Or just ignored it. 'The man is a journalist, after all, albeit only the editor of the local rag. It behoves all of us in the Force to be constantly on the alert to avoid revealing more than we properly should to the media.'

'I very much resent the implication that I might do that,' Kate said heatedly. 'If a male officer of my rank had a girlfriend who was a journalist, would you consider it necessary to issue such an elementary warning to him?'

Jolly stared at her in amazement, and his thoughts were transparent to Kate. *You just never know where the devil you are with a woman. They're liable to fly off the handle at the most trivial things.*

He reduced the tension with a diplomatic little laugh. 'Good heavens, you mustn't take everything so personally, you know. Now, how about that Berger fellow? From your earlier reports it seemed you had him earmarked as the Saxon woman's killer.'

'It may still turn out that he is, sir, but the Labrosse murder has thrown everything back into the melting pot.'

'Yes, yes, yes,' he said impatiently, then lumbered to his feet. 'You're tying up a high proportion of our manpower resources on this investigation, Chief Inspector. So for God's sake bring me some answers soon. Very soon.'

Kate remained at her desk until nearly eleven that night. But she had to wait until next morning for a breakthrough that promised to carry her forward.

Chapter Twelve

Frank Massey followed Kate into her office when she arrived at the Incident Room on Wednesday morning. He was carrying a bulky envelope, holding it by one corner between his finger and thumb. He put it down on the desk for her to see, address side up.

'This was in the mail delivered to the hotel this morning. We've been monitoring all their incoming post, of course.'

Kate looked without touching, although by now the envelope would have passed through too many hands to yield much under forensic examination. The name and address was typed. Mr Yves Labrosse, Streatfield Park Hotel. Above it, in capitals and underlined, was PERSONAL AND PRIVATE.

'Posted locally at twelve noon,' she commented.

With great care she slit the envelope open with a paper-knife and slid out a wad of used banknotes in an elastic band. Fifty-pound notes. Watched by Frank Massey, she counted them: forty-seven. Making £2,350. Kate held one up to the light from the window, checking for forgery. It seemed okay.

'What the hell was Labrosse up to, Kate?'

'Some kind of crooked dealing, for sure. Blackmail? But you'd expect that to be a round sum, wouldn't you? Payment for services rendered? A percentage of a nice fat contract pushed someone's way, perhaps?'

'I'd go for that one,' said Massey.

But Kate shook her head. 'I don't really see it, Frank. With Corinne Saxon in the picture, I doubt if Labrosse was allowed much influence in the placing of major contracts, and it would need to be a very fat contract to merit this level of payola.' She ruminated. 'I suppose it's just possible that Labrosse acted fast and fixed this after Corinne's death, but – no, I don't think that's the answer.'

'Someone was taking a chance sending it through the mail,' Massey remarked.

'They probably thought it was safer than to risk being seen handing over the cash in person.'

'We could check with the local banks to see what large withdrawals of fifties have been made just recently.'

Kate shot him a grim smile. 'You reckon the banks would play along? If so, we'd likely uncover a long list that Inland Revenue would be happy to see. But I somehow doubt that it would lead us to our chummy. How about fingerprints on these notes, though? If we find any, we'll have to take prints from all our suspects, to see if we can get a match. We might just get lucky, you never know.'

'Right, I'll give it a go, Kate.'

'And have someone get on to the Post Office and see if they can tell us in which particular box it was mailed. I don't suppose they can, but it's worth a try.'

'Will do.'

As Massey exited, Boulter came in. Wearing a big smile and carrying a manila folder stuffed with papers.

'Got something for me, Tim?'

'Have I just! I've spent hours on the phone to France and Switzerland. I'll say this for the lads over there, they can really move when they pull their fingers out.'

'Tell me what you've got.'

Boulter smacked down the file in front of her. 'It's all in there, guv. A fascinating story.'

'I'm sure it is, and I'll read it all later. Meantime, suppose you give me a rundown in your inimitable style?'

Handed a licence to dramatise, Boulter made full use of it. He plonked himself down on the chair across the desk from Kate, crossed his legs and loosed the button of his jacket.

'To start with, Corinne Saxon did give birth to a live child. A bonny bouncing boy. He'd have been seventeen now.'

'Would have been?'

'About eighteen months ago he took a header off his motor scooter and went under the wheels of a farm tractor. Curtains for the poor little bastard.'

'This was in France?'

'Yep, he lived there all through. In a village in the Haute Savoie. That,' he explained helpfully, 'is by Lake Geneva, on the Swiss border.'

'Kind of you, sergeant.'

'Actually, it was a stroke of luck getting the dope on this kid. My contact got on to the village gendarme in connection with the Labrosse name, and it turned out he knew all about Corinne Saxon's baby. It's the sort of little backwater where you can't do a pee without the local gendarme knowing.'

'Get on with it, Tim.'

'It seems that Corinne first got friendly with Mitzi Labrosse when they were just kids. Corinne's parents lived in the city – Lyons – but they had a weekend place in this village. As we already knew, when the parents were killed, Corinne's aunt brought her to England and raised her here. But the two girls always kept in touch, and when Corinne got into modelling she persuaded Mitzi to have a go too. She never hit the big time, though, not the way Corinne did.'

'Where's Mitzi now? Is it known?'

'Sure. She's back living in the same district. Married with three kids. It was from her the gendarme filled in the details he didn't already know.'

'And?'

'One day, when they were on a modelling assignment somewhere, Corinne confided to Mitzi that she was in the club. In a real state she was about it, half out of her wits. She was frantic with the thought of how being lumbered with a kid would mess up her life, but even more scared of having an abortion. Not from moral scruples, I don't mean. Just plain scared to death.' He grimaced. 'Funny, that, for a tough cookie like her.'

'Not funny at all. Abortion is never the easy option for a woman you men think it is.'

Boulter grunted. 'Anyway, Mitzi came up with a brilliant solution to the problem. It happened that she had an older married sister back home who was having problems in the

143

production department. When Corinne's pregnancy began to show, she went to stay with this couple – name of Chivac – and after the kid was born she left it with them.'

'They adopted the boy?'

'Nothing so formal. They just kept him. That sort of thing happens in rural communities. Even around here. You'd be surprised.'

'Not a lot surprises me these days,' said Kate dryly. 'Did Corinne keep in touch with her son?'

'Off and on. She sometimes remembered to send him presents for his birthday or at Christmas, and she'd occasionally visit if she happened to be within striking distance of that part of the world. But more often a whole year would go by without sight or sound of her. She was quite fond of the kid, it seems, when she remembered him. She went over from England specially to be at his funeral.'

'Did you discover who'd fathered the boy?'

'Unknown. Mitzi swore to the gendarme that Corinne never let on, even to her. Told him she couldn't make a guess.'

Kate dwelt on all that for a moment, then asked, 'Where does Yves Labrosse fit into all this?'

'He was Mitzi's cousin. His branch of the family lived just across the border in Switzerland. They used to exchange visits quite often, apparently, so that's how he and Corinne got to know one another.'

'You're not suggesting, are you, that Labrosse might have fathered the child? I rather doubt it; he was gay.'

'Oh! You've already discovered that, have you?' The look of disappointment on Boulter's face was comical. He'd been looking forward to bringing out this titbit.

'It was the hotel secretary who put me on to it. Not that she realised what she was saying. Then, later, Larkin confirmed it.'

'Larkin?'

'Yes. He and Labrosse were making it together.'

'Blow me! Talk about chalk and cheese.'

'Attraction of opposites.'

'Does that mean it was Larkin who did him in, guv?'

'Could be. Could very well be. But we're a long way off

144

bringing a charge yet, Tim. Tell me what else you've found out about Labrosse.'

'What you don't already know, you mean,' he said sourly.

'Now, now!'

Boulter hefted his shoulders. 'The guy was a crook. His history is this. He got a job straight from school as a kitchen boy in a local hotel. Within three years he'd been picked out as management potential and was made a trainee. The guy was a natural, by all accounts, and before he was thirty he was the assistant manager at a big five-star hotel in Geneva. But then, crash-bang-wallop, he was caught fiddling the wages. That old trick of having ghost employees on the payroll. And once they started delving they found he'd been up to all kinds of thievery. No probation for Yves, he landed a hefty stretch. He came out about three years ago, and without references nobody in the hotel trade would look at him. It's not quite clear how he made a living after that, but he didn't come up against the law again except for a couple of minor traffic offences.'

Kate mused. 'I wonder how it came about that Corinne Saxon offered him the job here? I guess she wasn't squeaky clean herself, but why employ a known crook as her assistant?'

'I've been wondering about that, guv. As far as I could trace, the last time those two met up was at the boy's funeral. Very close, the Labrosse family, even though Yves was their black sheep. It could be that Corinne saw him as a way of getting some top-class management at Streatfield Park, since she didn't really know the business herself.'

'She was taking a big risk, though. If it ever came out about Labrosse's past, or if he went back to playing his old tricks, she'd have trouble explaining why she'd given him the job in the first place.'

'Maybe,' Boulter suggested, 'they were in it together. They might have seen the chance of really milking Streatfield Park between them.'

Kate regarded her sergeant gloomily. 'It's all maybe, maybe. Not a solid bit of evidence in sight.' But she didn't want to be ungenerous, so she added, 'Not that you haven't done very well, Tim, gathering all this over the phone. As it turns out, you could easily have justified a trip across the Channel for a couple of days.'

'Now she tells me!'

Frank Massey stuck his head round the door. 'Got a little something for you, Kate. No prints worth a damn on those banknotes. But the typing of the name and address on the envelope looked pretty ropey to me, so I shot it over to Norman Riley at HQ to have a look at. Norman's a whizz when it comes to typewriters, he's got quite a museum of old ones at home. He's just rung me back. He reckons it's point one per cent short of a certainty that the typewriter used was a Remington model that went out of production over fifty years ago. Can't be many of them still around. So all we've got to do is find it.'

'My God!' Kate exclaimed. 'We got lucky after all.'

'How's that?'

'Tim, do you recall seeing an ancient Remington during the last few days?'

'Can't say I do, guv.' Then he did a double take and snapped his fingers triumphantly. 'At the Kenways' place. On the desk in their upstairs room.'

'Right.' Kate's mind went into fast forward, replaying all the evidence so far gathered. 'I never suspected any contact between Kenway and Labrosse. He must be quaking in his shoes right now, knowing that the money he mailed will have found its way into our hands, and wondering if there's any way we can trace it back to him.'

'D'you think he might scarper?' asked Massey.

'We'd better not give him the chance. Tim, get over to Ashecombe-in-the-Vale right away and fetch him in. And bring along that typewriter, too.'

Paul Kenway, when he arrived half an hour later, looked like a man who'd suddenly realised his length of rope had run out.

'Sit down, please,' Kate said briskly. 'Sergeant, will you caution Mr Kenway and explain his rights to him.'

'I don't undrestand,' Kenway protested weakly. 'Why am I here? What's this all about?'

146

'You're here because I need to question you concerning the death of Yves Labrosse.'

'But that's ridiculous. His death has nothing to do with me.'

'No? Then perhaps you will explain to me why you sent him a substantial sum of money. Two thousand three hundred and fifty pounds, to be exact.'

'I ... I don't know what you're talking about.'

'Mr Kenway,' Kate said wearily, 'didn't you wonder why the sergeant wanted to bring your typewriter in for forensic examintion?'

He shrugged, but made no reply.

'At this very moment we are having an expert comparison made between your machine and the typing on the envelope addressed to Yves Labrosse that arrived at Streatfield Park this morning. I haven't the slightest doubt they will match. So why persist in pretending?'

Kenway's shoulders drooped and his whole body seemed to sag. Yet he still didn't give up completely.

'Why shouldn't I send money to Labrosse? I'm an antiques dealer and I sold something for him. That was the proceeds.'

Kate regarded him sorrowfully. 'Which you passed over to him *in cash?* A large sum like that. Come on, Mr Kenway, don't waste my time.'

'He ... he wanted to put the money down on a new car, and he said it would be simpler for him to get cash than having to bother with cheques.'

'A good try, but when people ask to be paid large amounts in cash it's almost certainly because there's something shady about the deal. And you must have known it.'

'What I did, I did in good faith. You can't pin anything on me for that.'

Kate said impatiently, 'This is a murder I'm investigating. A double murder. You were once married to Corinne Saxon, and you had a motive for wanting her dead. It is now known that you had a connection with Yves Labrosse, who has also been brutally killed. So you can rest assured that I am going to get at the truth about this money you sent to him. It's up to you. Do I get answers the easy way or the hard way?'

147

Kenway stared at her, looking cornered. When he spoke the words came out in short, sharp bursts.

'You can't believe I had anything to do with Yves Labrosse's death. Good God, I'm not that sort of man. I couldn't kill anybody. Why should I want to kill Yves?' The light of inspiration came into his eyes as he thought of a reasoning that would save him. 'I wouldn't have sent him that money yesterday, would I, if I'd killed him?'

'I agree. Nor would you have sent it if you were *planning* to kill him. Which leads me to suppose that the murder was unpremeditated.' Kate stepped up the pressure. 'The way I see it is this. After posting the money, you decided to come and see Labrosse for some reason. The two of you quarrelled, and you struck him a heavy blow which killed him. That's what happened, isn't it?'

Kenway was shaking his head violently. 'No, listen, I didn't post that money until after Labrosse was dead. Everyone's saying he was killed some time between ten and eleven yesterday morning. Well, it must have been twenty minutes *past* eleven that I put that packet of money in the post box. I used the one in the village, just a few yards from home. We had several things for posting and I slipped out with them. My wife will tell you. It certainly couldn't have been earlier than twenty past eleven. When I heard on the radio later about Labrosse being killed, I wished to God that I'd never sent him the money, but there was no way I could get it out of the mail, was there?'

'Did anyone see you at the post box?'

He scowled. 'There was nobody around at the time.'

'Too bad! Sorry, but that line of defence isn't going to help you at all. We've checked with the Post Office and they say there are any number of boxes in the neighbourhood which have collections time-stamped noon. And since the previous collection at many of them is early morning, eight-thirty, there's no means of proving at what time that package of yours was actually posted.' Her glance sharpened. 'I presume you've been hoping and praying that we wouldn't be able to trace the money back to you?'

He gave a jerky little nod.

'Right. So now you can tell me all about it.'

148

Kenway closed his eyes against the unkindness of fate. He spoke in a monotone. 'It was about a month ago that I first met Yves Labrosse. I didn't know him from Adam, but he approached me with a business proposition.'

'This was at Corinne Saxon's instigation?'

'On, no. She had nothing to do with it. But Labrosse knew that I'd once been married to Corinne, and he also seemed to know that there was, well, bad blood between us. She wouldn't have told him, I'm sure, but I think he must have overheard us talking on the phone that time I rang Corinne asking to see her.'

Kate nodded. 'And Labrosse decided to capitalise on what he knew by inviting you to join him in a crooked deal? Which means, presumably, that Corinne was the one to be done down. What was the plan?'

Kenway made a gesture of surrender with his two hands. 'Labrosse told me that locked away in the attics at Streatfield Park was a whole mass of stuff — furniture, paintings, *objets d'art* — that wasn't suitable for using in the hotel. Admiral Fortescue wouldn't sell any because it was all family heirlooms, but Labrosse said he doubted if the old boy really knew what was up there. It would probably be years before anyone got around to realising anything was missing. And they still wouldn't know *when* it had disappeared. The risk was virtually nil, he said.'

'So you agreed to find a market for some of these stored items?'

'I didn't see why not. After all, it was Corinne's fault that I was in such a mess financially. If she hadn't been such a greedy bitch, if she hadn't insisted on my paying her that four hundred each month even though she didn't need the money, then Liz and I would have been okay. This seemed a good way of evening up the balance.'

'But at Admiral Foretscue's expense,' Kate pointed out. 'Not your ex-wife's.'

'I know. But those two, well, they were sort of partners in the hotel project, weren't they? In the circumstances it seemed fair enough. And it wasn't as if the admiral or his family were going to miss a few odd items. As I said, they'd probably never even realise that the stuff was gone.'

149

'That, Mr Kenway, is as tortured a rationale as I've ever heard in my entire police career. However, I'm not for the moment concerned with the sale of stolen antiques except in so far as it affects the murder of Yves Labrosse. And possibly the murder of Corinne Saxon, too. If, as you insist, you weren't responsible for those killings, then you'd better come up with a watertight alibi, or you'll be in deep trouble. This time, it won't be good enough to have your wife telling us you were at home with her.'

Kenway stared at Kate in dismay. 'But that's where I was, all yesterday morning. At home. Except for when I slipped out to the post. Liz will tell you, and you have to believe her. I was decorating the room that's going to be the nursery when the baby arrives.'

'You wouldn't have needed to be away for very long to kill Labrosse,' Kate observed. 'You could have been here at the hotel and back home again within an hour. It could even be possible that your wife didn't realise you were gone, if she was busy in the shop. Let's have the truth, Mr Kenway. Did you have some disagreement with Labrosse, and come here to have it out with him? You quarrelled, and in a fit of rage you struck him? Perhaps you hadn't meant to kill him. Is that it?'

'You've got it all wrong. Completely wrong. I've never even been to the hotel. He thought – we both thought it best for me not to be seen there.'

'But you could have come just this once. And very likely you were seen by somebody. We shall soon know, when we ask a few more questions among the staff and guests.'

Kenway was shaking his head vehemently. 'No, I wasn't there, I tell you. I wasn't there. I didn't quarrel with Yves, why should I? And I certainly didn't kill him.'

'Can you be so confident you didn't leave any telltale trace of your presence in Labrosse's room that our forensic experts can match up? What about fingerprints? However careful you might have been, it's easy to overlook something you touched. You wouldn't have been wearing gloves, would you, if you didn't set out to kill him? We shall require to take your fingerprints for comparison, of course.'

'Do whatever tests you like,' he cried, wild-eyed with

anguish, 'but you won't find any traces of me. Because I wasn't there. I'm telling you the truth, Chief Inspector. I admit to handling that stolen stuff for Labrosse, I won't try to deny it, but I didn't kill him.'

Kate was feeling less confident by the minute that she'd found her murderer. And, curiously, she wasn't all that disappointed. Kenway was a weak man, but he'd had a rough ride with Corinne. Perhaps he could still find happiness in his second marriage, if he and Liz could survive their present problems. Bloody fool to get entangled with a man like Yves Labrosse.

'That money you sent Labrosse,' she said. 'Do I gather it wasn't the first payment of its kind?'

'There'd been two lots before that. One for roughly the same amount, a bit over two thousand, the other just under.'

Hmm! In the search of Labrosse's room there had been no trace of that sort of money. A secret bank account in Zurich?

'Those amounts were a fifty-fifty split of the proceeds, right?'

'No, I had to send Labrosse two-thirds of what I got for the stuff, because he had to share with another man. So it was a third each.'

Kate leaned forward. 'Who was he, this third man?' She wondered fleetingly if Labrosse had been up to a new twist on his old 'ghost employee' racket, by inventing a fictitious partner in crime in order to gather in the lion's share of the proceeds for himself.

But Kenway said, 'It was a chap named Larkin. Admiral Fortescue's personal servant.'

Well, well! Kate and Boulter exchanged glances. 'Where did Larkin fit into the scheme?' she asked Kenway.

'He was the one who first told Labrosse about the stuff in the attics. Corinne and the admiral had decided between them which things were to be used to furnish the hotel and which were to be locked away for safety. That was all done before Labrosse arrived at Streatfield Park. The attics used as storerooms had special security locks fitted, but Larkin was able to get hold of the admiral's bunch of keys whenever he wanted so that Labrosse could select one or two items to

151

pass on to me. Not too many at any one time, because of
the difficulty of smuggling things out of the hotel without
being seen. Besides, I wouldn't have wanted to handle too
much hot stuff in one go. Safer altogether to do things bit
by bit.'

Kenway gave no sign that he was aware of the bedmate
relationship between his two fellow conspirators. Kate asked,
'Have you ever met this man Larkin?'

He shook his head. 'I told you, I never came to the hotel.
Anyway, there was no reason why he and I should meet.'

Could Kenway be lying? Had he and Larkin sided together
in a confrontation that resulted in Labrosse's death? Kate
doubted that. Rather, this new evidence about the theft
of antiques strengthened the probability in her mind that
Larkin had killed Labrosse. Kenway really had no motive
that she could discern, except the long shot that he had killed
Corinne, and that Labrosse had somehow found this out and
was blackmailing him. Thin!

Besides which, she had a strong gut feeling that she was
looking for two separate perpetrators. Her money was still
on Adrian Berger as Corinne's killer. And now, again, Larkin
seemed the best candidate for the Labrosse murder. But there
had to be a link between the two ... somewhere, somehow.
There had to be!

Get on with it, Kate! Gut feelings were all very fine, but
they needed the back-up of good, hard, solid evidence.

'You have insisted, Mr Kenway, that you were not responsible for the murder of either Labrosse or your ex-wife. Very
well, if I accept for the moment that you're telling the truth,
do you think it's possible that either Labrosse or Larkin –
or perhaps both of them acting together – could have killed
Corinne? Maybe she discovered about the stuff being stolen
from the attics, and they decided to silence her.'

Kenway didn't reply; he looked deeply thoughtful. Was he
giving serious consideration to the scenario she'd put to him?
Or was he wondering if this offered him an escape route?

Boulter prodded him. 'Well, Mr Kenway, what have you
to say about that suggestion?'

'I couldn't say about Larkin, one way or the other, but I
don't think it could have been Labrosse.'

'What makes you think that?' Kate asked.

He looked puzzled. 'Well, I can't be absolutely sure, of course. But the point is, the afternoon Corinne was killed, Labrosse and I had arranged to meet at a spot near North Chapel. He brought me two bronze figurines and a silver snuffbox to sell. But Yves couldn't tell you the truth about that, of course, when you asked him to account for his movements that afternoon. And neither could I.'

'What time did you meet him?'

'At two o'clock.'

'And you parted when?'

'We must have talked for about ten minutes. Longer, probably. We were discussing which sort of items were best for him to take next. Things that would fetch a good price, and that I could dispose of without too much risk.'

'Where, exactly, did this meeting take place?'

'It was at an old quarry that's not used now. There's room to park a couple of cars out of sight from the road.'

Kate stood up and crossed to where a large-scale map of the locality was Blu-Tacked to the wall.

'Come here, Mr Kenway, and show me the exact spot where you and Labrosse met that day.'

Kenway studied the map, getting his bearings, then stabbed his finger.

'Just there.'

Kate ringed the spot. 'Corinne Saxon was killed here,' she said, pointing to where a black cross had been drawn. Indicating another cross, she went on, 'And Streatfield Park is here. Labrosse's most direct route back to the hotel would have taken him along the lane through East Dean woods. He left you at, say, ten or fifteen minutes past two, and I remember it was established that he got back to the hotel at approximately three o'clock.' She glanced at Boulter. 'He'd have had time, all right. Remind me, sergeant, what was Labrosse's alibi for Wednesday afternoon immmediately prior to his arrival back here? How come we were satisfied with it?'

Boulter scratched his nose. 'He'd been to Gloucester on business for the hotel. Suppliers of catering equipment, I think it was. On his return, he went via Buriton and called in

153

at the market garden that provides a lot of the hotel's veggies. We checked that, and the timing seemed okay. Labrosse was well known there. He was always popping in to see what produce was ready for cutting.'

'But he wasn't there, was he? Not at the time he told us.' Kate frowned as she went on, 'I know old Mr Loxon at the market garden, I buy stuff from him myself. A charming old boy, but he's eighty if he's a day. He thinks of nothing but his free-range poultry and his muck-and-magic vegetables, and I can't imagine he'd be very precise about the exact hour of the day. If someone planted the idea in his head that they'd been with him at a certain time on a certain day, he'd be likely to accept that. Specially a good customer who saw him regularly.'

Black mark, Kate! Why didn't you spot this weakness?

'Get someone to have another chat with Mr Loxon, sergeant, and see what they can winkle out. We've got to get this cleared up.'

She waved Kenway back into his chair and sat down herself. 'Did you and Labrosse meet at any time since that afternoon?'

'No, we didn't meet. But he phoned me last Friday afternoon to tell me that Corinne had been found dead. He thought I ought to know, so that I'd be prepared in case the police came to see me. He said he didn't think it likely, but if they should start asking awkward questions about my exact whereabouts at all times since Corinne had last been seen alive – which was two-fifteen on Wednesday afternoon, he told me, when she'd set off from the hotel on a few days' leave – then on no account must I mention anything about my business arrangement with him, or let out that he and I had met at the quarry that afternoon.'

'I see! Which means, Mr Kenway, that you already knew about Corinne's death when we came to see you on Saturday morning. Your arrival home waving a newspaper that carried the story of the murder was just so much eyewash. I was suspicious at the time, but your wife seemed genuinely surprised. How come you hadn't told her the previous day, after Labrosse phoned you with the news?'

'It was difficult. Liz was out when Labrosse phoned. She'd

154

gone to the clinic about her pregnancy. When she arrived home she was telling me about what the doctor had said, about her having to rest more because her blood pressure was up. Liz was very upset. It just didn't seem the right moment to tell her about Corinne, and I kept putting it off. Then next morning, well, the truth is I went out early in the hope that Liz would hear it herself on the radio.'

'All right, all right, I get the picture.' Kate leaned back in her chair. 'Tell me, did you know about Labrosse's history before he took the job at Streatfield Park?'

'Well, only that he came from Switzerland.'

'You didn't know he had a criminal record there? That he'd spent some time in jail?'

'I had no idea. If I'd known that –'

'... you'd have been more cautious about getting involved with him? I'm quite sure you would. Does your wife know about your dealings with Labrosse?'

'She does now.'

'Now?'

'Well, I had to tell her. After you questioned me about where I was on the afternoon Corinne was killed, Liz wanted to know what I'd really been doing. She kept on and on at me until in the end I gave in. I didn't want to tell her, but it was better that having her think I killed Corinne.'

'Your wife must have had her suspicions when the police turned up and started questioning you about Wednesday afternoon. Why do you think she was prepared to give you an alibi?'

Kenway looked at her levelly, and she detected an upsurge of pride in the man.

'Because she loves me, that's why.' Suddenly he was beseeching. 'Please, you mustn't be too hard on Liz. She was only trying to protect me. And ... there's the baby to think of.'

Now he says it!

'I very much doubt that we'll find it necessary to bring any charges against your wife,' Kate said tiredly.

She could have added, rubbing it in, that the poor

155

woman would have more than enough trouble to contend with as a result of her husband's stupidity. But she didn't. The weak were supposed to be protected, weren't they?

Chapter Thirteen

'What now, guv?' Boulter asked, returning to Kate's office after he'd arranged for Paul Kenway to be driven home. 'Larkin again?'

'First things first, Tim. I came out this morning without any breakfast, and I'm ravenous. Let's have coffee and a sandwich while we recap what we've picked up from Kenway.'

The sergeant's face broke into a happy smile. 'So the guv's got a metabolism just like the rest of us. You make me wonder, sometimes, the way you can keep going for hours without sustenance.'

'When ten minutes is *your* limit?'

Grinning, Boulter picked up the phone and got through to the hotel kitchen. He launched into a detailed discussion about the filling of the sandwiches, then caught Kate's eye and said hastily, 'Whatever you've got will be fine.'

While they waited for the food to arrive, Kate ventured, 'How are things at home now, Tim? Any better?'

Mind your own bloody business, said the sudden scowl on his face. But deeper down, it seemed, he had a need to talk.

'Couldn't be more civilised. Julie and I are hardly on speaking terms. At least it's better than screaming at each other. She's threatening to go off again next weekend. What the hell does she expect of me? That's what I want to know. Am I supposed to tell my DCI to get lost when she needs me to stay late?'

'It must be hard for Julie to understand the demands of this job.' Kate saw his jaw harden, and knew she was perilously

157

close to the line she must not cross. 'Can we forget rank for a minute? Can I speak to you as a friend? As a woman?'

He shrugged, saying nothing.

'Listen, there's a limit to the amount we can give of ourselves to the job. When we're on a case like this, okay, we all have to be ready to work most of the hours God sends. But when you do get home, Tim, be a husband and father. Forget about work. Put it right out of your mind.'

'How can I? Do you?'

You walked right into that, Kate! She thought of Felix, who'd shrunk from bothering her with a personal problem because she was engaged on a murder enquiry. Of course she'd have dropped everything, temporarily, to go to her aunt's aid. But Felix hadn't been prepared to make a claim on her. That had to say something about Kate's own attitude.

'It's different for me,' she said evasively. 'I'm not married.'

Boulter was silent, but only for a moment. 'It's too late for good advice, Kate. I'll tell you something, the way things are going I shan't be married for much longer. Julie and I are pretty well all washed up.'

The arrival of the sandwiches ended the conversation. Thick-cut York ham with dill pickles, served with crisp salad.

'Right,' said Kate, 'back to work. First let's concentrate on who killed Labrosse. It certainly wasn't Berger. The only real suspects we've got are Kenway and Larkin.'

Boulter nodded. 'It could have been the both of them together. Thieves falling out. Say they quarrelled with Labrosse? Given his background it's likely he was trying to double-cross both of them in some way.'

'Kenway denies he ever met Larkin, and we haven't a shred of evidence to suggest otherwise. That doesn't rule it out, I agree, but it doesn't seem very likely to me.'

'Larkin on his own, then. Him and Labrosse in a lovers' quarrel. Crime of passion.'

'Could be. But in that case where's the connection between the two killings? Larkin was definitely at his gym club on the afternoon when Corinne was killed.' She pondered. 'Kenway, now, he certainly had a motive for killing Corinne. Bitterness

158

against his ex-wife, plus saving that big drain on his finances. But we have no good reason to think he'd kill Labrosse, have we, and anyway he doesn't strike me as the violent type.'

Boulter took another large bite of ham sandwich and chewed thoughtfully. 'We mustn't forget Kenway's wife. He admitted that she wormed out of him what was going on between him and Labrosse. Suppose she went to remon-strate with Labrosse for leading her husband astray, lost her temper and grabbed the first thing handy to hit him with? She could've, she's a big woman.'

'She'd have had to walk in and out of the hotel without being noticed. Just possible, but she certainly couldn't have *relied* on not being seen. Furthermore, a stranger to the hotel would have had a problem finding Labrosse's room without asking and drawing attention. The same would apply to her husband, too – if it's true he'd never come here to see Labrosse before. Get a couple of DCs asking the staff and guests if they saw anybody answering the description of either of the Kenways wandering around.'

Boulter jotted down a note while Kate mused.

'I don't think we're on the right track, Tim. It doesn't *feel* right. We're overlooking something important. There has to be a connection – a direct connection – between those two killings.'

'Maybe they *aren't* connected, guv. Maybe it's just a coincidence.'

Kate shook her head. 'Can't be. How about this? Suppose Labrosse knew the identity of Corinne's killer so had to be silenced? A man like Labrosse might have been trying a spot of blackmail. On the other hand that theory would rule out Berger, who couldn't have a more rock-solid alibi than being questioned by us at the time of the murder.'

'You're just not giving up on Berger as Corinne's killer, are you?'

'I'm not giving up on anyone. But Berger makes the best sense to me.'

'So what now, guv?' asked Boulter, his eye on the last remaining sandwich.

Kate pushed the plate in his direction. 'Let's have Larkin over here, and see what we can get out of him.'

Larkin was surlier than ever. 'The admiral is very upset by all this, miss. In his state of health he shouldn't have to be left on his own. I've already told you everything I know. Every bloody thing. It's not a bit of use keeping on asking me questions, you won't learn anything new.'

'I've already learned something new, Mr Larkin. A rather serious matter which you didn't see fit to reveal to me yourself.'

He tried not to show it, but his attitude changed. His truculence was smothered by unease about what was coming.

'I didn't hide anything from you.'

'No? How about being accessory to the plot to relieve Admiral Fortescue of a few valuable heirlooms? I wonder what he's going to think of his trusted steward cheating him behind his back.'

Larkin paled; even his thick lips lost colour. 'I don't know what the hell you're on about.'

'Then let me spell it out. You let drop to Labrosse at some point in your relationship that a large number of antique pieces were stored away in the attics here. This gave Labrosse a bright idea. He got you to "borrow" the admiral's keys, and he went up to the attics and selected a few choice items. Then a crooked dealer was wheeled in to dispose of the goodies. The plan worked smoothly, so it was repeated, and then again. What percentage of the proceeds did Labrosse hand over to you, I wonder?'

'I didn't get nothing from him. Whoever told you this, it's all lies. Nothing but bloody lies.'

Boulter snorted. 'Huh! What did you do with the money, Larkin? Pay it into your bank account? Or just keep it under the mattress? We're going to find out, you know, when we search your room.'

'You've got no right – '

'Withholding your permission, are you? That won't save you, Larkin. It just means you'll have to sit here for however long it takes us to get a search warrant.'

Under the sergeant's stony gaze, Larkin gave way with an angry shrug. 'Do what you bloody like, then. You won't find nothing to prove what you're trying to make out.'

Kate said, 'We have specific evidence that you were involved in these thefts. It's useless to go on acting the innocent.'

'I'm not acting. I haven't done nothing. Why should you take someone else's word against mine? Whatever Kenway might have told you, it's a load of crap.'

'Did I mention Mr Kenway's name?'

That brought him up with a squeal of brakes. He said slowly, warily, ''Course you did. You must've done. How else would I have known who you was talking about?'

'How, indeed? There's only one way you could have known about the criminal dealings going on between Labrosse and Kenway, and that's by being an accessory to them. I get very impatient with people who persist in denying their guilt when it's obvious the game is up.' Kate got to her feet. 'I'll leave you to think things over for a bit, while I go and have another talk with Admiral Fortescue.'

Larkin looked up at her in dismay. 'He's an old man, and he's sick, real bad. You've got no right to go worrying him on and on. It's not bloody fair.'

'Christ, look who's talking,' scoffed Boulter. 'You reckon it was fair to rob the admiral, who's been your employer for years and years? And you have the gall to make out you want to try and protect him from the police.'

'What he's doing, sergeant,' said Kate scathingly, 'is trying to protect his own skin. He doesn't want Admiral Fortescue to find out that his trusted steward is nothing but a common thief.'

'It's not like that at all.' Larkin's coarse-featured face was screwed up in helpless anger. 'Honest to God, the poor old chap's heart won't stand any more shocks. Oh, I know you think I'm scum, but – '

'You can say that again,' Boulter snapped back. This time Kate checked him with a tiny gesture of one finger. She wanted to let Larkin keep talking.

'The admiral's a good old stick. He's not like some of them high-and-mighty bastards in the navy who act like you're so much shit. All right, I'm not proud of what I did, but it didn't amount to nothing much, not really. He kept back all the things he specially likes, to have in his own rooms. What's up in the attics is just odds and ends that have been in the family longer than anyone can remember. They'll never even be missed.' Larkin warmed to his theme, spitting out the words. 'That bloody son of his in America, that bloody Dominic, he don't give a bugger. Did he bother to come over to see his dad when the old boy had his operation? Oh, no! It was only because he had some business to do in London that Master Dominic was here for the opening of the hotel. I was watching, and I could see him sizing up the place for the cash it'll fetch him one day. The admiral is always keeping on about saving Streatfield Park for the family. The Fortescue heritage, he calls it. But the minute he's gone the whole estate will be flogged off and everything in it, you mark my words.'

'So you felt justified in filching some of the stuff in the attics?' Kate rested her hands on the desk and leaned forward. 'Why then did you kill Labrosse, when you could have gone on and on with your nice little scheme? Did you think you could do better without him? Just you and Kenway working the racket together?'

'No, I never killed Yves. I never did.'

'Or was it,' she continued remorselessly, 'that you discovered he was cheating you? Not giving you your fair cut of the proceeds?'

'I tell you I never killed him. How could I have? I was with the admiral when Yves was done in, just like he told you I was.'

'I'll see what Admiral Fortescue has to say about that. He may remember things differently, in the light of your criminal activities.'

Larkin shot to his feet and clutched at Kate's sleeve. Boulter instantly sprang forward and yanked him off.

'Keep your filthy hands to yourself, Larkin.'

'I'm sorry, miss, I didn't mean ... ' He gulped. 'But don't you see, you'll be upsetting the admiral for no reason. No reason at all. He'll tell you just the same as he did before.'

'That remains to be seen.' Kate glanced at Boulter. 'Mr Larkin can mull things over before we ask him to make a formal statement. He might want to make a few changes to his story. Take him outside and get someone to keep an eye on him.'

'Where's Larkin?' the admiral asked in a querulous voice when he opened the door to Kate. 'What have you done with him?'

'We're keeping him over at the Incident Room, sir. I shall need to question him further, I'm afraid.'

'But why? What do you expect to learn from him? He knows nothing that he hasn't already told you.'

'Shall we sit down?' she suggested. 'There are one or two points I need you to clarify for me.'

He shuffled back to his usual armchair and sank down into it. He looked on the point of collapse, Kate thought with compassion. She'd treat him as gently as possible, but there was a limit to gentleness if she were to do her job properly.

'You and Larkin, sir, both stated that you were together in this suite for the whole of the period of time during which Labrosse was killed. I am now going to put the same question to you again, and I invite you to reconsider your answer. Between ten o'clock yesterday morning and a few minutes after eleven, can you vouch for Larkin's presence here? Can you confirm that he didn't at any time leave the suite, even for just a few minutes?'

A veined hand fluttered in protest. 'Yes, yes, Chief Inspector. It is exactly as I told you before.'

'But he wasn't actually in the same room with you for the whole of that time, was he?'

'Naturally not. But he was around. He wouldn't leave the suite without my permission.'

'So what you are really saying,' she pressed, 'is that you *assume* Larkin remained in the suite?'

'He *was* here, Chief Inspector.'

'How can you know that with certainty, sir, if he wasn't within your sight all the while?'

'He was in and out, attending to my needs. Several times I had occasion to ring for him, and he always came at once.'

'That still doesn't rule out the possibility that he left the suite briefly.'

163

'But he had no reason to. He never does in the morning unless to accompany me.'

'He might have had a very powerful reason to leave the suite *yesterday* morning.'

The admiral's skin seemed to shrink on his bones, giving him a skeletal appearance. 'You can't truly believe that Larkin had anything to do with ... with ...'

'Were you aware that Larkin had a close relationship with Labrosse?'

'I ... they knew one another, of course. They could scarcely not have done, both living here on the premises.'

'I mean rather more than that, sir. You do know that Larkin is homosexual?'

He frowned at her directness. 'The man has been in my service for many years, Chief Inspector, so I could hardly be unaware of such a thing. But Larkin has always been discreet in his behaviour. I've never held the fact against him, and I see no reason why you should.'

'I'm not raising this as a moral issue, sir. But in a murder enquiry I have to take any kind of intimate relationship into account.'

He gestured a reluctant acknowledgement of this. 'All the same, I cannot believe that Larkin and *Labrosse* were involved together.'

It all had to come out soon, not just the sexual aspect, but the thievery, too. So why not now?

'There was another connection between Larkin and Labrosse, sir. They were in league with a third person in the theft and sale of some of the valuable items that were stored in the attics here.'

'What?' The admiral was badly shaken, and Kate had qualms that she'd gone too far considering the dicky state of his heart. 'I cannot believe this. It's unthinkable. Not Larkin.'

'It's quite true, I'm afraid. Larkin has admitted his involvement to me.'

There was sorrow mixed with his obvious anger. 'I trusted that man. I have always thought of him as being completely loyal and honest.' He swept his two hands slowly back over his grey hair. 'Does this mean that he's been cheating me all these years?'

'My information only covers recent weeks, sir. It could be that Labrosse led him astray.'

'Labrosse! Yes, none of this would have happened but for Labrosse. He should never have come here. He was obviously quite unfitted for a post of such responsibility.'

'You were not aware, I take it, that Yves Labrosse had a criminal record in Switzerland?'

The admiral looked at her mutely for a moment, shaking his head. 'It doesn't surprise me, in the light of events. But how could Corinne have missed discovering about his record when she was considering his appointment?'

'Miss Saxon must almost certainly have known about his criminal past,' Kate told him. 'She and Labrosse knew one another over a period of many years. Since their childhood, in fact.'

'I see!' Another pause before he said, 'It was Labrosse who killed Corinne, wasn't it?'

'I don't know, but it's a possibility.'

'I believe he did. I believe it must have been him. And now he too is dead.' The admiral let out a long sigh. 'If only that could be the end of it all.'

'Are you in a position to tell us which items are missing from your attics, sir? Is there an inventory?'

He nodded. 'It will be held by my solicitor. I had better ask him to send someone here to try and establish the things that have gone.' The lines of strain on his face cut deep as he went on, 'This is an unfortunate business, Chief Inspector.'

'Unfortunate' was a mild adjective to describe two murders. Then it struck Kate that the admiral was merely referring to the loss of some of his family heirlooms.

'It may very well be,' she said, 'that there is a connection between the thefts and Labrosse's murder.'

He held up both his hands as if to ward off her persistence. 'It was not Larkin who killed him, I shall never believe that. I am very disappointed, naturally, by what you have told me about the man's dishonesty. Deeply distressed and disappointed. But that is quite a different matter from murder.

165

Please, Chief Inspector, put aside your suspicions concerning Larkin.'

'I can't do that, sir. I must follow wherever this investigation leads me.'

He gave her a beseeching look. 'Suppose ... suppose I decide not to press charges against Larkin? I could just dismiss him, perhaps.'

The admiral, it seemed, still hadn't grasped the full enormity of the situation. He was fretting because he'd been let down by a trusted servant.

'I shall be sending an officer very shortly to make a search of Larkin's room,' she told him.

He hardly seemed to take that in. 'Yes, I suppose it's necessary.'

If ever a man looked at the end of his tether, Admiral Fortescue did now. Kate felt concerned about him. He shouldn't be left alone, distressed like this and in his poor state of health.

'Might it not be best for you to detail one of the hotel staff to attend to your needs for the time being? You should have someone near at hand, I think.'

'Yes, yes, perhaps.'

On her feet, Kate hesitated. All the admiral had to do was to pick up the telephone and issue instructions for whatever he wanted. She herself had far more pressing matters to attend to. And yet the poor man looked so forlorn she hardly liked to walk out on him. Tender loving care was what he needed.

'Is there anything I can get for you?' she asked.

'Eh? Oh, no, no.'

'Have you had your lunch yet?'

'No, I ... I'm not hungry.'

'You should eat something, sir.'

But he only shook his head vaguely, lost in his unhappy thoughts. Kate felt sure he wasn't even aware of her leaving the room. On her way out, she stopped at the reception desk and suggested that someone should go along to the admiral's suite with a light lunch on a tray.

Boulter was eagerly awaiting Kate's return. There had been a positive result from the house-to-house enquiry made in the vicinity of Yew Tree Cottage at Larkhill, where June Elsted reported having seen Corinne Saxon and Adrian Berger together.

'The man is one of the gardeners at Streatfield Park, would you believe? An old chap name of Frederick Partridge. Which could hardly fit him better, considering he's a poacher. Seems he actually saw them at it, Berger and Corinne Saxon, through the window.'

'How come this wasn't picked up before, when the staff here were interrogated?' Kate asked sharply. 'This man must have been included in that.'

'Sure, he was. But there's a streak of touch-your-cap yokel in our Fred. Nosy as hell about what his betters get up to, but loyal, too. Wouldn't breathe a word against 'em to the likes of us. Told his missus all about the goings-on at Yew Tree Cottage, though, and his missus goes to church Sundays. Thought it were a proper disgrace, she told DC Farnham, especially with Berger being a married man. *And* his wife such a lady, from one of the best families round here.'

'Get on with it!'

'The first sighting was several weeks ago, just around dusk. A Thursday. Fred was setting his traps in the coppice at the back of Yew Tree Cottage. He saw two cars pull into the side driveway, and the lights were quickly dowsed. He could hear a male and a female voice, both subdued, and soft laughter. The instant the couple were through the front door, Fred creeps nearer to have a dekko. They couldn't wait to draw the curtains, could they, and he watched some heavy petting on the sofa. Then after a bit they gathered up their shoes and discarded apparel, and headed upstairs. I imagine,' Boulter continued, embroidering, 'Fred must have looked around for a ladder then, but — '

'Sergeant,' Kate warned. 'The facts.'

Boulter sighed. 'Fred kept his eyes and ears open, after that first evening. His bungalow is across the fields from Yew Tree Cottage — a mile away by road, but scarcely three hundred yards by crow-fly. He caught them at it several more times. But there was no more action since a Friday night three weeks ago.'

'Hmm! This old chap would have known Corinne by

167

sight, of course. But could he give a positive identification of Berger?'

'Oh, yes! Fred has seen Berger around lots of times at Streatfield Park. As often as not discussing plans with Corinne. There's no doubt about the identification, guv.'

'Will he be a good witness? He won't back down on us?'

Boulter laughed. 'Roy Farnham gave him the spiel about the penalties for wasting police time by not giving this info in the first place. If it didn't scare Fred overmuch, it certainly scared the shit out of his missus. She'll make damn sure he stands up and says his piece when we need him to.'

Kate tapped her desktop thoughtfully with a fingertip. 'We're getting closer, Tim. But Berger can still insist he didn't kill Corinne, and we have no proof to pin it on him. Unless we can get him to break.'

An enquiring tap at the door. Kate called to come in, and the excited face of a young DC appeared.

'Got something for you, ma'am.'

'Let's have it then, Ben.'

DC Ellery handed her a blue, cloth-covered booklet. 'Larkin's building-society account, ma'am. It makes interesting reading.'

Kate flicked it open at one of the fully completed pages. It took only the briefest glance to see that each month a regular amount had been paid in by cheque. Obviously Larkin's wages. Cash withdrawals were small – living at Streatfield Park as he did, he'd only need money for incidentals. So the balance was steadily growing. She swiftly turned to the page with the last entries. Of the most recent items on the credit side, two were sizeable deposits in cash. One for £551 and the other for £497.

She glanced up at Boulter, who was reading over her shoulder. 'Larkin's payoffs from Labrosse?'

The sergeant whistled through his teeth. 'A hell of a lot less than half of what Labrosse got from Paul Kenway. Larkin had a grievance there, all right, if he found out he was being swindled.'

'That's not all I've got for you, ma'am.' DC Ellery smirked triumphantly as he plucked from his jacket pocket a clear plastic bag containing some bloodstained fabric. 'I found this in the little kitchenette in Admiral Fortescue's suite, which Larkin uses for making hot drinks and so on. It struck me that I should look there.'

'Good thinking. Where exactly did you find it?'

'Stuffed down at the bottom of the wastebin liner, ma'am.'

Kate examined the handkerchief without removing it from the plastic bag. It was of fine-quality linen, hemstitched, with the initials YL embroidered in one corner. Suddenly she realised what had struck her as different about the dead Labrosse's attire. It was the absence of the customary white handkerchief at his breast pocket, that little affectation which had given an old-fashioned touch to his well-dressed image.

Labrosse's assailant, then, had pulled the handkerchief from his breast pocket, presumably to wipe off the fingerprints from the candlestick he'd used as a weapon. And had then disposed of it in what he thought would be a safe place. Larkin wouldn't have anticipated a search being made of the admiral's quarters.

'Nice work, Ben. This could be the clincher. Get it to the lab right away, to confirm that the blood matches the victim's. Not that I have any doubt about that. I take it you've sealed off Larkin's room and the kitchenette?'

'Oh yes, ma'am.'

When the DC had departed, Boulter said in a voice like the gleeful rubbing of hands, 'So, Berger for the one, and Larkin for t'other. Amen!'

'We've got a long way to go yet, Tim. And I still can't see the connection between the two murders. There *has* to be a connection.'

Boulter chuckled. 'You want it with bloody knobs on, guv!'

169

Chapter Fourteen

There was no cockiness about Sid Larkin now. His transfer to the starkly severe atmosphere of an interview room at DHQ plus the formality of the official caution conspired to put the fear of God into him. As Kate had intended.

She kicked off without preamble. 'We've found the handkerchief, Larkin.'

His expression was a fair approximation of total bafflement. 'What handkerchief, miss? I don't know what you're on about.'

'Labrosse's handkerchief. The one you used to wipe the candlestick with.'

His belligerence surfaced. 'You're crazy!'

'Why not admit the truth and save us all a lot of trouble? While the admiral was having his morning bath, you phoned Labrosse to meet you in his room. You'd found out somehow that he wasn't paying you your agreed share of the proceeds of the thefts, so you went to have it out with him. In the argument, you lost your temper and grabbed the nearest thing to hand – the candlestick – and hit Labrosse with it. Perhaps,' Kate added, 'you didn't intend to kill him.'

The slight hint that if he cooperated he might get away with a lesser charge than murder didn't work. Larkin was shaking his head violently. 'That's a load of crap. I didn't hit him. I didn't kill him. I didn't go to his room, not yesterday.'

'The first two sums received by Labrosse from Kenway,' she continued smoothly, 'each amounted to about two thousand pounds, and you – '

'No, that's not right,' he protested. '*One* thousand, you mean, not two thousand. Yves and I both pocketed about five hundred quid each time.'

'If that's what you received,' Kate said, 'and it tallies with the amounts you paid into your building society, then your friend was cheating you. According to Kenway, he paid Labrosse double what you claim. So Labrosse kept three-quarters of it for himself.'

'The bastard!' Larkin really did seem surprised, but his swift flare of anger quickly subsided into a sort of resigned acceptance. If it was just an act, it was a cleverer act than Kate would have thought the man capable of. A tiny seed of doubt about his guilt dropped into her mind. Although ...

'If you've only just this minute found out that Labrosse was cheating you, why are you taking it so calmly?'

He lifted his hefty shoulders. 'I thought I could trust Yves. But it don't come as no big shock that he was ready to do me down same as everyone else. You learn to expect it when you're one of the lower orders. They reckon you're just dirt to be trampled on.'

'He'll have me crying my eyes out,' Boulter broke in caustically.

'I suggest,' Kate persisted, 'that you didn't just find out from me that you'd been cheated. You learned of it before — how I don't yet know — and the resulting quarrel with Labrosse ended in his death. Why go on denying it?'

'Because it's not true. Not a bloody word of it.'

'So how do you account for the handkerchief?'

'I told you, I don't know nothing about any bleeding handkerchief.'

'It was the one Labrosse was wearing in his breast pocket when he was killed. We discovered it in the kitchen wastebin in Admiral Fortescue's suite. Stained with blood.'

Again his reaction really did look like genuine astonishment. The seed of doubt in Kate's mind began to sprout. She signalled to Boulter to take over the questioning.

'Listen to me, Larkin,' he said weightily. 'You can deny knowing anything about that handkerchief till you're blue in the face. You don't imagine we'll let it stop there? You were in Labrosse's room yesterday morning, and no way can you hide the fact. Right at this moment our forensic experts are busy analysing lots of samples that were taken at the scene of the crime. I'll tell you something: these days nobody can go anywhere without leaving a trace of his presence. I'm not just talking about fingerprints. You'll have left behind hairs from you head, flakes from your skin and fibres from your clothes. You didn't realise that, I bet?'

Larkin was white-faced, but he stuck to his guns. 'I've been in Yves' room plenty of times, but not yesterday. I don't care what you try to make out, I wasn't there and I didn't kill him. It wasn't me.'

'So who the hell else d'you reckon put that handkerchief into the wastebin?' Boulter demanded scornfully.

Kate felt her skin pricking with a sudden new insight. A dozen recollections were coalescing in her mind, all springing from Boulter's question.

Who the hell else d'you reckon put that handkerchief into the wastebin?

There was only one other person who could have done so without considerable difficulty. Only one other person to whom it might seem a convenient and safe place to dispose of what could prove to be a damning piece of evidence. Admiral Fortescue. He no more than Larkin would have expected the police to search in any part of his personal suite.

They had alibied for each other, those two. A conspiracy? Kate believed not. But just as she had pointed out to the admiral that he was in no position to swear Larkin hadn't left the suite for a brief time that morning, then no more had Larkin been able to swear the same thing about him. The admiral was supposed to be having his regular, leisurely morning bath. Where had Larkin been? In his own room tippling, most likely, and perhaps reading a newspaper. He wouldn't have noticed that the usual faint noises of swirling water were missing.

Motive? Fortescue believed that Labrosse had murdered Corinne, he had said so vehemently. But if this was his reason for killing Labrosse, then what had been his true relationship with Corinne? He had emphatically denied – and Kate had believed him – that Corinne's position at Streatfield Park was anything more than that of a partner

172

in the hotel project. But what of the past? Kate had always suspected that the admiral was concealing something. The story about Corinne's out-of-the-blue approach to him with irresistible ideas for converting his ancestral home into a hotel was implausible, to say the least.

Boulter was valiantly carrying on with the questioning, not giving Larkin any respite. But Kate knew that her sergeant was aware of her distraction. With a little jerk of the head she gestured that she wanted a word with him in private.

'Keep up the pressure on Larkin,' she told him, outside the door. 'He might reveal something. But I'm going back to Streatfield Park to talk to Admiral Fortescue again.'

He eyed her curiously. 'You onto something, guv? D'you reckon the old boy's been covering for Larkin?'

'No, Tim, that's not what I'm thinking.'

'Being cagey, aren't you? Not going to tell me?'

Kate smiled. 'Later.'

She drove fast the now familiar route to Streatfield Park, impelled by a growing conviction that she was on the right track. Could Fortescue have found the physical strength to deliver a mortal blow to Labrosse's head? Yes, just about. And when she'd seen him later, he was like a man who'd expended the last of his energy, both physically and mentally.

But she couldn't let the admiral shield behind his feeble state of health. There were answers she needed, needed now. There might be an innocent man, possibly even two innocent men, who had to be cleared of suspicion.

As Kate sped up the yew-lined driveway of the hotel, an ambulance passed her heading out. With a sense of foreboding, she braked the car at the hotel entrance and hurried inside.

June Elsted was at the reception desk. She looked shocked and distressed.

'What's happened?' Kate demanded. 'I saw an ambulance just leaving.'

'It's Admiral Fortescue. He's had some sort of heart attack. He seems in a pretty bad way.'

'How did it happen? When?'

'Well, I don't really know. Deirdre and I found him

173

collapsed on the floor in his sitting room. That was about twenty minutes ago. He was unconscious. I phoned for an ambulance right away.'

'What made you go along to him?' Kate asked. 'Had he called for help?'

'Oh, no. But when Larkin still hadn't come back by five-thirty we thought we ought to enquire if the admiral needed anything. I phoned his suite, and when there wasn't any answer we began to get worried. In the end we went along together to check he was all right, and that's when we found him.'

Kate nodded. 'He's been taken to the Peace Memorial Hospital at Marlingford, I suppose?'

'Yes, that's right. And he wants to see you, Chief Inspector.'

'Wants to see me? You said he was unconscious.'

'He came to a little before they took him away. And his very first words were to ask for you. He seemed ever so weak, poor man, and the paramedics told him not to talk. But he kept insisting that he must speak to you urgently. I phoned to your office right away, just a minute ago, and they told me you'd gone to Marlingford yourself and that they'd get a message to you.'

'Thanks, June. I'll go back to Marlingford now and see him.'

The radio was beeping when she got back to her car. Frank Massey. She told him she'd got the message and was heading straight to the hospital.

But, frustratingly, when she arrived there she was informed that she'd have to wait to see Admiral Fortescue because the doctors were with him.

'How long will they be?' she asked, masking her impatience.

'I can't say,' the staff nurse said briskly. 'It might be some time, I'm afraid.'

Kate gritted her teeth. 'In that case I'll go along and visit my aunt who's a patient in Nightingale Ward. Perhaps you'll send for me at once if I'm not back before the doctors are through.'

Richard was with her aunt. He immediately vacated the

bedside chair for Kate, who sat down and bent forward to kiss Felix. Damn it! She wished desperately that Richard hadn't been here. He was a complication she could do without just now. When this investigation was all over, as she hoped it soon would be, then perhaps the two of them could get back together without images of Corinne Saxon intruding between them. On Monday night, when she stayed over at Richard's flat, she had let herself believe that Corinne's ghost had been laid. But after leaving him, she knew it hadn't been. And couldn't be yet.

'How are you feeling now?' she asked Felix.

'Pretty fair. It's sweet of you to find the time to visit me each day, considering all you've got on your plate. I'm not on the critical list any longer.'

After that, how could Kate announce that she was just filling in a few odd minutes? She wished now that she hadn't been so urgent about being informed the moment it was possible to see Admiral Fortescue.

Richard caught her gaze and held it. 'How is the investigation going, Kate?'

'Progressing.'

'You don't have to be so cagey on my account,' he said bitterly. 'This is Wednesday evening, don't forget, and this week's *Gazette* is already printed and out on the streets. When you come to read it, by the way, you'll find it's a masterpiece of making bloody little seem a bloody lot. Every word is based on the official police handouts. There's not a whisper that the *Gazette*'s editor gave the Chief Investigating Officer considerable help on the case.'

'So I should hope,' Kate retorted. But his thrust had gone home. She knew it must have sounded as if she didn't trust Richard with the smallest scrap of confidential information. She did trust him, she trusted him completely, but his personal involvement with Corinne Saxon made her ridiculously edgy.

Felix asked interestedly, 'What's all this about Richard helping you, Kate?'

'Oh, he gave me some information that was useful. A photograph, actually. It provided us with a vital link.'

The door opened and a nurse looked in to summon Kate.

175

'When Admiral Fortescue heard you were here at the hospital and waiting to see him, Chief Inspector, he was very anxious that you should come at once.'

'Sorry about this, Felix,' Kate said embarrassedly, getting to her feet. 'It's something very important.'

Richard made no attempt to hide his reproach in the scathing look he threw her. Her aunt's easy acceptance, though, made Kate feel even worse.

'Don't worry about it, girl. I've got Richard to keep me company.'

Never before had Kate seen Admiral Fortescue looking as pale and wraithlike as now. It was nearly impossible to visualise those limp arms of his lifting a heavy silver-gilt candlestick and smashing it down on Labrosse's skull. But somehow he had found the strength. She had no doubts at all now.

'Chief Inspector, thank God you're here!' His whispered words scarcely ruffled the overwarm air of the small hospital room. 'I have a great deal to tell you, and there isn't much time left to me.'

Kate drew a chair up close so that she could hear him. 'You mustn't overtax yourself, sir.'

A faint stirring of his fingers brushed her warning aside. 'Larkin . . . have you arrested him?'

'No. He's – ' The conventional phrase about helping the police with their enquiries would sound flippant in the circumstances. Kate substituted, 'He's being held to answer further questions.'

The admiral rocked his head from side to side on the pillow, the most vehement gesture he was capable of making in his weakened state.

'Larkin did not kill Labrosse, Chief Inspector. I cannot die in peace if I allow an innocent man to be punished for a crime that I committed.'

'What exactly are you telling me, sir?' asked Kate. She needed to commit him to an unequivocal statement.

'I struck the blow that killed Labrosse.'

Kate didn't pretend surprise. 'Why did you kill him?'

'He was an evil man.'

'You mean, because you believe he killed Corinne Saxon?'

'I do believe that, yes.'

'But you had some other reason for killing him?'

'He was a murderer, a thief, an extortionist, a blackmailer.'

'A blackmailer? He was blackmailing you?'

The tiniest nod of his head, as if he were ashamed.

'On what grounds?' Kate asked.

The admiral said slowly, 'He was in possession of knowledge that could bring great distress and embarrassment to me and my family.'

'Will you tell me about it, please?'

'Yes, yes, I shall tell you everything. Everything. I ask of you only that you use no more of this information than is necessary in order to complete your investigation. I shall never be brought to trial, you realise that? I am dying.'

What point was there in murmuring comforting words of hope to a man who had just confessed to murder? Besides, whatever the medical prognosis, Douglas Fortescue had lost the will to live.

Kate gave him what she could of the promise he had asked for. 'I shall respect your confidence, Admiral, as far as it is within my power to do so.'

He closed his eyes slowly, as if in relief. Then he opened them again, and his gaze focused upon Kate's face.

'You asked me how it came about that Corinne decided to approach me with the suggestion of turning Streatfield Park into an hotel. The explanation I gave you was the truth, but it was not the whole truth. You see, when I met Corinne all those years ago, our friendship was rather more than I admitted to.'

'You and she had an intimate relationship, sir?'

He managed a smile, weak and strained. 'That would be putting it mildly. Of course she was many years younger than me, and I was a married man with a son. But ... I'm not attempting to make excuses for what happened, but Corinne was so fresh and lovely. So vivacious. It was a delight just to be in her company. I was completely infatuated with her. Our liaison was very brief, only ten days in all, but unfortunately it resulted in Corinne becoming pregnant.'

His baby!

177

'When she became aware of her condition,' the admiral continued, 'she somehow found out where I was at the time – the ship had put in to Hong Kong – and she telephoned me from London. She was overwrought, in a very distressed state. She was so very young, poor thing, little more than a child herself, and that added to my feelings of guilt and responsibility. I managed to contrive some leave, and I flew home in order to see her and make plans. It was a most embarrassing situation. It could have ruined my marriage, and my prospects of promotion in the navy would have been seriously damaged if my wife had sued for divorce on those grounds and the tabloid papers had got hold of the story. In the end, to my great relief, Corinne agreed to accept a sum of money which would cover the cost of an abortion and see her through the difficult time.'

'But she didn't go ahead with the abortion?'

His tired eyes sharpened. 'How did you guess? I returned to Hong Kong and my ship, and I confidently believed that the whole foolish episode was behind me. Years passed and I neither saw nor heard anything from Corinne. Though many was the time I saw her photograph in *Vogue* and other fashion magazines my wife subscribed to, and I thanked heaven that her career had prospered despite the setback of her pregnancy. Corinne was outstandingly lovely as a model, if you remember, and her success was richly deserved.' He closed his eyes and drew several deep breaths, gathering his strength. 'You can imagine my astonishment, Chief Inspector, when Corinne wrote to me last autumn, recalling our past association.'

'And telling you that the pregnancy you believed to have been terminated had in fact resulted in a child being born?'

'That revelation was made later,' he said, 'when Corinne came to visit me.'

'And she used the fact that you'd fathered her child to put pressure on you to agree to her hotel scheme?'

'Not pressure, no, not exactly. Corinne merely informed me that she and I had a son. Robert. She showed me several photographs of the boy at different ages, and the resemblance to myself was very striking. I couldn't doubt that the child was mine. She assured me that he was being well cared for by good people, though she wouldn't say where that was. I could have insisted upon knowing, I suppose, but at the time I was in a state of shock, and later it seemed best not to involve myself any more closely. So many years had gone by during which I hadn't even known of the boy's existence. My feelings were ambiguous. To some extent I wanted to meet Robert, as any father would. But it was an immensely difficult situation. I already had a son, Chief Inspector, my legitimate son Dominic. The sudden appearance of an unsuspected half-brother would have been very distressful to him and his family. It might also have complicated the inheritance when the time came, and I so dearly wanted Streatfield Park and all it represents to pass in its entirety to Dominic. And in due course of time to my grandson, Winston.'

'Did Corinne explain to you why she had decided against having an abortion?'

'Yes, she did. She told me that when she'd had more time to think about it, she realised that an abortion would be wickedly wrong. And so she went ahead with having the child, despite all the difficulties it would inevitably mean for her. Bravely, she did it on her own without troubling me again and risking a threat to my marriage and my career. I had to feel most grateful to Corinne for that. When she enthusiastically outlined her scheme for turning Streatfield Park into a hotel, it seemed almost as though I were being given a chance to recompense her for the wrong I'd done her. And by helping Corinne, I would be helping the son I had fathered.'

Anxiety sharpened his gaze. 'But now Corinne is dead, and I am about to follow her to the grave. I must make some kind of provision for that boy. May I ask a favour of you, Chief Inspector, When you leave here, will you contact my solicitor and ask him to come and see me without delay? Somehow Robert must be traced, and funds made available to him.'

Kate pondered briefly, but she knew it had to be said. 'Your son Robert is dead, sir. He died in a road accident some eighteen months ago.'

'Dead? But . . . that cannot be true. Corinne was in regular touch with the boy. In fact ... ' He paused. 'I could not admit this to you before, but Corinne told me it was to visit Robert that she needed those few days off.'

'My information is undoubtedly correct, sir. We had it only this morning from the French police, who had talked to a close relative of the people who brought the boy up. He was killed in a motorcycle accident.'

The old man looked at her in bewildered appeal. 'The French police? How ... ?'

'I had learned in the course of my investigation, you see, that at one time Corinne Saxon gave birth to a child, and this was being followed up. When the boy was born, Corinne handed him over to a French couple who couldn't have children of their own. The wife was the sister of a close friend of Corinne's. Corinne did visit the boy from time to time, and she attended his funeral. So there is no possible question of a mistake. Our enquiries, however, did not bring to light the name of the child's father. It seems that Corinne had always refused to reveal that.'

Observing the frail old man lying limply in the hospital bed, Kate wondered what he was feeling about Corinne's deception. And how much did he care about the sudden snatching away of a son he'd never met, of whose very existence he was unaware until quite recently? How much emotional energy did the admiral have to spare? He had killed a man, and now he himself was dying. What Kate had just told him at least removed the tug at his conscience that dictated he ought to make provision for his unacknowledged son.

'You said that Labrosse was blackmailing you,' she prompted him.

'He had somehow discovered about my affair with Corinne, and about the boy. His demands were quite outrageous. It went much against the grain to give in to a blackmailer, as I'm sure you can imagine; but I had so much to lose if Labrosse were allowed to broadcast the facts of my past indiscretion that I was prepared to make a deal with him. Against my better judgement I agreed to let him run the hotel for me for the time being, on generous terms. But Labrosse wasn't satisfied with that.'

'What exactly did he want from you?'

'He threatened me. He said that if I wanted to ensure that the paternity of Corinne's son Robert was never revealed, then I was to let him have complete control of the hotel. He demanded a long-term contract giving him full power, and the salary he wanted was beyond all reason.' The admiral sighed deeply. 'If only I'd known that Robert was dead, I'd have dismissed the wretched man on the spot.'

'Labrosse knew that your son was dead,' Kate said, not sure if the admiral would have realised this. 'He too attended the boy's funeral. He was related to the couple who brought Robert up, and that's how Corinne knew him.'

There was pain in the old man's eyes. 'So he and Corinne were in league against me. They set out together to cheat me.'

'I have no evidence to suggest that, sir. I think it's possible,' she added gently, 'that in her own way Corinne was playing straight with you. She needed a good assistant manager for the hotel, and she might have thought that Labrosse could do a first-class job. Despite his criminal activities she might have thought she could control him. The fact that you overheard them quarrelling suggests to me that Corinne might have been having more of a problem with him that she'd anticipated. In my view she applied unfair moral pressure on you to begin with, and she was undoubtedly wrong to mislead you about your son still being alive. But perhaps, once established here, she was genuinely working hard to ensure the success of the hotel.'

Kate's intention in saying all this was purely to comfort a dying man. To her surprise, though, she found that she believed it – at least partly. Life could be very tough for women in what was still a man's world; she knew that from her own struggles. Corinne Saxon, too, had managed to build a successful career for herself by putting her assets to good use – in her case, exceptional beauty and vivacious charm. There was nothing to be condemned in that. But like all modelling careers, even the most eminent, Corinne's had proved short-lived. For some years she had been out of the limelight. To find a niche for herself that brought her an assured income and carried with it an aura of celebrity and glamour must have been very tempting.

Corinne could have argued to herself that Admiral Fortescue was benefiting equally from their arrangement; she had saved the ancestral home of the Fortescues. Probably she'd never seen her approach to him as blackmail. She merely had a weapon to wield to gain her end. And the fact that the weapon was a phantom one, that their son was dead, would scarcely have seemed relevant to Corinne. A situation with no losers; everyone a winner.

Admiral Fortescue said wonderingly, 'I need not have killed Labrosse after all. I could just have sent him packing.'

Kate asked, 'How did you kill him, sir?'

His eyes held surprise. 'But you must already know.'

'I'd like you to tell me.'

'I went to remonstrate with the man, to tell him that what he demanded of me was preposterous. I didn't intend to kill him. Not, of course, that my intentions matter now.'

'I need to know everything, sir, for the record.'

'Yes, yes. Labrosse had given me an ultimatum. I was to agree to what he asked, or suffer the consequences. I telephoned him in his office yesterday morning and said I wanted to see him, in his room. I chose the hour of my habitual morning bath. Larkin would then be in his own part of the suite, on call if needed, so I was able to slip away without his being aware of it. Labrosse was already there in his room when I arrived. I had the foolish notion that by offering him a sufficient sum of money I could buy him off and rid myself of him once and for all.'

'You just said that you didn't intend to kill Labrosse when you went to his room. In that case, why the secrecy? Why should it matter if Larkin knew you had left the suite?'

He regarded her helplessly, having no answer.

'I have no wish to harry you, sir,' Kate went on, 'but I think you *did* intend to kill Labrosse. As an intelligent man, you must have known that a blackmailer cannot be bought off. He will always return for more.'

The admiral nodded slowly. 'Killing him was not a settled plan in my mind, Chief Inspector. But yes, I think you are right. The actual blow I struck was on the spur of the

182

moment, but I am sure I knew in my heart that Labrosse could not be allowed to continue living.'

Premeditated or unpremeditated? Did it really matter? The murderer in this case would never survive to stand trial.

Kate merely said, 'Please go on, sir.'

'As I said, I offered Labrosse money for his silence and his immediate departure. He seemed highly entertained by the suggestion, and said that he much preferred his own plan. He told me that he'd prepared a contract he wanted me to sign, and went to his writing table to get it. As he sat down to unlock the drawer his contemptuous manner enraged me. It was as if by turning his back on me like that the man was deliberately taunting me with my powerlessness. I'm afraid I lost all control. I snatched up the candlestick from the mantelpiece and brought it crashing down on his head. Instantly his whole body went limp, and he slithered from the chair down to the floor. I knew that I had killed him. I felt alarm, but no remorse.'

He fell silent, no doubt reliving the horror of those moments.

Kate said, 'Please continue. What happened next?'

'I dropped the weapon, instinctively, then I realised that it would bear my fingerprints. So I wiped it clean before discarding it again.'

'What did you wipe it with?' She knew, but she wanted him to say it.

'I used the handkerchief from Labrosse's breast pocket. I was reluctant to use my own.'

'What did you do with the handkerchief?'

'I took it away with me. You will find it in the kitchen wastebin in my suite.'

'We have already found it, sir. Presumably you also took away the draft contract?'

'Yes, I couldn't let you discover that in Labrosse's room. I locked it away in a drawer in my bureau, intending to destroy it later.'

'Did you destroy it?'

'No, it will still be there.'

Kate paused, wondering if she ought to continue. Admiral Fortescue looked almost at death's door. She guessed that he'd screwed himself up for this confession, and she doubted he'd find the strength to rally again. Any remaining questions that needed answering had better be asked now.

'Do you still believe that Labrosse killed Corinne Saxon?'

'I do. Is that not what you think, Chief Inspector?'

'What do you suppose his motive would have been?'

A scarcely discernible gesture of his hands where they lay limply on the bed cover. 'To put into action his plan of obtaining full control of the hotel. He knew that as long as Corinne remained at the helm he would only be a secondary figure. So he disposed of her. I am convinced he was sufficiently ruthless to do that. And even though it was not a matter of raping her first — as you tell me — the way he desecrated her body was unspeakably vile.' His tired eyes became keener. 'I can see you do not agree that he killed Corinne.'

'I have reason to think otherwise,' Kate said. 'I believe that in blackmailing you Labrosse merely took advantage of a situation that Corinne's death presented to him.'

'Then who . . . ?'

Kate shook her head. 'I can't answer that yet. I have my suspicions, strong suspicions, but so far I lack sufficient evidence to bring a charge.'

'I hope you find it. I most sincerely hope you find it. Corinne's murderer must pay for his crime, just as I am paying for mine.' The old man took a juddering breath. 'I'm so thankful to have confessed the truth to you and removed all suspicion from Larkin. The knowledge that an innocent man might suffer for what was my responsibility would have been a heavy burden to carry with me into eternity.'

'Larkin will almost certainly be charged with complicity in the thefts, sir.'

'Yes, he deserves that. He failed me badly. He has been with me for many years, and I always believed that I could trust him.' His face twisted in a wry grimace. 'Who am I to speak of failing a person to whom one owes loyalty and trustworthiness? My son — my firstborn son, Dominic — will doubtless fly over from America as soon as he learns that I'm in hospital and severely ill. I should find it difficult to face him in view of what has happened. So it is all to

184

the good that I shall almost certainly be dead before he arrives.'

Douglas Fortescue had decided that the time had come for him to die. It was pointless to try to persuade him to cling to life. He was a man with an iron-strong resolve. Kate returned his gaze directly and steadily.

'Would you like me to stay with you for a while, Admiral?'

'You're a kind woman, Mrs Maddox, but no. I'd prefer you to leave me now. I want a little time to collect my thoughts and make my mental farewells.' The ghost of a smile again. 'To prepare myself to meet my maker.'

Kate rose to her feet. 'I'm sorry, sir, for the way things have turned out.'

'No, my dear lady, you have no cause to be sorry. Leave the regrets to me.'

Chapter Fifteen

Returning to DHQ and enquiring for Boulter, Kate found that her sergeant was taking a meal break in the canteen, having laid on yet more food for Larkin in the interview room. This concern for the suspect, Kate translated, sprang from the needs of Boulter's own stomach.

Unfeelingly, she sent for him forthwith.

'I couldn't get anything more out of Larkin,' he said defensively, 'so there didn't seem any point keeping on at him.' Then, on a note of accusation, because he felt excluded, 'How about you? I hear you've been talking to Admiral Fortescue at the hospital.'

Kate filled him in, and sheer surprise at this outcome cheered Boulter's mood.

'My God,' he said, when she came to an end. 'I had Larkin tagged for the Labrosse job. He seemed a sure bet. You thought so too, guv, I reckon?'

'So far as I let myself feel sure about anything,' she agreed. *Bloody pompous you must sound, Kate Maddox!* 'Anyway, Tim, let's go and break the good news to Sid Larkin that he's off the hook on the murder rap. But I think he might still be able to help us make the connection between the two killings.'

'Aren't you ever going to let up on that angle, guv? We must have got it right this time — the old admiral for Labrosse, Berger for Corinne Saxon.'

'Amen, as I remember you saying when you got it wrong before.'

In the interview room, the debris of the meal Larkin had

186

been served was still on the table. Understandably, he hadn't had much appetite. The PC at the door took the tray away with him as he departed. Kate sat down opposite Larkin. Boulter remained standing.

'Why did you tell me, Larkin, that Admiral Fortescue didn't leave his suite between ten o'clock and eleven yesterday morning?'

'Well, he didn't, did he?'

'The admiral has now confessed to the murder of Yves Labrosse, so on that charge you are in the clear. But I believe you're guilty of seriously misleading us. I think you knew that he was absent for a while. Didn't you?'

'I couldn't be sure.' Relief had replaced anxiety and Larkin's sulky confidence was returning. 'I told you the truth, you can't make out any different. I didn't hear him go out.'

'Now you listen to me,' Boulter cut in roughly. 'You're in a very dicey position, Larkin. Apart from all that thievery you were up to with Labrosse and Kenway, there's the question of what information you withheld from the police on the matter of Labrosse's murder. So I advise you to listen very carefully to the chief inspector's questions, and to give her truthful answers.'

Kate continued, spelling it out, 'You knew – or you guessed – that the admiral had left the suite for a short time. Right?'

'Well, I suppose I might have done.'

'Yes or no?'

'Yes, then. I mean, I thought he must have gone out. But I weren't positive.'

And when you heard Labrosse had been murdered, you believed that it was Admiral Fortescue who had killed him?'

'I guessed he could've done it.'

'What motive did you think he had?'

Larkin hesitated, caught Boulter's hard gaze and said hurriedly, 'Yves had got something on him, I knew that. I don't know what it was, though. Yves wouldn't tell me.'

That, Kate could accept. For Labrosse to have shared what he knew about the admiral would have been to relinquish some of his power. Larkin might have tried to apply some leverage himself.

'Labrosse was blackmailing Admiral Fortescue, you're saying?'

'Well, I suppose so. If you put it like that.'

'If you believed that the admiral might have killed Labrosse, why did you keep quiet when you yourself came under suspicion for the crime?'

He shrugged, cockily confident. 'You couldn't never have pinned it on me, because I didn't do it.'

While he was feeling pleased with himself, Kate went straight on, 'Admiral Fortescue is of the opinion that Labrosse killed Miss Saxon.'

'No, he never,' Larkin protested. 'He never!'

'You sound very sure of that.'

He knew that he'd said too much and tried to retract. 'Well, I don't reckon Yves could've done.'

'Larkin,' Boulter barked out, 'are you forgetting what I just told you? Don't mess us about.'

Kate waited in silence, giving him time to think about it.

'Okay,' he muttered reluctantly. 'It won't make no difference to Yves now if I do tell. It wasn't him who killed that Saxon woman. She were already dead.'

'Keep going.'

'That Wednesday, Yves had been for a meet with that Kenway bloke. They went to an old quarry over by North Chapel. On the way back to Streatfield Park he drove along that lane where it happened. Up ahead he saw two cars pulled in at the side. One was bright red and he recognised it straight off as Miss Saxon's. A man was just getting out of it on the passenger side, but when he heard Yves' car coming he dashed to his own car and drove off like crazy. Yves wondered what the hell was going on. He pulled up alongside Miss Saxon's car and he could see her sitting there behind the wheel, but she looked all slumped, like. He got out to take a closer look, and he could see she was dead. Strangled.'

'This is a load of crap,' said Boulter gruffly.

'No, honest, it's God's truth.'

'So why didn't Labrosse call the police?'

'He thought it'd be safer not to get himself involved, that's why. Yves couldn't afford to be asked questions about how he came to be at that spot, and have you coppers on his tail.

Could he? And another thing, he'd had a hell of a row with the Saxon woman about some missing receipts a couple of days before that, and people had heard them at it. Anyway, he was just about to drive off and keep his mouth shut, when it suddenly hit him that if she was found right away he'd still have a lot of explaining to do about where he was at the time she'd been done in. So Yves hauled her body out of the car and carried it into the woods. Miss Saxon was just setting off somewhere on a few days' leave, and Yves knew she wouldn't be missed till she was due back after the weekend. So he reckoned that if she wasn't found right off, the cops wouldn't know exactly when she was killed, so you wouldn't be badgering him with questions about where he'd been Wednesday afternoon.'

'Are you telling us that Labrosse just carried the body into the woods, then dumped it and left?' asked Kate.

'Well, no. What he thought was ... maybe if he made it look as if she'd been raped, like, it would confuse things a bit more. He said you people wouldn't be so likely to suspect him, not with him being gay.'

'So he ripped her clothes and faked a rape?' Boulter demanded disgustedly. 'A charming character, your lover boy.'

Larkin shrugged and looked away.

Kate said, 'What about Miss Saxon's car? Labrosse must have known that when it was found abandoned, there'd be a search for her and questions asked.'

''Course he did. He was planning to drive it somewhere out of sight. There's lots of tracks in them woods. But then he heard the sound of another car or something coming along, and he got scared. So he jumped back in his own car and drove off sharpish. When he got back to the hotel he was very busy what with her being away, and he couldn't go out again without it looking funny like. So he kept an eye out for me round about sixish when I was due back from my gym club and nipped round the garage before I'd put the car away. He said to get over to them woods pronto and shift her car in among the trees. But when I got there, where he said I'd find the car, it was gone. We couldn't figure it out, no ways, and Yves proper got the wind up. Then later, on Sunday, I

189

heard you tell the admiral about some bloke coming along and nicking it.'

'Did Labrosse give you any details about the man he saw getting out of Miss Saxon's car?' Kate asked. 'Either about him *or* his car? Anything that might help us identify him?'

'Oh, he knew who it was, all right.'

Kate could hardly believe such luck. 'Who was it, then?'

Larkin made a what-the-hell gesture. 'It were that architect bloke, what's his name? Berger, that's it. The one who done all the alterations to Streatfield Park.'

'Labrosse definitely recognised him?'

'Yes, I told you. It was Berger, no doubt about that.'

'You don't look all that chuffed, guv,' said Boulter, closing the door of the interview room behind them and walking with Kate along the corridor. 'You've every cause to be.'

She gave the sergeant an absent smile. 'Early on in this case, Tim, you said something about opening up cans of worms. You weren't wrong.'

'Just think,' he ruminated, 'if the old admiral hadn't jumped in and killed Labrosse, Berger might easily have done the job for him. He must've had just as strong a motive. I can't believe that Labrosse would miss such a perfect chance to apply another spot of blackmail.'

'You're probably right.'

'I feel a bit sorry about old Fortescue, don't you, guv? In his hoity-toity way he wasn't such a bad old stick.'

'No, he wasn't.' Already, they were talking about him in the past. 'Listen, Tim, I want to make a phone call. Get Berger pulled in, will you, and let me know when he's here.'

In her office she punched out the hospital's number. The Sister answered when she was through to the right ward.

'This is Chief Inspector Maddox. How is Admiral Fortescue, please?'

'He's very weak, Chief Inspector, and we can't hold out much hope. But he's sleeping peacefully at the moment.'

Not to wake again? That would be best. Kate replaced the phone, feeling depressed in a way she couldn't immediately pin down. Of course! Phoning the Peace Memorial Hospital had brought back her feelings of guilt about not paying Felix a proper visit today. She picked up the phone again and pressed redial.

'Please put me through to Miss Felicity Moore on Nightingale Ward.'

'Kate!' exclaimed her aunt a moment later. 'I was just thinking about you, girl.'

Hard thoughts? 'Felix, I'm really sorry about popping in like that earlier, then dashing off again after only a couple of minutes, but – '

'Don't worry, you couldn't help it, could you? Duty called.'

If only her aunt wasn't being so damned understanding and forgiving.

'I'll be in tomorrow for a nice long visit. That's a promise.'

'You've got the case all wrapped up, then?'

'I didn't say that, Felix.'

'Oh, pooh! I can hear it in your voice, girl. I know you too well. I shall want to hear all the gory details.'

'You'll be lucky.'

This was better, chucking it back at each other. Funny, she felt a deep affection for Felix and knew it was mutual; but in normal circumstances they shied away from any hint of sentimentality. They were independent, self-reliant women, both.

'Let's have no more games,' Kate told Adrian Berger, after Boulter had performed the preliminaries. 'Make no mistake about it, you're going to be charged in connection with the death of Corinne Saxon. The precise nature of the charge will depend on what you have to tell me. Or rather, what I believe of what you tell me. So I want the whole story, please, with nothing left out.'

She hadn't really expected Berger to crumble instantly at this headlong approach, and he didn't. Instead, he adopted an attitude of pained and weary protest.

'I've already told you all there is to tell,' he said. 'I had nothing whatever to do with Corinne Saxon's death. I was elsewhere at the time it occurred.'

'That's right, you told me you were with another woman.

But I'm not going to demand her identity, Mr Berger, because I know very well that the Wednesday afternoon ladyfriend is just a figment of your imagination. Furthermore, I have definite evidence that you were at the scene of Corinne Saxon's murder that afternoon.'

'How can you possibly — '

'You were seen.'

'Seen!' Berger caught his breath, badly rattled by this. But he rallied. Kate almost admired him. 'That's absurd. Who is it saying they saw me?'

'Oh, come on! You know who it was. You've been blackmailed about it, haven't you?'

'Blackmailed?' He looked astonished. 'I don't know what you mean.'

His reaction seemed genuine, and Kate could only suppose that Labrosse had been too busy putting the screws on Admiral Fortescue to start demanding money from Berger. No doubt he'd have got around to it in time.

'The fact remains that you were seen.'

Berger opened his mouth as if with another denial, then changed his mind. 'I have nothing more to say.'

'That is your right, of course. However, I thought you might like the opportunity to give me your version of what happened.'

'I tell you nothing happened.'

'Oh, something happened, Mr Berger. Let me give you one scenario. You deliberately set out to kill Corinne Saxon in the vilest way imaginable. After brutally strangling her, you carried her into the woods where you ripped her clothing and desecrated her body to make it appear that she'd been raped. Then you abandoned her there to rot in the undergrowth.'

That got to him, as she had intended. For moments he stared at Kate, his eyes seeming glazed. Then with a sound that was something between a moan and a cry of despair. he buried his face in his hands.

'No, you mustn't think that. It's not true. I didn't ...'

'You didn't what?'

His hands dropped away. He was shivering. 'It was an accident. I ... I couldn't believe it when I realised Corinne was dead. I was in a rage. She made me so angry.' His voice gathered strength against Kate's accusation. 'But I didn't dump her in the woods and tear her clothes. I *couldn't* do a thing like that to her.'

'Why not?' asked Boulter, with deliberate callousness. 'After throttling the life out of a woman, what's the difference if you go on and mess about with her corpse? If she's dead, she wouldn't feel a thing.'

Berger started protesting again, almost incoherent with distress now. Kate said quietly. 'Tell us all about it, Mr Berger. Everything.'

He was silent for a minute, then began disjointedly, 'I loved Corinne. I was crazy about her. But I don't believe she ever felt anything much for me. She couldn't have done. I thought she did, at first. It was wonderful, and I began making plans for us to go away together and start a new life. For Corinne's sake I was ready to divorce my wife and give up everything I'd worked for so hard. But she just laughed when I told her. It was dreadful. I couldn't stand her laughing at me.'

His voice had taken on a plaintive, begging-for-understanding note. Kate saw now that Adrian Berger was essentially a weak man hiding behind a façade of arrogant self-confidence. A woman like Corinne Saxon, she guessed, would have felt nothing but contempt for him if he'd pleaded with her in this craven way. And Corinne's contempt would have had a cruel cutting edge. Kate began to feel a sneaking sympathy for him; one of the pitfalls of being a female in this job! She forced her mind to remain open, nonjudgemental.

'When did your affair with her begin?' she asked. 'And how?'

Berger shook his head slowly, as if wondering how his life could have fallen apart in this way.

'From the very first moment I saw Corinne I knew that I wanted her. I'd seen photographs of her, of course, when she used to be a model, and naturally I'd thought she was very attractive. But I thought that about other models, too. Meeting her in the flesh, though ... I can't really explain it. She was fantastic. Not just beautiful – the most beautiful woman I'd ever seen in my life. The first time we met was just after Christmas when I was called in to discuss the conversion of

193

Streatfield Park. Corinne had been given full control by Admiral Fortescue, and she knew exactly what she wanted. She always did know exactly what she wanted. Then in the spring, when the actual work commenced, we were having a drink together and I happened to mention a cottage belonging to my brother-in-law that I'm remodelling for him. Corinne said she'd like to see it, and we went there one afternoon and, well, we ended up making love.'

Which had been Corinne's game plan, no question. She had decided that the architect working on the conversion would serve to amuse her for a while. Then when she'd grown bored with him, he was expected meekly to vanish out of her life.

'You used the cottage regularly after that first time?'

Berger nodded. 'Whenever Corinne could get away.'

'And when did she break the news to you that it was all over?'

The memory made him shudder visibly. 'I'll never forget that day. It was three weeks ago last Friday. Corinne said it so casually, while we were getting dressed. I asked her about the next time, and she said, "There won't be a next time, Ram." Just like that! I couldn't believe it, I thought she was teasing me, but she wasn't. She'd decided, and that was it. I kept on trying to make her change her mind, but after that, whenever I had to go to the hotel to oversee work on the new chalets and the squash courts, she'd arrange it so we were never alone together. I kept phoning her on some pretext or other, and the last time I did she was really nasty to me. She told me to get lost, then slammed the phone down.'

'How was it you knew where and when to waylay her last Wednesday? Had Corinne told you of her plans?'

'No, it was the admiral. He happened to mention that Corinne was going away for a few days, but that she'd be there up until lunchtime on Wednesday, if I needed to check anything with her. I guessed at once that Corinne would be spending the time with some man, and the thought drove me out of my mind.'

'Going to plead insanity now, are we?' said Boulter, in his hard-man role. 'You chose a nice quiet spot on the route you knew she'd have to take, with the deliberate intention

194

of killing her and making sure no other man could have her. You were no more out of your mind than I am, Berger.'

'Hang on, sergeant,' said Kate, with the voice of sweet reason. 'How can we know the state of Mr Berger's mind at the time?'

Berger shot her a grateful look. 'I suppose, in a way, that I *was* insane. It's a terrible thing to be in love with a woman who can treat you so callously. It seemed like the end of the world when she finished with me. The end of everything that made my life worth living.'

'So you went to plead with Corinne one last time?' Kate suggested.

'Yes, that's right. I should have known better, but I thought I might persuade her when she realised how much I truly loved her. It seemed impossible to believe that she could go off with some other man when she could have me, who was willing to make all kinds of sacrifices for her sake.'

Kate didn't need to glance at Boulter for him to keep silent. Her own voice was low and steady, almost gentle. 'Tell us exactly what happened.'

'I got to Streatfield Park about half past one, and I waited a few yards along from the entrance gates. Corinne drove out just after a quarter past two, and I followed her. She must have realised it was me, but she didn't stop. So when she turned along that lane – she'd always claimed it was a good short cut to the motorway – I accelerated past her and cut in, forcing her to stop. She was furious with me, but I still thought I might somehow get through to her. I got in beside her and said straight out that I knew she was going away with a man. She didn't deny it. She suddenly started laughing. "That's right," she said, "I'm off to gay Paree for a few days – with someone who's a hell of a better lover than you ever were, Ram." In his misery and indignation at the memory, Kate knew he was telling the exact and shaming truth.

'What did you do then?' she asked softly.

Berger gave her a lost look. 'Do? I reached out and grabbed her by the shoulders. I wanted to shake some sense into her. She knocked my hands away – Corinne was a strong woman – and she told me to get out of the car and stay out

195

of her life. I saw red, a blinding red, and after that everything
went hazy. Next thing I knew my hands were around her neck.
I suppose she must have struggled. I remember she grabbed a
torch from the dump bin on the door and tried to hit me with
it. Then suddenly she went limp. I didn't mean to kill her,
you've got to believe me.' He was looking not at Kate but
at the man who seemed to be his disbelieving enemy.

'Nevertheless,' Kate pointed out, 'you did kill her. You
can't escape the consequences of that.'

'I know, I know. But I didn't do all the rest of it. Not
dragging her into the woods and ripping her clothes and
making it look like rape. That wasn't me. I swear to God
it wasn't.'

Why should it matter so much to a man who faced a
murder charge that he shouldn't be blamed for this final
degradation of his victim's dead body? Kate felt a tug of
pity for Berger.

Not so Boulter, who said harshly, 'Maybe not. But you
didn't try to resuscitate her or summon help, did you? No,
you just beat it and left her there.'

'I didn't mean to leave her like that. I was going to try and
revive her ... give her the kiss of life or something. Only
before I could do anything I heard a car coming. I was in a
blind panic. I ran to my own car and drove off fast. I had
to go past the other car, there was no time to swing round
and go back. But I kept my face away and I just hoped and
prayed it wasn't anyone who'd recognise me.'

'Unfortunately for you, it was.'

'Who?' he demanded, but then rushed straight on without
waiting for an answer. 'Was it him who did those other beastly
things? Why did he, what was it all for? When I heard about
Corinne's body being found in the woods and that she'd been
raped, I was totally stunned. I couldn't make any sense out
of it. Or was it someone else who did that? And why, for
God's sake? *Why?*' He was in a ferment, reliving the past
days of horror, fear and bewilderment.

'You'll know the answers to all those questions soon
enough,' Kate told him, 'when we compile the case against
you.'

Again, Berger buried his face in his two hands. 'I'm done

196

for, aren't I? I had so much, and I've lost it all. Thrown it all away.'

Why the hell, Kate, do people only value what they've got when it's too late?

Chapter Sixteen

It was just on ten when Kate decided to pack it in for the day. Tomorrow there would be the winding-down of the investigation, starting on the huge mass of paperwork that still faced her, standing drinks all round as a thank you to the men and women on the squad. She hoped that by tomorrow evening she'd feel less tired and more in a mood for celebrating.

The phone on her desk rang. Boulter picked it up, spoke, then glanced at his chief inspector apologetically. 'It's a personal call for me, guv. I'll take it somewhere else.'

'No need, Tim.' She stood up, easing the taut muscles of her neck, and reached for her bag. 'I'm going to freshen up now, then it's off home for both of us.'

When she returned, Boulter had finished his phone call. There was a grim look on his face.

'Fancy a drink, Kate?' he asked, taking her by surprise. That hadn't been on their agenda.

Why not? She needed to unwind. Besides, she had a feeling that Boulter was in need of a shoulder to cry on.

'Okay, Tim. Just one. The Market Inn suit you?'

He shrugged, indifferent about where they went.

Downstairs, as they reached the vestibule, the man at the desk glanced up.

'Ah, ma'am, I thought I'd missed you. Message just received from the hospital. Admiral Fortescue passed away fifteen minutes ago. Peacefully, they said to tell you, in his sleep.'

'Thanks, Barry.'

She and Boulter left the building, to walk the short distance to the pub.

'The old boy willed himself dead, Tim,' she observed sombrely as they fell into step. 'It almost amounts to suicide.'

'Sensible man!' Boulter's voice was bitter. 'Saved himself from facing a murder rap, hasn't he?'

'I doubt if it was for himself, Tim. By nature the admiral was a fighter. More likely he was thinking of his son – the embarrassment a prolonged trial would cause Dominic and his family.'

'And now, I suppose, the son and heir will flog off the ancestral home for an almighty packet, like Larkin said he would, and hot-foot it back to the USA. Sod the precious Fortescue inheritance his old man was trying to save for him. The lucky bastard!'

Kate waited until they were seated, with the drinks Boulter had fetched from the bar in front of them. Then she said, 'Okay, Tim, let's have it. What's eating you?'

'Julie's bloody walked out and left me, hasn't she?' he burst out.

'You mean,' Kate said, dismayed by the rage boiling inside him, 'that she's gone to stay with her sister again?'

'Yep. That was her on the phone just now. But this time she's not coming back. A trial separation, she calls it.' He snorted. 'Trial is about right when those two sisters get their heads together – with me in the dock! I've never done a damn thing right, according to that bloody Brenda. Her and her prick of a husband who's got a cosy little nine-to-fiver at the Town Hall. They're who put Julie up to it, that's for sure.'

'What suddenly brought this on?' Kate asked in a carefully neutral voice.

'She's been thinking things over all day, she said, and she's realised that coming back was a mistake. There was no future for us together.' Boulter gave a hollow laugh. 'It's all down to me, according to her. All my bloody fault. Just because I'm a normal human being and don't match up to the crazy fantasy she's got in her head of the perfect husband. I can't ever be relied on, I'm always getting home late, I hardly see

199

the children, I never take her out, I forget birthdays and anniversaries, I'm bad-tempered and slovenly. You name it, I've bloody got it or done it.'

'I'm very sorry, Tim. Really sorry. But don't you think it's possible that Julie has a point? I mean, do you ever try to see things from her point of view?'

The black look he shot her said, *You too! Traitor.*

Kate went on, 'Okay, if you want to be left alone and nurse your grievances, go right ahead. But if you want to get your wife and children back, you'd better do some hard thinking. Some of Julie's criticisms you can't do much about, they come with the job, but she's intelligent enough to know that. With other things, though, I think you could make a bit more effort to match up to what Julie wants — what every woman wants — from her husband. A bit more understanding. A bit more attention. A bit more romance in your relationship.'

Kate wondered if she'd pushed her nose in too far where it wasn't wanted, but when he didn't smack her down she felt emboldened to continue. She was fond of Tim Boulter. She liked his wife, too, even though Julie had made it very clear that she disliked and resented Chief Inspector Kate Maddox. As for the two children, Mandy and Sharon, they were really nice youngsters. The Boulters had all the ingredients to be a happy little family. Kate, having lost her own chance of family happiness through a cruel stroke of fate, hated to see so much potential thrown away for want of effort.

'Your marriage is worth saving, Tim. Worth fighting for. Why not give it a try?'

He shrugged petulantly. 'It's not up to me, is it? Julie's the one who walked out.'

'I know, but you can go and see her, can't you? You'll want to see the children, anyway. Talk things over with Julie and try to sort out your differences. Be reasonable, and —'

'Reasonable! She doesn't know the meaning of the word.'

'I think you'll find she does. I think you'll find that Julie will respond if you show her that you're willing to try, too. Always assuming, of course, that you really do want her back.'

There was pain and darkness in his eyes. 'Sometimes I

think I hate her guts. That if I don't ever see her again it'll be too soon. But then, oh, I don't know. It's going to be hell without her and the kids.'

Fretting over the Boulters' problems as she drove home, Kate reflected irritably that any of her male colleagues would take the sensible view that so long as his work wasn't affected, the sergeant's personal life was entirely his own business.

She'd been busy handing out sage advice to Tim Boulter, but she still had a repair job to do on her own relationship. As things were, she faced going back to an empty home, when she might have been returning to the welcoming arms of someone she loved. The word caught Kate by surprise and she thrust it out of her mind. She was in no mood to analyse her feelings towards Richard just now.

She turned in at the gates of the stable conversion, and rolled to a standstill. Getting out, she spotted among the cars parked in the forecourt one that was joltingly familiar. Richard's blue Volvo. What did this mean? She went over to investigate and found Richard sitting behind the wheel, fast asleep.

She reached in through the open window and shook him by the shoulder.

'What the hell are you doing here?' she demanded as he woke, her voice belligerent.

He blinked at her in the dim light that seeped out from behind the drawn curtains of the other flats. 'Waiting for you, what else?'

'But why?' Fear gripped her suddenly. 'Has something happened to Felix?'

'Calm down,' said Richard, climbing out of the car. 'Felix is doing fine, as you saw for yourself this evening. But she phoned me about an hour ago to say she thought I'd like to know that you've solved your case.'

'Felix says altogether too much.'

'But is she right?'

'As a matter of fact, yes. That's why I'm so late home, wrapping things up.'

Richard was silent for a countable number of seconds. Then he put a hand up and laid it against her cheek.

'We can't talk out here,' he said. 'Let's go inside.'

Unsteadily, Kate found her key and opened the front door. Richard waited without speaking while she switched on lights and drew the curtains in her living room. When at length he spoke Kate could read an underlying challenge in his voice, a hint of lingering anger and resentment.

'Are you going to tell me about it now? Who was it killed Corinne?'

Did he have to pressure her like this? It wasn't the right moment. And then Kate suddenly knew it never would be the right moment. Ought she to admit to Richard that she'd felt jealous of Corinne Saxon ever since he'd first told her of their former relationship? Or did he already know that; had he guessed? What he couldn't know about was the shaming spark of satisfaction she'd felt on recognising the murder victim as her imagined rival. She had carried the guilt of that with her all through this enquiry. It would take a long time to erase it from her mind.

'It was Adrian Berger, the architect,' she said, and then, 'I need a drink, Richard.'

'I'll get it. You sit down.'

Kate flopped onto one end of the long sofa, kicking off her shoes, while Richard fetched the whisky bottle and two glasses, putting them on the low coffee table in easy reach. He poured a good measure for them each, handed Kate hers, then sat down too – but at the far end, away from her.

'Adrian Berger,' he said. 'I never guessed it would turn out to be him. *Why,* for God's sake?'

'Jealousy. He was crazy about her. They'd been lovers, and Corinne dropped him for another man.'

Richard nodded, accepting that. 'But why the disgusting farce of making it look like rape?'

'No, that wasn't him, that was Labrosse.'

'What?'

Kate told him the whole story. The only significant detail she omitted was a report from London's Met that had come in that evening in response to a request for any information about Corinne Saxon's recent life prior to her turning up at Streatfield Park. It appeared that for the past few years she had worked as a high-class call girl. Telling Richard that would only distress him.

By the time Kate had finished they were on their third whisky. More time went by as they sat there, still well apart on the sofa. But the emotional distance that had separated them was gone, Kate knew that.

Relaxed, suddenly feeling happy, she stretched her arms above her head and gave a huge yawn.

'Bed is the place for tired people,' Richard suggested.

'Mmm!' she sighed dreamily.

He pushed himself to his feet, a slightly awkward movement with his stiff leg.

'Want me to carry you?'

She grinned. 'Oh, very macho! I'm supposed to be a liberated woman, buster.'

'Have it your way.'

She lugged herself up. Richard crossed to her bookshelves and spent a minute selecting a few volumes.

'What's that in aid of?' Kate demanded.

'A few works of reference, to see you through the night.'

'Put them down at once,' she ordered sternly, 'and come to bed. Hurry up!'

Richard dropped the handful of books onto the sofa and followed her into the bedroom.